RISE: LAST CHANCE

NOT EVEN DEATH CAN KILL YOU.

KT HANNA

Author: K.T. Hanna
Cover Artist: Caitlin Greer
Typography: Bonnie Price
Layout & Design: Caitlin Greer

Disclaimer: This is a work of fiction.
Names, characters, businesses, places, events, and incidents are either the products of
the author's imagination or used in a fictitious manner. Any resemblance to actual
people, living or dead, or actual events is purely coincidental.

Copyright © 2020 Katie Hanna
All rights reserved.

Ebook ISBN-13: 978-1-948983-24-2
Paperback ISBN-13: 978-1-948983-23-5
Hardback ISBN-13: 978-1-948983-25-9

ALSO BY KT HANNA

Last Chance:

Rise

Somnia Online:

Initializing
Anomaly
Fragments
Dissonance
Distortion
Fusion

The Domino Project:

Chameleon
Hybrid
Parasite

Dedication:

Andie

For becoming so much more than I ever imagined

DEATH

Electricity doesn't taste like you think it will. The only thing that stands out about it is the smell of burnt flesh, down through into the bones. It tastes more in line with its scent, like charred chicken without the barbecue sauce.

It lingers in the back of your throat, pulsing like an electric eel while it strangles the life from your body.

The drone of the ambulance siren pulled me out of the haze.

I blinked, my eyes sticky with something, probably blood. Knowing my luck though, it could be something worse. The throbbing in my head wouldn't abate, and voices leaked through to me like I was floating through some sort of abyss and they were miles away.

"I've got a pulse." The shock in that voice almost made me laugh, only oxygen didn't seem to too fond of me right then, and I dragged in a ragged breath, surprising myself with the pain that echoed through my chest.

Something flickered behind my eyelids. Like when you look at the sun too long only to have that damned circle of blazing light stuck with you no matter where you look, with open eyes or not.

"That can't be." The second voice was deeper, filled with confusion that struggled to remain professional. "I could have sworn they were gone."

I got it though. It felt like I should be dead. Brief images flashed through my mind. Pain so searing it took my hard-earned breath away again. So, either I was having a hell of a ride straight up to the not-so-pearly gates, or I was still alive.

Somehow.

The light flashed again behind my eyelids, momentarily distracting me from the EMS attendants I'd managed to stump with whatever had happened. It'd come to me eventually; I just couldn't quite remember at that moment.

Amidst the prodding at my arms, there was a mild sting as they inserted what I assumed to be an IV, underscored by rash movement as the ambulance sped through crowded streets. They should be crowded unless I'd somehow jumped dimensions in a Tardis.

This time when the light returned behind my eyelids that still weren't cooperating with me, it rippled across my lack of vision reminding me of the older computer screens when they booted up, flickering into their 8-bit glory.

Please wait while the system adjusts to your confinements. This won't take long.

I blinked. Literally. Disconcerting as it was, I was as thrown off balance for a few seconds. With the influx of light from the stark white interior, the message I thought I'd seen vanished in a haze of brightness. Whatever it was had to have hit me in the head a lot harder than I realized.

Or burned me to a crisp as the electrical line collapsed on top of me.

That explained the taste. Images came rushing back, and I squeezed my eyes shut not eager to relive my near demise. Except there it was again, when I shut my eyes. In silver white letters like it was tattooed on the back of my eyelids in spider silk:

Core rebooting in… 5, 4, 3, 2, 1,
Second Chance System enabled.

Species: Human
Ability: Electricity
Designation: Runner
Rank: Junior
Skills: To Be Determined
Data analysis processing…
And I had no fucking idea what it meant.

"… your eyes?"

The deeper, first voice seemed to be waiting for an answer from me, only I wasn't entirely sure what the question had been. Obviously, it was something like can you open your eyes. In fabulous fashion, I decided to simply force my eyes open again instead of giving an answer. Although in hindsight, the screech of pain that escaped me when the bright light pierced my vision once again was probably enough of one.

At least the words disappeared for a while. A very short while. Once the brightness faded, they were there again, but subtler. They'd only become obvious if I tried to focus on them, but they lingered at the corner of my vision when I didn't. Since I didn't wear contacts, it wasn't as though someone could play a practical joke on me. There was writing in my eyes and lightning in my veins, apparently. Not a nightmare, but I wasn't sure I could trust this as reality either.

This trip to the hospital was going to be super fun. The ambulance rattled over a pothole and made me groan.

"That's a yes." Slowly the deeper voice came into focus. He wore his EMS uniform like an honor badge, sandy brown hair dusted just below his eyebrows, and it swayed in time with the vehicle's movements. "Don't sit up yet."

He continued marking off several things on a chart, a frown tugging at his lips. His name badge declared to everyone who could read that his name was Shane.

"Well, in good news, you seem to be alive."

"Shouldn't we check with the doctor first?" was what I tried to say, but my voice wouldn't work yet. It felt like fire was busy rushing down my throat to burn whatever remained of my body to cinders.

"No talking. We're almost there." Shane's gaze lingered on me for another moment, a thoughtful gleam in his eyes.

No talking. No problem. Wasn't like I could say much. I closed my eyes again and instantly regretted it. Except this time the initial message was relegated to the side. This time it told me something else.

Calibrating your current location. Assessing your abilities. You, Dare Harvey, have been gifted with the power of electricity and have been raised from the dead. You are hereby conscripted by the system to aid in the war against humanity. Stand by.

My brain reeled even as the vehicle slowed. Maybe I'd hit my head harder than I thought. War against humanity? I *was* human last time I checked. However, perhaps I was a zombie now. My head hurt thinking about it.

Hospitals never held a feeling of well-being for me. All they demonstrated was death. My grandfather, my auntie, even a cousin...all of them went to the hospital and didn't come back out. Granted, my brain realized this was because they were ill and the hospital itself didn't kill them. But a part of me always wondered, because how can we ever know? Not to mention that I was apparently hallucinating words in front of my eyes.

I'm sure I could have walked myself inside the death trap, but good old Shane decided it was better for me to remain on my gurney as they pushed me in through the ER entrance and into chaos. Considering they'd thought I was dead, he was probably right to be cautious. My muscles ached in ways that made me question if they'd be able to support my weight right now.

The cold hit me as soon as we entered the structure. No one else appeared to be shivering. I think the electrocution short circuited my eyes or something, because everything not up close and personal seemed blurred and whacky.

What were the odds there'd be a clown standing in the hall with a blue balloon otherwise?

I shook my head and tried to get comfortable on the rolling bed, but the mattress section was hard and cold through the sheets. In a way it resembled the hard sidewalk I could barely remember falling on. Guess they didn't hit the warmer when they thought I was a corpse. How the fuck was I alive? If I was to believe the floating information, I'd been brought back from the dead. A hysterical giggle began to form in the back of my throat and I choked it down lest they think I needed a different hospital.

They wheeled me into a room. An actual room and not just one partitioned with curtains. The other EMT left after swapping my plugins over to the ones in the room where they picked up an even beat. The bass of the sound hummed through my body, relaxing me.

Shane stayed, pausing at the door hesitantly. It looked like he wanted to say something, but the words weren't bypassing the block in his brain. Probably not something I wanted to hear given the circumstances, and yet something I might need. I waited, impatiently, uncomfortably, while I tried to ignore the sterile feeling of death as the underlying scent of antiseptic permeated my senses.

"Dr. Caroline will be with you shortly." He paused again and softened the next words preemptively with a smile. "She's a bit of a character. Don't let her brusque manner get you down. You're pretty damned lucky."

And with that, before I could even say *thank you*—or *what the fuck do you mean*—Shane was gone. The examination room I was in was small and had no windows. Even the soft glow of the X-Ray boxes on one side of the room wasn't enough to make it comfortable. It was the only light in the room, casting shadows of the equipment against the other walls. If I were still five years old, I might think they were all monsters, but they weren't. I wasn't. That period of time felt like another life.

I snorted a laugh, because in a way, I guess it was. New lease on life? Check. Rid of weird phobias about hospitals and claustrophobia? Big nope there. I went to pull myself up, and gripped the side of my gurney, only to yelp as static shock ran up my arm.

Visibly. What the hell? Small flashes of blue sparked under my skin, and I just knew I had to be hallucinating.

There was a clicking noise in the room, and I closed my eyes, blocking out the shadows, blocking out the sound, and tried to convince myself it was nothing. And yet, at the bottom corners of my eyelids were small swirling circles, like my brain was waiting for something to load. Counting down.

"Dare Harvey?"

The crisp and cool way the words were spoken made me sit up despite my resolution to stay lying down. This time I didn't reach for anything, engaging those trusty core muscles, and managed to avoid that display of electrical current I wasn't ready for.

Even as I tried to nod, my head spun with the sudden movement, and the doctor who entered swam into vision. It was odd in itself, wasn't it? That I didn't have a nurse or PA check me over first? After all, doctors were always the last stop, just to confirm there was nothing wrong. Perhaps the EMTs counted for that. Maybe.

"Yeah." I found myself squeezing the word out between clenched teeth as I tried desperately to fight against the vertigo spell that wouldn't abate. Shocking myself, head spinning, I wasn't right and I knew it.

Input. Gathering data. Calculating surroundings. Piping in allocations.
What the everliving...

This was going to get annoying if my head had really decided a computer lived in it. Years of therapy, that's what this accident was going to cause. Years of debt because of the cost of therapy which presumably would continue after my parent's insurance no longer carried me. Fan-fucking-tastic.

Finally, the doctor came to stand in front of me. She was tall, a little taller than me, probably around five nine without the heels. Her no-nonsense black hair was pulled back into a tight bun and her eyes hid behind black rimmed spectacles so much that the faint light in the room reflected in the lenses, obscuring her eye color.

Doctor Leigh Caroline
Designation: Healer
Rank: Mentor
Skills: Mind/Spirit/Water
Second Chance Affiliate
Point of Contact. Supervisor.

I blinked, still trying to figure out what the hell was happening to my mind. Surely it wasn't just my imagination? Apparently it thought I should just accept the fact that I was obviously going insane.

"Leigh Caroline." She nodded and her smile was as tight as her bun. All business, like I'd interrupted something important. "Though I assume you already know this."

Maybe this wasn't crazy after all. Fear bubbled in my throat, trying to make me throw up. But I choked it down before speaking in defiance. "What is this thing in my head?"

Had the electricity somehow implanted me with…nope, I was drawing a blank. I had no fucking clue. And my voice sounded like my vocal folds were made of sandpaper.

She cocked her head to one side, like she was trying to figure out if I was kidding or not. Coming down on the latter, she sighed. "Looks like it's bugging again then. It does that sometimes. You've been given a second chance. At life."

She spoke the words like I was supposed to just laugh and go, *Oh! How silly of me*. Except I didn't, and I'm pretty sure my blank stare at her said exactly that.

Swiping her finger across the tablet she held in her hand, she bit her lip before speaking. "You were hit by a dislodged electrical cable. In the moment of your death, it was determined that you and your skillset could be of use to the program." She spoke slowly and deliberately, like I was a five-year-old. Which was ultimately fine by me, because I didn't understand anything.

"So, while I was lying there on the pavement dead for all intents and purposes, someone came along, dodged the sparking wires, and injected me with a microchip, using their invisibility cloak so no one standing around would think something was up?" Incredulous though it sounded, I'm quite proud to say I think I delivered the question with a deadpan face. No pun intended. Not really anyway.

I actually managed to get the good doctor to crack a smile, even if it barely covered her irritation.

"No. No. Don't be silly. There's a failsafe built into the human body. Has been for thousands of years, beginning of the species type thing. If the program needs the power of potential skills gained through the cause of our death, then we receive a second chance." She continued the smile, and if I could have done so without my head spinning, I would have patted myself on the back.

"What's the catch?" Because I've always found cutting right to the center of things helped. That whole tiptoeing around shit never got anyone anywhere. There was always a catch.

She appeared to be relieved by the question, but didn't look at me. Instead, as she spoke, her fingers flew across the tablet in her hands. "There is a terms of service agreement you'll be able to access. You have to read through those and accept them. Should you break any of them, your program access will be terminated. Should you—"

"Wait. Terminated? You mean, my Second Chance thing will be gone, and I'll be dead?" Like how the hell did she try to gloss over that?

This time she wouldn't meet my eyes. I couldn't blame her; in fact, I felt a bit of pity for her. Who wanted to be the person breaking the news to newbies that if you didn't abide by the terms of service, your connection would be literally severed? Shivers that felt like minor convulsions shook me for a few moments.

"Technically, this is borrowed time. You were meant to die. And while bending those terms or not following your assignments as given can result in punishment, breaking the rules jeopardizes the program itself. Since you were meant to be dead anyway..." She shrugged at me, and put her screen down.

"I get it." I did, but I couldn't help the cold ball of fear in my gut. "What does this program do?"

She brightened at that question, and the smile dropped years off her age as it reached her eyes. They glinted oddly silver for a moment, but then it was gone. "It helps us prevent the human race from destroying itself."

"Don't suppose we help the world in the process? You know, extinction, murder, and whatnot." I half joked, but the serious side wouldn't let me go further than that.

Dr. Caroline nodded, her seriousness back on like a mask as she fished a device out of her pocket. In a way it reminded me of one of those infant nose suckers I'd seen my eldest sister use on my niece. "In a way. If there's no world left, there's nowhere for us to exist."

"That's a relief." I tried to joke, but the air felt so thick, I couldn't breathe properly. The monitor behind me seemed to disagree and maintained its monotonous beeping without change.

"Hold still." I did as told and she punched in a series of buttons on the device before stepping back to look at me with a frown. "While your body is mostly okay, this will help promote and speed up the healing process."

Whatever that thing in her hand was, it was definitely not a nose sucker. Thin tendrils escaped from the front of it, glowing like dull white lasers. Everywhere it touched my body, I felt a breeze of cold rejuvenation blow through, somehow under my skin.

The doctor frowned as she got to my left shoulder, and paused. "I can't fix that scar."

Though I wasn't comfortable with the device that reminded me of a tiny space octopus, I glanced down. My left bicep down to the top of my forearm, and for all I knew all the way up my shoulder under my shirt, was covered in what looked like a tree root system.

"Lichtenberg scar." Dr Caronline murmured. "Not even this can heal that."

"What is that?" I asked softly, still trying to take in the plethora of information that was swimming around in my head.

Her smile was tight this time. Not giving in the slightest. "Classified." Was all she said. I didn't push any further as she finished her examination of sorts.

When she was done Dr. Caroline reached behind me to unhook the chords. "Your body is in super healing mode right now, so you might find yourself short of breath, perhaps a little tired. I've boosted your cellular regeneration levels, but your body needs the rest of your energy to continue healing fatal wounds. When you get home, the system will help you master the skills you've gained."

"Wait." The gears in my brain began to turn, finally having caught onto the whole thinking aspect of the problem. "What skills? I'm an IT major. I work with technology. What am I, a super hacker now?"

She laughed, but I could tell a bit of it was forced. Maybe I hit too close for comfort or something. "You were killed by electricity, so your initial ability comes from that element."

A billion questions flooded my mind, so many that I felt overwhelmed, and it was enough time for her to move on, even if I didn't want her to.

"I'm your mentor. You can come to me with any questions. Just make sure the system can't answer them for you first. I'll activate the terms of service for you now. Read through them carefully. It's not legalese. I'll wait while you familiarize yourself with them."

I might have been mistaken, but her tone sounded like she understood the confusion, like she sympathized with all the information coming at me at once. But that she was also busier than I could fathom.

Considering she too would be on borrowed time, I guess that made sense. I wanted to know how long she'd been here and was about to ask when my vision was flooded with script.

Second Chance Organization—Terms of Service

1. *You (hereto after referred to as the "SC Agent") must perform the tasks as set out for you.*
2. *There is no right of appeal by the SC Agent. All SC Headquarters Decisions made are final.*
3. *The SC Agent must satisfy their own alibi should the need arise. The SC organization will not be responsible should such a measure be required.*
4. *Only discuss SC with fellow cleared SC Agents.*
5. *Do not get caught in the process of completing any SC Tasks.*
6. *Do maintain your life as it was prior to entry into the SC program as best you can.*
7. *Compensation is based on the type of task, and quality of performance. This will be delivered in the form of experience gained (allows you to progress in the organization's ranks and your personal skills), and in monetary compensation.*

Violation of any of the above can result in warnings, punishment, and even termination of the Second Chance Program.

She was right. It was straightforward as hell. Blunt even. No tact there. What the fuck had I gotten myself into?

2

SECOND CHANCE

The thin plastic water bottle Dr. Caroline gave me before I left the hospital weighed heavily in my hand. I couldn't even bring myself to drink from it. Didn't water conduct electricity? What if I took a swig, and electrocuted myself all over again?

Everywhere I turned, symbols and writing popped up in my peripheral vision, taunting me with information and numeric references I didn't know how to interpret yet. Despite the good, weird technology wielding doctor's lack of reassurances, I felt a tingle of excitement. Electricity. It had said electricity, hadn't it?

Ability: Electricity

"Thanks," I murmured out loud, realizing belatedly that it probably wasn't the best idea. The voice in my head, or the words in front of my eyes, didn't respond further. So, I guess my power was electricity.

What even the fuck did that mean?

Late afternoon cast long shadows between buildings, keeping the concrete cold. It was a longer walk to my share house than I would have liked. Even though I didn't feel quite steady on my feet, I needed the fresh air.

Although the irony of the levels of pollution in the city wasn't lost on me. *Fresh* wasn't exactly the right word to describe the air around here. Maybe I just needed to clear my head amidst the comforting smells of smog and sounds of traffic.

Yeah, I'd go with that.

My cell phone felt heavy in my pocket as it rang, yet again. Probably Mom checking in on me. She always worried. I was the youngest, the last to leave the nest. Now I lived in a big city, more than two hours away from her and if she didn't get frequent updates from me, she panicked.

What would she have done if I hadn't entered this Second Chance thing? What if I were just dead?

I shivered again, irritated at myself for not bringing a thicker coat. But then I hadn't expected to be out this late. Instead of my usual layered hoodie, all I had with me was my track gear. I pulled my flimsy University of Pennsylvania jacket around my shoulders while I clutched the bag the doctor gave me. Discharge paperwork made the life-after-death portion of my day seem like a dream. It said that I didn't need to check in with my GP. I wasn't sure I could ever see my GP again.

Callibrating…

The eerie word streamed across my sight, the echo of the voice in my head; it made all of this so dream-like. All I'd done was sneak in an extra track practice.

Here, between the tall brick buildings, sunlight didn't quite reach the street level. The stench of exhaust fumes, cigarettes, and fast food littered the air so much I could practically taste it even breathing through my nose. I'd call Mom when I got home. Or maybe my brother, Davin.

Even the TOS made little sense to me. Why on earth give me this life, but threaten to take it away if I disagreed? That was some fucked up shit there. It left me wondering if I really did die.

Death occurred at 12:40:22pm eastern standard time.

Revitalization followed at 12:42:42

The little green man on the pedestrian sign hopped to life but I barely noticed at first. 12:40:22. I legitimately died. Was dead, in fact, for two minutes and twenty seconds. I shook myself, barely setting a foot onto Spruce before the little man told me to stop. I lagged behind the throng of people who presumably didn't have a doomsday computer in their heads.

It was easier to walk home. I didn't have to pay attention, just let my feet walk me there, doing my best to ignore the flashes of script constantly inundating me with information.

I was so focused on paying attention to my steps that I didn't see the man until it was too late. He barreled into me, swearing at me as I fell to the ground, and felt the skin on my knee scrape even through the fabric of my jeans.

Today was turning out to be superb.

And they say sarcasm doesn't pay. It sure as hell brightened my day.

Pushing myself back up, I barely made it to the opposite side of the road in time. The hot air of the vehicles revving past me sent goose bumps up my legs. I just wanted to get home and collapse, to get home and try to make sense of this. Perhaps if I fell asleep, I'd realize this was all a bad dream, but the throbbing graze on my knee made me sincerely doubt that was the case.

Electricity. How was I going to use electricity as a power? That didn't even make sense, did it? I frowned, wondering how this whole system worked. Implying it was a program meant there had to be a hub somewhere. But who ran it, and what was its actual purpose? Thousands of questions flooded my brain.

Electrical Skill Affinity

Please wait until you are somewhere quiet, and out of visual range of anyone not in the SC program before activating the tutorial. Failure to comply will result in punishment.

Well, then. I guess that told me. So, it could hear my thoughts too?

Anything projected without a specific target is subject to interpretation by the SC system. Please note that thoughts are permitted, but any actions that could damage the success of the operation will result in dire consequences.

Oh great, I could think my own thoughts then.

Please note that thoughts are permitted, but any...

I only just managed to stop the growl building in my throat. This was going to get irritating very fast if I couldn't figure out a way for it to stop reacting to my thoughts. Given the amount of script it was throwing at me, and the strange soft electric voice it projected into my thoughts, avoiding what it told me was difficult.

There had to be reasonable explanations for this. No one was ever "discovered" on the news as having electrocuted an entire building or whatnot. This whole electrical power thing was likely way overinflated. Though Dr. Caroline hadn't seemed like the type of person who would exaggerate that much. Maybe I could bring our electricity bill down to zero. I laughed at my own joke, but the system didn't seem inclined to respond.

I glanced down at my knee to see if I was bleeding, but noticed it wasn't hurting much anymore. Stopping, I flexed it, but it didn't even hurt like stretching skin normally did. I'd have to check when I got home.

Finally, I made it to the section of row houses that were mostly cheaper rentals. You could tell that by the way their facades weren't quite as nice as the ones a few blocks closer to campus. Where the window panes were chipped with no sign of care in recent years, and the metal banisters going up the outside stairs flaked off, revealing rusty spots all over them.

The huge double doors that led into the hastily-converted apartments I called home boasted a deadlock, but the doors jangled so loosely I was pretty sure the locks weren't effective. Each floor resulted in a three-bedroom apartment. The clothes washers and dryers were in the basement, along with a storage unit for each floor. While I wished I lived on the entry level so I could strategically avoid carrying groceries up stairs, I was sort of glad we were on the second floor. It wasn't as high as it went, but at least it would make it more difficult for people to steal our shit if they bothered to break in.

I trudged up, my energy slowly ebbing. Though I was kidding myself. I'd felt zapped ever since I died. Funny that.

The door to our apartment jangled almost as much as the main entry door, and I realized I'd forgotten to check the mail, which wasn't all that typical of me. I'd get the mail later.

Each apartment had three bedrooms. One was a master suite, and the other two smaller rooms shared the general bathroom. I had the smallest room, and therefore the smallest payment per month. Considering I also had the lowest paying work, I thought that was a good thing. Mom and Dad couldn't afford to pay my board; they were barely afloat as it was. With three other siblings, I'd learned to use the hand-me-downs and make do with what I had a long time ago.

The living area, as usual, was full of geeky tech crap. Motherboards littered the workspaces, our TV even lay in pieces, and I swore it was functional yesterday. It was probably Orion tinkering as usual. Speaking of Orion, how the hell was I supposed to explain all this to my best friend?

Pushing the thought aside, I passed the kitchen, surprised to see Jacob in there.

"Hey, Dare. Mail for you," was all he said before turning back to whatever website he was browsing on his tablet, while he sipped at his late afternoon coffee. He worked the nightshift at an IT support place. Coffee around four p.m. was just asking not to sleep otherwise.

"Thanks." I picked up the three envelopes, frowning at them. Jacob had the master suite, and he was actually working on his postgraduate in engineering before diving into his masters. Hence, he could afford the higher rent.

I headed to my room, plunked down the bag the hospital gave me, eyed my stack of ramen that I kept in my room, and threw myself down on the bed. Shitballs.

What had I gotten myself into?

As if in response, the SC program booted up in my vision, again.

Second Chance Program

Initiative of the Second Chance Organization

Tutorial Program—Electrical Skill Affinity

It is recommended that you take this tutorial as soon as possible. Being recruited into the Second Chance Program is an excellent opportunity. The future of humanity is up to you.

Oh great. No pressure there then. The future was up to little old me. We were all fucked if that were really true.

I resisted the urge to roll my eyes and figured now was as good a time as any. Plus, it had the added bonus of delaying the opening of my mail.

I closed my eyes to get a better look at the script on the dark backdrop of the inside of my eyelids, and mentally chose to move the tutorial forward.

The same feeling of vertigo I'd had upon sitting up in the hospital spread through me, like I was floating while watching a screen. Perhaps an IMAX experience, or even virtual reality or something. But certainly not what I'd been expecting.

And far more lecture-esque than I'd wanted. I slogged through enough of those a week, couldn't this be a bit different?

Second Chance Program
Electrical Skill Affinity
Product: Mental Direction
Initial Designation: Runner
Correlation: Electrical/Space/Time

Maybe if I just kept quiet in my head, it'd think I understood everything it was going on about. I really hoped so, because I was confused as could be.

Suddenly, my head slammed into my pillow, and I couldn't move my legs or arms. The pressure against my chest made me gasp for air, and for a moment, I thought I was actually going to suffocate. Which would be so typical for me. Ha ha, you're alive! Nope, now you're dead. Again.

Except I didn't. I couldn't open my eyes, but it felt like I was moving on a rollercoaster I couldn't see. If I thought about it, that made it even scarier.

It took me a few seconds to figure out that the scene being shown to me was from earlier that day. From my electrocution to be precise. I could see myself standing on the corner, dressed just as I was now in my running gear with my jacket slung over my shoulder. I was watching the sports car as it careened out of control, could see the people running from the scene.

The bright green of the vehicle mesmerized me like a pinwheel, hypnotizing as it jumped the curb so much faster than I backpedaled. My mind screamed at me to move faster, but all I did was step back too slowly. The car side swiped one of the three electricity poles that hadn't yet been buried.

I experienced it again. Blinking slowly as I looked up and watched the poles fall, their cables ripping from their mounts. Flailing electric cables hissed with power as they plummeted down on top of me. The searing pain running through my body as it electrocuted the life out of me.

The image paused, right as the electricity hit me allowing the pain to linger. I could see myself lit up, forks of power cascading through my body, through my brain, leaving a Lichtenberg scar down my left side. It glowed blue before turning bright red. I'd not even noticed it before the doctor mentioned it. Smoke emanated from the soles of my shoes and drifted into the wind. Damn it, I'd need to get another pair. I hadn't even noticed that gummy feeling wasn't just my legs.

All I could think was how did they film this? How was it that they had this perfect vision of me in that situation? Furthermore, if they could see it was about to happen, why the hell didn't they stop it?

The image spun in front of me, singling out different aspects of my body, attaching markers to my fingers, to my brain, with long explanations I needed to process and work through. Initial extraction points, compounded ability potential, designation determination. The words swirled in my mind, threatening to overwhelm.

The whole time my body was filled with that first instant of electric shock.

Then the movie of my demise continued. Electricity spread through my body, activating what appeared to be a switch at the base of my brain stem. An infinite amount of possibilities ran through my mind as I watched just how I'd died, as I accepted the fact that I had to have died, because there was no other explanation for it.

The system does not make errors. Your cells and body were revitalized at 12:42:42. You have entered Second Chance.

A knock at the door startled me enough that whatever gravitational force had confined me to the bed let up, and I opened my eyes, able to blink the current vision away. Damn it. All I wanted to do was learn what it was I could do so I didn't accidentally, I don't know, fry my roommates. Unless this was a nightmare, in which case I'd like to wake up now.

Jacob stood outside my door, his head stuck in a book as usual, a purse to his lips. "Hey, are you okay?"

I looked up at him. He rarely came to check on me. So I lied through my teeth. "Sure I am. Why do you ask?"

He shrugged and raised his gaze to meet mine. "Just saw a video of an accident that happened around midday. The picture makes it look like you, or at least what you're wearing. I was worried."

He smiled, but I could still see the concern in his eyes. He'd promised my older brother he'd look out for me. Davin was out at the University of Pittsburgh, insisting he needed more space from our parents. He spoke with Jacob all the time, and they always got together in the summer.

Analysis complete. Target is not a member of the Second Chance program. Please limit contact or risk punishment.

Define fucking punishment, I thought at it, irritated.

Fucking punishment is not an option. Please rephrase inquiry.

I had to stop myself from speaking out loud. *Say what now? Define punishment.*

Incomplete parameters.

I managed to swallow my sigh, not wanting to worry Jacob more than he already was. *Define punishment within the bounds of the Second Chance program.*

The Second Chance program reserves the right to terminate your contract should you be found in breach of its TOC. This includes, but is not limited to, revealing the nature of the program, your missions, or the fact that you should be dead. Please read the TOC in full for more information.

I wasn't going to anyway. I grumbled at it before trying to soften my irritated expression.

"I'm good, Jacob. Thanks, though. It looked far worse than it was. Just had to go get checked out." I hope my smile seemed genuine and I shrugged into my jacket more hoping to conceal the scar.

I couldn't very well tell him that I was great after my brain restarted and plunged me straight into bizarro land. He'd have me over to the counseling office in no time flat.

"Okay, but let me know if you need anything. You might still be in shock." He reached forward and ruffled my hair. It wasn't my fault he was taller than me. Stupid genetics. He'd done that since I was about ten, so I couldn't really complain. "I have to head into work in a few. Will you be okay alone here tonight?"

I glanced at my watch, trying to brush off his concern. I wasn't that fragile, I just got electrocuted, that's all. But I didn't say that out loud. Instead, I began to wonder where Orion was. I usually knew what was going on, but today had been an odd day. "I'll be fine. Just going to lie down, probably sleep a bit."

I could dream, right? Jacob nodded and wandered back to the living area, leaving me to stand there watching him. People always seemed to salivate after the good-looking people. Jacob wasn't ugly, but he wasn't gorgeous. Soft brown hair with a hint of curl, amber brown eyes that sometimes looked gold in the sunlight. Just tall enough to annoy me at around six feet tall, yet short enough that he got irritated when he couldn't reach something.

Absentminded though he was, Jacob was a good guy. More beautiful than ninety percent of the world because of his heart.

My heart, on the other hand, had stopped today. Literally. With both of my roommates out of the house, now was the perfect time for me to figure out how it had started again, and just what I had to do to keep it that way. Because apparently the system's judgement was beyond reproach.

3
TUTORIAL

Resuming Tutorial

This information is vital to your participation in the Second Chance Program. It would be best to remain undisturbed.

The words weren't ominous in themselves, but their context, that the program was watching my every move. That was pretty bloody spooky. Since I was fairly sure now that I wasn't having a weird dream, this whole situation left me with an overwhelming sense of curiosity tempered by the fact that I hadn't asked to be brought back to life. Consent obviously wasn't its consideration.

I took a deep breath and figured I may as well get it over with. As if reading my thoughts, which it likely was, the tutorial began again, but this time it skipped over the accident, and went back to the diagram.

Fingers. Okay, I could live with that. I could activate electrical impulses through touch. At least theoretically. It would allow me to circumvent electrical locks, bypass computer protections, and basically disrupt anything that relied on either of those for monitoring and security.

Great. I was going to be a master thief. It felt a little anti-climactic, and I had to wonder if it was going to interfere with my IT career. I'd been fighting through my studies for over two years already. For this to halt my progress—that would piss me off.

As if to answer my disgruntled question, the next prompt showed how to control this power.

I had to will it to happen. No one ever wished for anything bad when they were feeling hot headed, did they now? This meant I was going to have to get a better handle on my temper, which my parents had been trying to get me to do for the last almost twenty-one years, so good luck on that, Second Chance Program.

Willing, and specifically focusing. I had to touch the object I needed to access and will the energy through my fingers to perform whatever action was needed. It felt so rudimentary, like it wasn't a special power at all, but a sort of stopgap measure. I guess getting electrocuted to death didn't make me a superhero. The disappointment was real.

Frowning, I motioned with my mind, if that's even a thing, for more information. But the next section had a lock hanging over it, like I needed to go and learn how to use what it had taught me first before it would allow me to access other tutorials for my more advanced abilities. Pay to play in my head. Fantastic.

Here I was going to college and having courses about electricity manipulation in my head at the same time. Unlocking new chapters felt like I had to study. What if I accidentally triggered something they hadn't taught me yet? Brilliant idea, right?

I sighed and gave in to reviewing the information available to me. If I concentrated, I could turn the image around and view my body from all different angles, visualize the flow of power as it accumulated in my fingertips. I frowned. While technically it made sense, there seemed to be other avenues that it could travel, other ways for me to expel that force. Didn't the human body run on electricity? A minuscule amount, at any rate. I wasn't an electrical engineer or pre-med student though, so my thoughts on the matter were purely speculative.

The electricity in the human body might only be low voltage and small, but that didn't negate the fact that neurons and synapse function relied on the element. Surely that gave rise to far more fascinating things than had been in the tutorial so far.

Skill acquired: Rudimentary Electrical Pulse Control

Still. I couldn't help feeling underwhelmed at the whole idea. This computer in my head acted like it knew everything, yet this whole Second Chance thing was decidedly duller than anticipated. Electricity ran everything. Whether it was solar powered, wind or water powered, or even coal… electricity was life. Now it had effectively saved mine. Food for brain thought.

Saving the world from itself. What a crock of crap.

Second Chance Terms of Service Accepted. Please direct any inquiries in specific terms.

I raised an eyebrow and opened my eyes, the words now hazier, but still present. Specific terms, eh? Apart from asking it what the hell type of practical joke it thought it was, I did actually have questions about mechanics and development.

"Do the powers increase? Or is this all they are?"

Please rephrase the inquiry.

Rolling my eyes wasn't going to work against whatever this was, but oh how I wanted it to. "Is this all there is to my powers?"

In order to prevent fatal errors, SC has determined that starting with basic releases of power is the best course of action. Some abilities, when used before control has been gained, can burn their host from the inside out.

Well, I guess I was lucky the system was on my side. It wasn't exactly something I'd thought of in my few hours of a second life.

"Thanks," I said awkwardly, not really expecting a response but not sure of what else to say.

Silence followed, and I thought it best to get up so I could rummage around the kitchen before I gave in and made ramen to appease my grumbling stomach. Whatever anyone else said, apparently dying made me really hungry.

You are welcome.

Somehow the voice in my head, the words in front of my eyes, they sounded hesitant. Like the program wasn't sure what to make of someone thanking it. I didn't respond further—it wasn't necessary—but since this whole thing started, it was the first moment I thought things might turn out okay.

The kitchen was clean, again. Jacob often got into bouts of insomnia and spent all of his time cleaning. I wished I could say the same for Orion, and yet cleanliness wasn't in the top of my criteria for being a best friend. Being there to talk to was, and right now I couldn't even share anything with Orion, so it was better for him not to be here.

Peanut butter and jelly for a very late lunch. Good ole PB&J. It was my go-to, along with a small, elementary school lunch-box-sized gala apple that I could get for a whopping fifty cents each. Dinner would be the ramen stacked in my room that I got on sale when Jacob's parents took us all to the local bulk order store. Their use by date was well into the future, although now that I'd died, I did wonder if anything could kill me.

You can technically die again. Be cautious.

Gee, thanks, system.

Second Chance doesn't provide invulnerability. It might take more to kill you, but you can still die.

I bent my knee and straightened it again, noticing that the scrape I got on the way can home was non-existent now. At least insofar as feeling it went. I hadn't had the courage to look yet. That was a better explanation than I'd had for most of anything since entering this, second state of my life. So I smiled, sending thanking thoughts. Perhaps it was a machine, a computer, a chip, or I was losing my shit, but either way, it seemed to react well to being treated with respect. That and it appeared we were quite literally stuck together.

PB&Js should have some sort of award. The way it mingles in my mouth, triggering saliva and generally making me a happy person for a few moments. Usually that small glee lasts a lot longer, but not every day involves death, learning you have powers, and then the words: *FIRST ASSIGNMENT* flashing across your eyes.

What the—

Location: Heavenly Dough on the corner of West and Main.

Objective: This task must be performed without being noticed before, during, or after. Do not disturb anything unnecessarily. You will be required to utilize your abilities for the first time. Leave the target object in your apartment mailbox once you are done.

Target: Retrieve a file from the office marked "Accounts Receivable: Dionce"

Time Limit: 7:30pm today.

Reward: Progression experience. Monetary compensation. Both of these are dependent on the quality of performance.

My thoughts rushed through my head so fast it was hard to grab hold of one. The most astonishing thing to me was: wait, what? Why the fuck was I breaking into a bakery? Then I focused on the fact that I might get paid for this. So while I had to keep up appearances in my normal life, I'd be getting paid for my work in the program. Or maybe I'd gain Second Chance coins I could save and use to unlock abilities.

Sometimes sarcasm was my only friend.

Stealing a file sounded far more like petty theft, and less like: oh hi, you have superpowers. Make sure you pursue a life of crime. It made even less sense to be stealing something from a bakery.

Assignments are allocated based on the skills required to perform them. The lock will require that you unlock it using your abilities. It is an initial test of your control. This task must be completed, not questioned.

What, so I have to make sure the dough rises? But the system gave me no response. Obviously it didn't have a sense of humor. I guess that told me. I didn't thank the system this time but glanced at my phone to see what time it was. Didn't the program know anything about me? Don't tell me not to do something; it's paramount to egging me on to do that exact thing.

It was already four o'clock in the afternoon. Damn it. If I didn't want to fail my first task, I was going to have to leave shortly. Just to make sure I made it with plenty of time to spare. Being late to anything was one of my pet peeves.

In the back of my mind I couldn't help thinking this was a test. A test of what, I had no idea. How this file was going to save humanity from itself and other threats wasn't obvious in any way either. If I could do this, they'd let me stay in the program, they'd let me live.

No, that wasn't creepy at all.

It also didn't make any sense. I finished shoving the sandwich into my mouth, not taking the time to enjoy the texture or taste. Next I grabbed a damned light jacket. It was only going to get colder between the concrete buildings, and the dip in temperature that accompanied the close onset of spring in the evening. It was light weight, and yet zipped up into a black hoodie. The extra paneling on the outside would help me stay warm and hopefully incognito. Although, depending on how badly I did, it could yield the opposite results. Still, I didn't have another option.

My phone was at fifty percent battery, which gave me a good few hours even if I practiced my nervous habit of surfing on it all the way to my destination. I needed to keep my fingers busy. Maybe the program knew that; perhaps that's why it made them the channeling source for my ability, skill, whatever.

I had no clue, and if the system could hear my inner monologue it wasn't giving me any signs of it. It left me alone. With my thoughts. Running rampant through my mind.

Fantastic.

Grabbing my wallet, I pulled the zipper up on my jacket and shoved my hands into my pockets. No, I didn't look suspicious at all. Maybe the system was ignoring me because of the constant sarcasm in my head.

Closing my door, I headed out into the living area, checking myself for the keys. How I wished I could have coded entry like I knew some of the newer apartment complexes had. Still, I loved the charm of this old brick townhome. Just as I was reaching for the door, it opened toward me.

I had a moment of panic, of complete surety that I was about to get robbed, that I was here at the wrong time. My fingers crackled, and I glanced down at them, shocked to see tiny remnants of what appeared to be mini lightning strikes coating them.

I had to clench my fingers into fists when I realized that it wasn't a robber—it was Orion.

He glanced up at me, surprise on his face. His almost black hair fell forward from the sides of his head where I knew he'd pushed it impatiently behind his ears. "Aren't you usually at the library?"

"Yeah." I didn't know what to say. He sounded so concerned, and I was drawing a blank. Then I remembered Jacob's worry. Clutching to it like a lifeline, I forced a smile. "Had a bit of an accident, but they took me to the hospital and had me checked out, so I'm okay. Hungry though, so I'm off to grab some food."

Orion raised an eyebrow, and I could see the cogs whirring in his brain. Knowing my luck, I probably had the remnants of that damned PB&J on my face. Or else, he'd known me since I could remember and knew my budgetary requirements were definitely on a par with his. He also knew about my ramen stash, because he had an almost identical one. Eating out just wasn't my thing. It was a luxury I wouldn't usually afford.

Well done with the thinking on my feet there, self.

"Are you sure you're okay?" His voice was softer than usual. Lulling with the concern that was so real it was poignant. "You seem pale. You should sit down. I can order us something in."

"No. It's okay." The words almost choked me, because I realized as he asked that question, I was anything but okay. There was nothing right then that I didn't want more than to sit down with him and feel safe. But I couldn't tell him, I couldn't tell anyone. So I forced another smile. "It's just been one of those days, you know? I think I deserve a treat."

His eyes lit up, like he understood that sentiment, and he probably did, because I knew he'd had a good few of those days himself. Always there for me, like I tried to be for him. One of the most selfless people I knew, as he demonstrated with his next words. "If you wait a few minutes, I'll come with you."

It took all my strength to deny him, all my strength to force myself to make hurt appear in those blue eyes. From the reflection of our entire history together, to the intelligence in them. "I kind of just want to be alone right now. Lots of mortality shit taking up my mind. But can we hang when I get back?"

I desperately wanted that pain to go away, wanted to make sure he realized I wasn't just blowing him off. That I'd rather sit down and goof off discussing our days and the latest fads we'd grown too old for.

He nodded, even though his expression was more wary than usual. I knew he'd come around eventually. He just had to.

"Sure thing. Just be careful out there. No more accidents. Stay sharp out there."

"Like a knife." I said, pushing my way out of the apartment before I could change my mind. *No more accidents* was my fucking middle name from now on.

FIRST

I'm not sure why I still felt chilly as I stepped out onto the street. With my jacket pulled tightly around me, it should have warded off most of it. While it wasn't quite spring yet, the days weren't cold as such. Perhaps the shadows exacerbated the fact that I hate the cold. Or that whole death thing. Give me sunshine any day of the week. Cold and dreary made me want to sleep and never wake up. And today there seemed to be shadows at every corner.

Even those thoughts felt too close to home, and I glanced at the cheap step counter my older brother, Davin, had gotten me for Christmas. It did the job, even had an app thing it could hook to on my phone, but it wasn't working. Hell, I think I was lucky my phone was working after being hit by that much electricity.

I still had a few hours before the deadline, but the sense of urgency I felt tried to choke me. Heavenly Dough was one of the best bakeries in town. In the afternoons it swapped over to shepherd pies, casseroles, stews, and other amazing food for those who didn't have time to cook or had stayed late at work. It was perilously close to the areas that gentrification wasn't quite brave enough to tackle yet. Of course, it wasn't as bad as the open air drug market up in

Kensington, but you could still mostly tell where the boundary lines were drawn.

It was a good twenty-minute walk north, and right then I didn't feel like taking anything powered by electricity. Call me paranoid, but I thought I'd avoid subways and cable cars for a while lest some random power surges derailed them.

My fingers crackled at the thought, and I hugged my arms around my chest, wishing my jeans were warmer and that I'd chosen a winter jacket instead of my hoodie. Maybe the cold seeping through to me was a remnant of death.

I was more than half way to the bakery before I realized the one big flaw in my rushed exit. I didn't bring a backpack, so this file folder thing, which sounded very papery and not as digital as I'd expected, was going to have to fit under my jacket. Maybe I could stuff it in the waistband of my jeans. Next time, if I made it through this time, I'd have to brain more.

Still though, this task, mission, whatever it was, bothered me. Maybe the system would react to a direct question.

What's so important about this file?

Nothing. Impatience was one of my strongest traits. I could be stubborn along with the best of them.

Why do I have to steal something?

It was probably my imagination, but it felt like the system sighed. *SC requires that you obtain this file. You must not take anything else. Retrieve this file and do not be discovered. It's a simple task.*

I took the fact that it answered as a win, and didn't ask anything else. I could feel lines underneath my skin as they crackled with pent up energy, and focused on those instead.

Evening rush time was no joke at Heavenly. I could see the crush of bodies from outside. Luckily, it was far enough from my house that I wasn't a regular. Popping into the crowded small bakery at rush hour was more distracting than I thought it would be. There had to be at least thirty people crowding the tiny space in front of the service counter, and easily half that again wedged into the small tables lining the opposite wall. Definitely more than the partially hidden fire code sign on the wall suggested should be allowed.

There were undoubtedly more than forty-eight people in here.

How did they enforce that sort of shit anyway?

I'd never been stealthy. Maybe it was because I hadn't had a reason. However, as a track athlete I was light on my feet. So, I slipped through the throng of people muttering apologies as I made my way to the counter to grab a number. No one blinked an eye as I did. It was how the system worked, and right now it was working for me.

Being way back in the service numbers meant that no one took any notice of me as I made my way to the bathroom. My breath hitched as I walked past the single stall restrooms. A faint hint of artificial citrus wafted out as I did.

I steeled myself and walked as purposefully as possible toward the employee only area just beyond the restrooms. My heart beat faster than ever, my palms sweaty, and I belatedly wondered if they'd dust for prints.

A split second before I reached for the handle, I pulled my hoodie's sleeve over my hand. Couldn't leave anything incriminating behind. That was in the Terms of Service. Don't let anyone else know about second chance. My breath caught again, and it was difficult to breathe. My skin tingled like the branches of my Lichtenberg were extending their tendrils and threatening to strangle me.

Through the door, there was a round table with several cheap plastic chairs. On the right wall a well-stocked set of shelves with buckets and cleaning supplies took up most of the space. On closer inspection they were green cleaning supplies. It made me like the place even more. Damn it. I couldn't afford emotions right now.

Ahead, on the far wall, was a door marked *Office*. Trying to keep the time in mind I headed toward it, purposefully, like I belonged there. In the busiest hour of the bakery's day, it was unlikely anyone would come back here. Still, it was better to be safe than dead. Again.

The door knob didn't turn in my jacket-covered hand. I frowned. Of course it would be locked. What had I been thinking? My fingers sparked and I withdrew my hand hurriedly.

Only then did I notice the flat stainless steel panel to the side of the door. I had the sneaking suspicion that touching it was not a good idea. *Is that a print reader?*

It took a moment, but the system replied. *Yes. Best to circumvent it.*

But it didn't give me any specifics, nor did it try to give me advice. In all honestly I was relieved it didn't have a finger hidden somewhere in this room for me to use. Which meant it wanted me to use my ability.

I waited for a moment after the thought, but either it wasn't there, or it was ignoring my statement of the obvious. What's the worst that could happen anyway? I hadn't stolen anything. I could say I got turned around trying to find the bathroom.

I placed my thumb against the sliver of wall between the panel and the door, breathing deeply as I did so. Electricity, right? Just a small shock should do it. Not that I knew how to do more than handle this power theoretically.

My first attempt yielded a spectacular nothing. Just a tiny spark that would have been lucky to statically shock someone. My nerves made my hands clammy. Best not to have damp hands while conducting this stuff.

So, I tried again. This time I tried to imagine a trickle of electricity filtering through into the wiring in the minuscule space between the wall and the panel. The tendril of power that flickered out from my pointer finger wasn't exactly small. I jumped back as it escaped my body, or maybe I was pushed back a bit by the force—I really had no idea.

But it did the trick, and I could hear the lock of the door click.

Successful execution of: Rudimentary Electrical Pulse Control
You have gained field experience.

I didn't have time to figure that out. Without giving it any further thought, I twisted the handle and entered the office.

The fluorescent lights inside the room were blinding and it took a while for my eyes to adjust. Once they did, I felt somewhat let down. The room was tiny, like it was the cleaning supplies closet before being turned into an office. The desk only just fit with about two feet to one side. Filing cabinets lined the back wall, haphazard drawers half open and closed. Nothing seemed locked.

I took a deep breath and moved to the back, careful not to upset anything on the desk. The filing cabinets were old fashioned grey metal and had letters on them. I search for Dionce, but my joy in finding the drawer containing the Ds disappeared as I heard a door creak.

Fuck.

I whirled around and watched the office door, frantically trying to figure out somewhere to hide. There were no windows, so there was no escape. My well thought out plans came back to bite me. I was so sure this was the way to go.

Think, damn it, think.

I ducked behind the desk. I was barely flexible enough to curl up into the tiny hole in front of the chair. It was cramped as hell, but I could sit there and wait. It's all I could do. Could I go to jail for breaking in here? Surely not, right?

This time the creak was slightly closer, and I realized it wasn't the doors, because the door didn't creak when I opened it. It was probably the person's shoes. My heart sat right in my mouth, like it though it a better cavity than my chest.

I heard whoever it was move. They cursed softly under their breath. Though that might have been my wishful thinking, because I wanted to curse so badly. They were flipping through the small shelf almost directly behind the door if my hearing directionality was correct.

I couldn't hear their shoes creak again, but a shadow flickered in my peripheral vision, edging off to the side. No matter what I did, my eyes couldn't focus on it. The muttering continued and wasn't in sync with the movement I couldn't quite see. The chill that crawled down my throat threatened to choke me. My imagination had been running wild since I'd died.

Finally, the sound of paper crumpling reached my ears, and the person at the shelves made an exasperated tsking noise. They exited the room, shutting the door loudly behind them. The shadows fled in their wake.

Taking a deep breath, I counted to ten before moving. I half expected the person to have lulled me into a trap and to be standing there, but they weren't. Not wasting any time, I dove into the draw marked D. Dionce, Dionce...

Found it. The file appeared to be thicker than anticipated and I didn't have time to go through it. They wanted the file with that name, I guess that meant that Second Chance got the file with that name. I reached in and grabbed the file.

A grating noise almost made me shit my pants. It wasn't that loud, only unexpected. But not nearly as surprising as the cabinets pulling in on themselves like a Babushka doll. The wall behind it rose up into the ceiling, its tatty appearance making way for a solid steel door set in dark red brick.

Alrighty then.

I shoved the thick file into the waistband of my pants. Obviously it was some sort of key. Did they mean me to find this entrance?

Do not give away the existence of Second Chance.

The system whispered the words into my head, because I might have forgotten them in the last thirty or so minutes. I rolled my eyes. Surely it wasn't giving away SC if I just took a peek right? I mean, there was a door there, and doors are there for opening.

Nerves firing brightly, I was scared to look at my hand. And yet as I reached for the panel at the side of the door, the same type of panel that I cracked on the office door, I could see lines of white and pale blue flashing under my skin, escaping from my fingertips. Almost like the electricity inside me was alive and excited all on its own.

Since SC remained quiet in my head, I simply assumed I was okay to look. Surely it would warn me if not. I took the lack of response as agreement and focused on releasing the electrical charge. Convincing this massive door that I had the right fingerprint was somehow much more impressive than the entry to the office.

Sparks jumped, sliding into the minuscule crack with eager abandon. My fingers tingled as the light above the door flashed green, and swung inwards.

It opened onto a metal staircase, and I took a few steps in. I stood at the top of the railing looking down on long metal walkway. Other paths branched off it, going to places I couldn't quite see. I glanced behind me and noticed the door had a print pad on this side too. Surely I had a bit of time to look around?

Taking a deep breath, I began to descend the stairs as quietly as I could, arriving at the next platform, which brought me about ten feet closer to the activity below. I could make out cages. No, not cages. Like thick plastic or glass soldered together with steel. They receded into the walls at the end of the walkways that branched off the main thoroughfare. While I could just make out people and clipboards, I couldn't quite see what was in those containers.

A soft crescendo of beeps filtered up to me, as if medical monitors were everywhere. Maybe one more platform down would tell me more without giving away my presence. Although, what would they do if they found me? And who the hell were they?

Be cautious.

And it fell silent again. Thanks SC old buddy, old pal. Curiosity won me over though. This was far too surreal. Surely I was imagining shit. Death, it seemed, had gifted me with a need to know more.

Only two more descents stood between myself and the bottom level. Anxiety crept up, yelling at me inside my head. Didn't I know I'd probably be killed if I was discovered? What if they were cooking meth down here? I wouldn't know until I was too high to act.

But what if they weren't? I crouched down low on my new platform, watching everything I could. The people down there wore lab coats. The few I could see had devices set over their eyes. I'd think they were night vision goggles, but they looked even heavier and somehow far more complex.

What I'd taken for soft music, startled me when it turned into a loud screech that echoed up through the opening, before returning to the soft and whimpering moan. The more I studied them, the more they appeared mechanical in movement, like they'd been programmed to behave in a certain way.

Almost like it heard my thoughts, one of them looked straight up at where I crouched. It took every semblance of control I possessed not to move, to let the dark colors I wore blend me into the background.

The shadows up here in the metal stairway began to gather around me, like they were moving of their own accord. I counted to ten, but they kept getting closer. Finally the person looking at me looked back down at what they were doing, and their mechanical movements began again.

However, my shadows didn't give in. They stalked me, sticking to the solid surfaces and not the stairs themselves. I took a gamble and ran. Taking the steps two at a time, as softly as I could, I dashed up the two flights of stairs only to come face to face with a closed steel door. Without thinking, I pointed at the finger print pad and released a burst of energy in desperation. The door swung toward me so fast, it almost hit me. But I didn't care.

I dived through it and back into the bakery's excuse for an office, clutching the folder against my abdomen as the door swung shut.

A shadowy tendril got stuck between the metal and the brick, falling to the ground in a clump of noise I hadn't expected. For a brief second I glimpsed a flash of metal through the dissipating gloom before the file cabinets slipped back into place.

ONE DOWN

Successful execution of: Rudimentary Electrical Pulse Control
You have gained field experience.
You have increased your skill to: General Electrical Pulse Control

Great, that was good to know. I took stock of myself, calmed my breathing down, and tried to regulate my heart rate. My mom always did that to prevent panic attacks, and I'd grown up knowing how to calm myself down. Not that I thought she'd ever imagined I'd be calming myself down from… whatever that was.

Speaking of which. After another deep breath I angled a thought at SC. *What the hell was that down there?*

Crickets. I glowered and focused on getting myself out of that room instead of dealing with the system. It gave me the distinct impression that everything was currently on a need to know basis.

I approached the office door counting to three in my head. A sense of urgency yelled at me to move faster, but that would only lead to unnecessary mistakes. I twisted the knob with my covered hand, relieved that office didn't require me to cheat my way out of it. No one was in the staff room. At least that was some luck.

I decided to lower the hoodie since usually that made it seem more suspicious. Brown hair wasn't exactly noteworthy. Dark jeans and my layered hoodie weren't overly descriptive.

It's a pity electricity couldn't make me invisible, at least not without shorting the wiring and plummeting the shop into darkness. So far I'd broken into dog knew what with my new fangled superpower. Wait. Did that make me a super villain?

I got out of the room as fast as I could.

The noise from the front of the shop hadn't lessened even slightly. By my calculations, and by the few numbers it appeared had been called since I went in there, it had only been about ten minutes. Yet, they seemed like some of the longest moments of my life.

Some of the longest, most adrenaline pumped moments.

And it was still coursing through my veins.

I was starving. I looked longingly at the food behind the counter. With three dollars in my wallet, I wasn't exactly rolling in it, but I was sure I could afford a small something. Fuck it. I deserved this.

My number was three away. Even as nervous as I was, as loud as the oh my hell what the crap voice was trying to be in my mind, the sheer excitement drowned it out. Right now, it felt like I could do anything, and my ability egged me on. Like it was telling me to use it, to fling it out.

Be cautious of giving into your power. Pull it back.

I blinked, and the server called out number forty-one. SC was right, I guess. Even though I tried to quell it, a small part of me didn't want to. That portion of my brain rebelled against my common sense. It wanted to release my power, to see what I could really do. To be honest, so did I. But maybe not in a crowded bakery that doubled as a hideout for whatever the fuck was beneath it.

I took my turn at the counter and grabbed a cheddar bagel. Doughy and cheesy. Exactly the carb fix I needed to soak up that excess buzz.

As I stepped outside the bakery, the wind tousled my hair, and the smell of freshly cooked goods drifted out with me.

A dark spot flickered in front of my vision briefly, causing me to take a step backward. Maybe it was a fly or bug, but it had seemed larger. I turned to look at it, but it disappeared. What had those shadows been downstairs. Or else, what had they pretended to be. Because I was pretty sure there was something mechanical under them.

Instead, I turned my attention to Heavenly Dough's security? What the crap was up with the filing cabinet. Come to think of it, what was in that file. I munched on my bagel as I attempted to resist taking it out and checking. The system hadn't expressly told me not to look at it now, had it?

But the file felt heavy against my shirt, like a weight I might have to bear.

Maybe I should go to the hospital and talk to Dr. Caroline again. That would be nice, but she had basically said to only visit as a last resort.

If I was supposed to die, shouldn't I be dead?

Those were some big heavy thoughts right there.

My feet automatically led me home. I was just over halfway through the third year of my degree. I'd lived here for a long time, and it really had become home. The soft yellow light that only sort of illuminated the entryway through the half glass door felt welcoming and cozy as I walked up the seven steps to unlock it. The yellowing walls weren't helped by the partial lack of light either.

Three letterboxes hung loosely on the wall. No matter what the landlord did, no matter how many times he moved them or tried to tighten their hold, the old house seemed to prefer leaving them jangling just that bit.

I pulled out the folder, feeling sick to my stomach. Was a file really such a huge cost to exchange for my life? My inner conscience helpfully supplied the answer: that depends what they do with the information. Had it wanted me to see that underground facility? The wall didn't move until I pulled this specific file. So many damned questions. I needed time to sort through them.

I took a deep breath and flicked open the front cover. Frowning, I flipped through the first few pages. Whatever this was, it was in a language I couldn't understand. All that did was make me curiouser.

Opening the mailbox, I retrieved the mail for our little unit only to find a manila envelope in there as well. Just the right size to fit the damned folder into. May as well be useful and give no one else a chance to see that I was putting something else in there. I mean, this was the task right?

I didn't even want to think about who had come to drop this envelope off. It was all I could do not to look around and see if I could find them. Shoving my stolen goods into their pale tomb, I slammed the mailbox shut and glared at it, holding our mail in my hands so hard I began to crease it.

Objective Complete. First mission accomplished. Process and analyze what you learned while completing it.

Gee. Homework too. Great. I sort of just stared at the now-closed mailbox with our letters clutched in my hands.

"What did the mailbox do to you this time?" Orion stood on the stairs, looking down at me, a lopsided grin on his face. His dark brown hair dangled loosely, and he reached up absent-mindedly to push it behind his ears again.

Thinking quickly was usually my thing, but I never really lied. Lies were pretty much my pet hate. "It delivered us bills."

I held them up as if to prove my point, but more so I was doing something, anything.

He raised an eyebrow at me as I began to climb the stairs up to him. One of those I'd come to know over the years that meant he didn't really believe me, but that it was okay for now. "Damned bills. How much better would life be if we didn't have any of those?"

Guilt boiled in the bottom of my gut and I forced a smile at him. "I don't know. I gave up living in fairy tales when I was a kid."

Orion eyed me skeptically. "Bullshit. You never liked them then either."

I had to laugh. He had a knack to call me on my crap. "Good point. Guess I never believed in the make believe after all."

"That's kind of sad." His tone took me by surprise, as did the thoughtfulness in the words. If I didn't know better, I'd say he had robot eyes with the way they gleamed even in the low light of the stairwell.

"Well, I'm not sad." There, I lied, and it tasted like bile.

He smirked at me. "Pull the other one. I know you better than that. Are you really okay after the accident?"

I hesitated, which probably sealed my doom, because Orion knew me better than I knew myself sometimes. "I'll be okay."

And I wasn't sure if I was trying to convince him or myself.

The next morning took its damn time arriving. I barely slept. Every time I thought I was about to doze off, the sensation of electricity rushing through me jolted me awake. Or else, robots clad in shadows reached for me just before I woke up.

At five-thirty, I stood up, about ten minutes before my alarm. I had to be at the track by six thirty, may as well get up a few minutes before I usually would.

Stumbling into the bathroom, I rubbed my scarred shoulder. The contact with my other hand made all of the veins tingle. For a split second the reflection in the mirror made it seem like my Lichtenberg was on fire, but it was gone as soon as I blinked. I really needed more sleep.

How I was going to make it around the damned track today, I had no idea. My teeth felt gritty, and I couldn't remember if I'd brushed them before bed, so I attacked them with what little energy I felt, blinking blearily at the mirror.

Glasses. I'd left my glasses in the damned bedroom, and my eyes felt too itchy and clogged to risk putting in my contacts. Stupid eyesight. Couldn't have had death fix that in the process.

Death doesn't cure what ailed you in life. Second Chance allows you to live. Not to become immortal.

Fine. Be completely and utterly analytical. I wasn't entirely sure, but it seemed like the system in my head had gained a bit of attitude.

Your first task is marked as completed. You will receive compensation directly into your bank account.

I got paid? It was weird directing a thought at a part of my brain. But I knew speaking out loud to myself wasn't going to go down well.

The TOS you agreed to stated as much. You will gain experience in order to move up to higher ranks within the organization, and you will be compensated.

Maybe that made up for the crazy shit from last night. But it sure as hell didn't quite my curiosity. Frankly, it just fed it. I shut my jaw, realizing belatedly that I'd been staring at myself in the mirror. Well, sort of past myself really. I finished brushing my teeth, mulling over the information in my mind, and tried desperately to wake up properly.

"Uh. Dare?"

Orion stood at the threshold of the bathroom, entirely awake, and focused completely on my left side.

Shit. I should have thought of that since I usually slept in tank top or shirts. I'd kept it covered yesterday.

My thoughts converged, rushing to give information that sounded plausible. "The accident yesterday involved a bit of electricity."

My best friend frowned and took a couple of steps closer. It wasn't like the bathroom was large, and feeling his breath so close made it seem like he could see all my secrets. His fingers traced down my scar, lighting me up with electricity again, making it thrum through each little tendril.

"You don't get these from a *little* bit of electricity." His tone was soft, filled with worry for me, but was edged with steel. If only he knew.

"Yeah, I know." It was difficult to force a smile. Orion had enough shit to worry about. He didn't need to add me to the list. "I'm good though. Heading out to practice."

"Sure you're up for it?" He glanced over the scar again, a frown tugging at his lips. "I'm sure Coach Marth would let you off the hook. One look at that scar, and you won't even need a doctor's note."

He was right of course. Coach Marth told it like it was when you needed to hear it, but he was also the first to advocate self care, and I knew what he'd do with this. "I'm fine. The fresh morning air will help."

The frown stayed on Orion's face though. "I don't think it's wise to push yourself. That's a mega shit ton of electricity if it gave you a Lichtenberg."

He wasn't about to let it go, so I scowled. The urge to use the electricity inside me seemed to grow when I got irritated or scared. It flared with emotion. Fantastic. "I don't want to be late, and I'll be fine."

"Whatever you say." Orion shrugged and crossed his arms, but I could tell he was irritated with me. "Now hurry up. I need to brush my teeth too."

I laughed, finally awake enough to go over the words I'd spoken already. Nothing I'd said should have given anything away.

"Yeah, you really have stank breath," I teased as I stepped out of the room.

My only answer was him slamming the door behind me.

Face washed, clean clothes on, I walked into the kitchen to grab some peanut butter on toast. Fantastic meal that one. Protein was key. I'd be warmed up by the time I got to the track, because there was no way I was taking the trolley. Checking my backpack, I threw my tablet inside—thanking my stars I'd not had it on me yesterday—and made sure my digital pen was in with it. Everything, including text books, was on there. This tablet thing made it possible for me to run with a backpack on and not break my back.

I sorted through the terms I'd agreed to in my head while I ran. Slow at first so as to warm up in the chilly, almost spring air. The normal scents of Philly assaulted my senses. Gas exhaust, cheap weed, and piss lingered underneath the damp of the morning breeze. As far as I'd understood, I was to maintain my lifestyle as it had been before my afterlife began. Easier said than done. There was no way I could keep the scar hidden. The fractal patterns looked gorgeous, but damned if I couldn't remember the searing pain before the nothingness.

Jogging in the city was quite common, and other pedestrians automatically parted ways so I could keep going. Not that there were many people around just after six in the morning.

Do you have any questions?

The sound of the system's voice took me by surprise. I wonder if it was really speaking to me or if I'd supplied my own version of it speaking the words my head sees. *Are you really speaking, or am I just reading?*

A bit of both.

Fantastic answer. Still, it was good to know it wasn't all in my...well, I guess it *was* all in my head. I glanced down at my empty wrist and grunted in frustration. My step counter was gone. I'd taken it off last night because it was fried, but damn if I hadn't gotten used to it in the last few months.

Yes, I had questions for Second Chance, but that could wait until I'd navigated the city streets and gotten to my destination in one piece.

I do, but I have to figure out how to ask them.

It paused for a moment before replying. *Very well.*

The athletics fields and arenas were on the outskirts of the university's grounds, near the Schuykill River. I pushed myself more than I usually would have, or I'd not have made it on time. Considering I got to the locker room with only five minutes to spare, I needed to get my shit together, or else wake up earlier.

I'd warmed up enough to take my jacket off, although the cool air tickled at the hairs on my arms, taunting me with goose bumps. My endorphins laughed at nature's attempts to make me cover up. Complete with training pants and a school t-shirt that incidentally revealed less of my scar than a tank would have, I made sure my shoes were tied and headed out to see the coach and the rest of my team.

It was the only way I could afford to go to this school. Full athletic scholarship. Long distance specialist. Anything under one thousand meters, and I sucked. Make me run a few miles though, and I was in seventh heaven.

The best thing about running though? Freeing my mind. Letting everything else around me melt away. No thoughts of electrocution. No thoughts of money troubles. And no worries about turning into a thief in the night.

My first class on a Monday didn't start until nine. Which left me extra time for running around in circles. I could feel the coach's eyes on me, like he was trying to read my mind. Well, I had news for him. I already had a friend in my head, talking to me whether I liked it or not.

You seem uncomfortable.

No shit, I shot back at the intrusive bloody system.

Are none of my thoughts my own?

Sometimes you are quiet, other times you are loud. I read the volume. If I can't hear you, I do not respond.

Odd. Sometimes it spoke like it was an individual instead of a program. No time like the present to figure out what I'd actually gotten myself in for.

Is the assignment I went on last night typical of tasks I'll be given? There we go, let's see where this got me.

After a short pause, the system piped up, but this time it was more formal, and less concerned. Maybe there were two sides to it.

At Junior Rank, yes. You will be given trivial tasks that may or may not require your abilities.

Wait. How was that a trivial task last night? I mean… I ran the words over in my mind, deliberately choosing them. *How was that weird science lab thing behind that hidden door, trivial?*

Not to mention running from what appeared to be a programmed shadow. But I waited for an answer instead of adding to my initial question.

You retrieved the necessarily file. As long as you weren't observed, you were successful.

Did it just avoid my question? *Did you intend for me to find that door?*

The object of these tasks is to test your aptitude and put you on the correct path for your specific gifts.

Apparently it wasn't about to give me a straight answer. Stupid thought activated system. Why couldn't I talk to a real person? Correct path? Well, that sounded ominous. *Isn't my aptitude with electricity?*

Yes. Your skill is based on the cause of your death. As you were electrocuted, you have an affinity to that element. However, if you cannot act in a stealthy manner, or make split second decisions, how is your ability to enhance or control electricity of any use?

I'm not sure if the question was rhetorical, but it made sense to me, so I didn't reply. The steady beat of my feet against the rubber-like track beneath me timed like a metronome. It helped the thoughts tick steadily through my head as if they were musical notes.

This is like basic training then? Was all I could come up with, despite the synchronicity my body currently felt. At least the electricity hadn't interfered with that.

Yes. Junior rank does one of two things. You either pass your tests and move onto the next level, or else you fail them, and your TOS is terminated.

A chill that had nothing to do with the early morning swept through me. At the far end of the field a breeze picked up, whipping some errant leaves left over from autumn into a frenzy. Shapes like shadows danced on the wind, at once there and then gone. I shook my head and focused on what SC had said to me. They didn't seem to mind culling their herd if the system had miscalculated and pulled the wrong person into the program.

The Second Chance program does not make mistakes.

Again with the eavesdropping. *Thanks.*

I didn't want to talk to it anymore and tried to direct my thoughts inward to avoid alerting its presence. Maybe it caught on, or maybe I was successful. I wasn't sure at all. But it was almost eight-thirty, and I'd been running for over two hours if I counted the run to the school.

Coach Marth walked out to meet me as I slowed down. He threw me a towel and crossed his arms. What was it with people taking that stance around me today?

"You looked calm out there. Steady paced. Solid. A few weeks to go until State. Are you ready?" There was something else he wasn't asking, because the most important questions came first.

I grinned. "Of course I'm ready." I was proud of my resistance. *Born ready* just sounded so presumptuous.

He smiled. "Good. Now are you going to tell me why you either got a very convincing tattoo, or why you have a Lichtenberg scar on your left arm?"

Yeah, there it was. The other shoe. I didn't think I'd favored my left side, but I could be wrong. Still he wouldn't have said I looked solid if I hadn't. So it must just be that he wanted to know where the scar came from. "Was in an accident yesterday. Got lucky."

"You were in an accident and all you got was that scar, eh? No injury. No hospital stay. Just jumped straight to a scar then?" His tone sounded skeptical, and I couldn't blame him. "Does it hurt?"

I shrugged. "It stings a bit, aches every now and again. Nothing I can't handle."

Hell, I'd run with blisters before. This was nothing. With every word I spoke or action I took, I wondered if the system was watching. How many agents did it have and how much multitasking did it have to do?

"Did you get it checked out?"

Ah, now I got it. He was worried that I hadn't gone to a doctor and got a release. That it might impact my ability to perform at the State championships. "I'm good to go, coach. Don't worry. Got checked out at the hospital and everything."

The relief he felt spread across his face. "Good. Can't have my number one runner down for the count. Need to get you to Nationals again. You were robbed last year."

I laughed, because he was right. No one was tripping me this year. Fuck that shit. I'd been naïve in my sophomore year. Now I was a junior, and I wasn't taking shit from anyone. "We've got this, coach."

And I headed into the locker room before he could keep chatting to me. Right now I only had about twenty minutes to shower quickly and then make it to my class on time. At least Ethics and Internet Data would let me relax a bit.

The hot water was divine. I don't know how people had lukewarm showers, or even cold ones. Hot was where it was at, and it even helped soothe the ache that wouldn't quite stop in my shoulder. The tiredness that eluded me during the night had decided to set upon me with abandon. Pretty typical, yet annoying. Every time I closed my eyes I felt like I was being watched and jolted back to full wakefulness.

I toweled myself off and flicked my hair out of my face. Drying it was just a waste of time, it never did what it was told anyway. As I reached for my locker shadows flickered in each side of my peripheral vision, and I felt a strange sort of surge inside me, like I'd eaten tingly crunch bites or something and was going to be sick.

Darkness continued to linger at the edges of my sight, and I couldn't help the feeling of déjà vu, like I should know these things. That I should understand them. It didn't have the same vibe as the ones I'd seen last night. Close, but only similar.

The headiness almost made me stumble with recognition that floated just out of reach, and I had to shake myself out of the stupor and pull back into the now. The now where I didn't have long before my next class, and I needed to hurry up even more.

I reached for my locker, but the moment my hand touched it to pull it open a rush of power began to pool at the contact point. It couldn't have been more than a microsecond, but it felt like an age. I could see my skin make contact with the metal, watch the tiny shots of electricity bubble over and out of my skin, making definitive contact with the locker.

All I could think in that split second was: oh shit. Then time came rushing back, and I was pushed away with such force that I flew into the lockers behind me, before falling to the ground.

It momentarily knocked the wind out of me, and the darkness in my vision disappeared while I tried to catch my breath.

Ill-advised usage of your skill. Please be warned, when lay people are present, limiting of power usage is advised.

I didn't use it deliberately! I threw the words at my stupid interior voice. My lungs hurt and as they began to calm down, so did my back. It had better be temporary. I had shit I need to do, races I needed to win.

Be more cautious. You may need to practice so the electricity doesn't bottle up and require an outlet. Releasing pent up and unused power is paramount to maintaining your health.

Gee, thanks for telling me sooner. I couldn't keep the sarcasm from my voice as I picked myself up gingerly and tested to see if anything was broken.

It seemed okay, and I really hoped it was. At least my locker was open now. I grabbed my day clothes and pulled them on, stuffing my athletic gear haphazardly into my backpack. It was difficult not to think about how much worse that discharge could have been had I still been in the shower. With the water to conduct my outburst.

The system was quiet, like it didn't know how to deal with sarcasm. We were going to get along just famously. I could already tell.

FRIENDS

It was all I could do to not throw myself into the seat in my lecture hall. I was so not in the mood for this subject today. Ethics and I were on shaky footing. Call me stubborn, but I wasn't sure bringing me back to life and asking me to break into nice little mom and pop shops so I didn't die again was entirely ethical. Not to mention baiting me with a perfectly disguised secret door and then pretending it didn't exist? No, that was unforgivable.

Ethics has nothing to do with it. We are preserving humanity. For this, some sacrifices must be made.

Oh, because humanity is so worth preserving. This was a sore point with me. It always had been. Humans destroyed as much as they created. Sometimes I wondered if we were sent here because someone else got fed up with us.

Humanity must not be permitted to kill itself, or the world around us. Checks and balances must exist.

Odd. The phrasing didn't sound quite right, and it made me think the system had missed a few moments in our history. *Why did you let the second world war happen then? Hell with that, what about the first?*

There was a pause, and it went on so long, I didn't think it was going to answer me again, but it finally did, only a moment before my teacher entered the room. I never thought it would be able to sound sad. But even SC surprised me with the amount of remorse in its voice.

Those were the best possible outcomes.

Wait what? *How?*

Trust us when we say WWI and WWII were not intended. It was simply the best possible outcome at the time.

Talk about chills. How was that possible though? The best outcome couldn't be remotely true. The sheer number of lives lost, the cruelty. Not to mention the high count of civilians caught in the crossfire, and the genocide. Fuck. How could it purport to be protecting humanity and do this? It carried on like I'd asked it my thoughts.

Ultimately, we settled for the best possible outcome at the time. We always do. The least lives lost, the most integrity preserved.

Integrity? If it were tangible right now, I'd punch it. It was back to using we again. And I guess that was all the answer I was going to get. I had to think about this later. Right now I needed to pay attention to my class. My scholarship didn't only depend on athletic performance. Try as I might, I couldn't get the system's sadness out of my head. It sounded almost human, complete with failed logic. I wasn't sure that was a good thing.

It was so difficult to focus on the subject matter of the lecture that it got annoying. I'm not sure how I managed to make any notes at all. It certainly wasn't going to help my note taking job. It sounded odd, but for each lecture there was a student note taker whose notes were sent out to any students with disabilities who could benefit from said notes. Mine were usually organized perfection, and I did it for each lecture in every one of my subjects. That and training a high school track team two times a week was how I paid for my expenses. Note taking paid for my food. Training paid for my rent.

I pushed the haunting words of the system to a corner of my mind and pulled out my cell phone to bring up my bank's app. I didn't get paid until next week, so I was expecting it to contain about forty dollars. But it didn't. I'd received a payment from SC Corp. One hundred dollars. It took me more than two weeks to earn that much with note taking.

I'd broken the law, stolen a file, found a secret laboratory, and they paid me one hundred dollars. Seriously? No wonder they wanted us to maintain and hold down our previous lives. When it mentioned compensation, I'd assumed it wouldn't be much, but I'd secretly been hoping I was wrong. Guess they had more overheads than I thought.

With the lecture over I finally glanced down at my notes and ran through them. They were better than I'd expected. Maybe a part of my brain just kept writing down what it was hearing. Since I'd already read the materials covered in this lecture, I was sure that I'd detailed everything included in those. Fifteen dollars was fifteen dollars, especially considering I was already attending. If I played it right, it could feed me for up to five days.

I pushed my tablet into my backpack and slung it over my shoulder. Heading out to lunch after the two hour lecture, my legs were seizing up. I didn't stretch enough after all the running I did. I was going to pay tomorrow. On the bright side, my back wasn't hurting anymore, so that had been more shock than smashing into a row of metal lockers. Still, I could feel this buzzing on the surface, bouncing from fingertip to fingertip as I walked. Glancing down I could see a spark of blue jump from one of my digits to another. I needed some way to stave off this nervous energy without killing myself or others.

Cyan surprising me as I exited the room was not one of those ways.

"Hey, Dare!" She grinned at me, nudging my side with her elbow in that infuriatingly co-conspirator way of hers. It made everyone around her think we were in on something.

"Hi, Cyan." I could only imagine her parents named her after the bright color when they saw her eyes. They were alarmingly blue. Unsettling even. Not like Orion's, whose were calming and soft. No, hers were a blue that no one believed weren't contacts. Yet I'd known her for the last few years of my life, and sure as shit, her eyes had always been that disconcerting color.

To compensate, and probably to irritate people, especially her parents, she'd taken to dying her hair cyan blue since the senior year of high school.

Her personality matched her clothes: today, a white shirt with a dancing blue cloud on it, and a pair of bright blue leggings. Bright. Bubbly. And slightly blinding. That was Cyan. "Come on! You're slow today. What happened, did you hurt yourself?"

She linked her arm through mine and dragged me off to the coffee shop at the corner of the IT building. I had two hours before my next class, so I didn't bother trying to escape. That took far too much energy when it involved Cyan.

Please make sure you maintain your regular way of life as much as possible. This is a part of the TOS you agreed to.

Luckily, Cyan was bubbly enough that she took my mind off the scathing retort I wanted to mentally scream at SC. Of course I knew it was in the bloody TOS. I'd read the damned thing.

I slouched into one of the couch chairs, and pulled out a very squished ham and cheese sandwich with a wince. Ham would be better cold straight out of the fridge in the morning, and peanut butter didn't have to stay cold to taste good. Had to remember that for next time.

My other friends filed in, dumping their bags at the seating area we snagged, and headed over to grab themselves food from the cafeteria. A small voice in the back of my head that actually belonged to me reminded me that I had some spare money for once. But I wasn't sure I wanted to touch it, and my sandwich was good enough, as was the apple I'd eat after.

Orion threw himself into the seat next to me. He reached into his bag to fish out his own sandwich, and the smell of peanut butter drifted over to me, making me regret my choice anew.

"I'll remind you to make it with peanut butter tomorrow. Again. I think you've just fallen into a high school habit." Orion grinned at me like he could read my mind, except he couldn't. It was just that I'd told him so many times that I really should follow his example.

"What did you get up to last night?" he asked. And I wasn't sure if there was a hint of suspicion I saw in his eyes, or genuine curiosity.

"Went out for food, only got a bagel. Ate ramen, tried to sleep." And I didn't even lie.

"You forgot *beat up the mailbox.*"

"I didn't forget. I was deliberately omitting it." I grinned and popped the last bite of my sandwich into my mouth before retrieving my apple. It seemed he'd forgotten about my scar.

Orion's laugh was silvery. It was the only way to describe it. When he laughed, people couldn't help but smile with him. Lucky bastard.

I wasn't in the mood to talk though. I was in the mood to give the Second Chance system a bit of a third degree, but I wasn't sure how to. It was in my head. While I was glad to be alive, I didn't ask it to save me, and now I was beholden to its whims? *How often and when will I get the assignments?*

I waited, trying to see if I could sense a presence in the back of my mind, but nothing was there. And it didn't answer me. Maybe it wasn't listening in. It was infuriating. I didn't even realize I was tapping my foot impatiently until Orion leaned over from his seat next to me.

"What's got you so worked up?"

His expression held an earnest look, one I wasn't willing to meet, so for one of the first times in our friendship, I avoided eye contact. "Just have a meet coming up in a couple of weeks, lots of exams are looming on the horizon." I shrugged, hoping he thought it just the usual.

His frown was anything but believing. "Oh, so you mean like you've had to do for the last, say three years of school?"

He was right, and I knew it. "Yeah, like I've had to do for the last three years. And like I always do and never complain about. Sometimes you can be insensitive, Ry."

He cringed and offered me a grape as a peace maker. "Sorry. I know you like to keep shit to yourself, but you should know better than to count me out of it."

"If I lumped all my crap on you constantly, you'd be buried in a matter of minutes." I chewed down on the grape, letting the juicy insides explode in my mouth. Grapes should be classified as drugs. You could never have just one. I held out my hand for another.

Orion eyed me suspiciously. "Is this just another ploy to eat all of my grapes?"

"You know me too well," I said, forcing my laugh.

He used to know me well, maybe that had changed now. We hadn't been as close lately as we used to be in high school. He was always so busy. But then who was I kidding? So was I. And with this new being dead thing, it was only going to get worse.

About to sigh, because fuck knows I needed to expend some of the pent-up woe, the system finally woke back up.

Next Assignment.

Immediately it had my attention, because you know, that wasn't terrifying at all. The thing was, it was difficult for me to divide my attention. I still had no idea how I'd managed to take notes earlier. And I'd never got parts in the school plays because acting and I didn't mesh.

Orion's expression could only be defined as quizzical. He knew I wasn't actually paying attention, even though I looked at him. His brows pinched ever so slightly exhibiting annoyance. He scrunched his nose sort of like a rabbit, except it wasn't cute; it meant he was about to get pissed. And right then there wasn't a damned thing I could do about it.

"Sorry," I ventured to say when the stupid system delayed whatever it was about to tell me. "Totally spaced out."

He raised an eyebrow.

"Sure," he said, and I knew from his tone he'd believe the sky was purple before he believed that I'd only spaced out.

This whole living in secret thing was going to get really complicated, fast. Even though his demeanor said that I didn't deserve for him to repeat himself, he began to speak again.

ASSIGNMENT

Location: Professor Chapman, Head of Anthropology Department's Office, anthropology department, your campus

Objective: Do not get noticed in the performing of this task. Leave the target in your apartment mailbox at the end of the day.

Target: Retrieve Professor Chapman's Day Planner.

Time Limit: By the end of the day tomorrow (11:59p.m.).

Reward: Progression experience. Monetary compensation. Both dependent on the quality of performance.

Seriously. *So now I'm a common thief?* I directed my thoughts angrily at the sky, at somewhere in my head that could hear them.

Please repeat the inquiry. Your question does not make sense.

I blinked and noticed that Orion had turned his back to me and was talking to Neale, one of our other friends. Cyan sat, perched on the arm of his chair, leaning forward and eagerly listening to the conversation they all had while I spent time conversing with myself. I felt a flash of jealously rise in me, like bile in my throat threatening to overwhelm my senses.

Swallowing it down, I opted not to analyze it too much. That would only lead to rampant confusion and irritation. I couldn't put my finger on just what I was jealous of. Was I jealous of Cyan being close to Orion, or vice versa? Or was it just that I wanted to talk to them all like yesterday had never happened?

Rephrase the question, huh? I'd give it rephrase the damned question. *Why resurrect me, if all I'm doing is being a common thief?*

Your manner of death gifted you with an ability the program requires. The decision went in your favor. You are performing duties required to maintain a status quo, to keep the balance.

My manner of death, huh. We still had to discuss how it had footage of my death from outside of myself, but I'd figure out how to approach that later. I grit my teeth, trying not to yell in my brain for fear that it'd come out of my mouth instead. *Is this how the rest of my life will be?*

Your life is still your own. As you perform these tasks, you will grow in experience and control. As you do so, your rank will increase. Higher ranks receive more complex tasks. Does this answer your initial inquiry?

How could I have forgotten that I have a rank? *What was my rank again?*

Junior. This is the rank that all Second Chance agents begin with. Should you not perform in a satisfactory enough manner, your rank will not increase, and the odds are that therefore Second Chance will no longer have an agreement with you.

Panic began to rise in me. Well, panic and anger. The sensation didn't sit well. It made me want to vomit while I punched things. I wondered if the system could sense that because it followed with the most soothing words I've ever heard a computer, or system, or whatever it was utter:

So far, you are not in danger of this.

At least that was one piece of danger I'd manage to avoid. With my whole whopping one mission behind me.

Thank you, I said again.

My reply was silence, but a heavy one, like the system was trying to figure out just what it could say to me and ended up giving up. I got the distinct impression that being polite confused it. Considering I could understand it receiving irate responses, I'd take every advantage I could muster.

It was too late in the day for me to worry about performing the task. Considering all of its demands, if it wanted me to keep my existing schedule, it needed to be better about when I got advised of assignments. I had to coach this afternoon, straight after class. For the first time, I didn't feel like it. These kids looked up to me. I wanted to go home and hide in my room. Maybe punch a brick wall on the way. I don't know. Maybe this way the system could just let me die in my sleep and what should have happened would have. It was still difficult to wrap my head around the fact that I'd died.

There was that part of me that didn't question it. A part of me wanted to live. Stubbornly, perhaps not even in my own interests, but I was young, and I'd clawed my way toward my dream. Disregarding a chance to maintain that life—that was foolhardy, wasn't it?

Excellent observation.

I waited for it to say more, but the damned thing was picky about when it spoke and when it didn't. I wished it was corporeal so I could punch it instead of a wall. The amount of catharsis involved in physical combat about something that annoyed me was unbelievable.

Track kids were ferried from a couple of the local high schools to our field. The program was meant to keep kids out of gangs and drugs, and it pulled kids from all over the city, but mostly low-income areas. This university donated its facilities to the cause. Running was cheap. All you needed were halfway okay shoes, and the will to work. If I'd grown up with more money, perhaps I'd have pursued a different athletic avenue, but as it was, running always worked for me.

I ran when I was sad. I ran when I was happy. And everything in between. With the wind in my hair and my eyes on the road, there was nothing I couldn't conquer. Except, apparently, death. For which I needed the assistance of a demanding voice in my head.

"Dare?" Coach Marth startled me, and I whirled around from watching a group of teens finish their stretches.

"Yes?" Maybe I looked worried, or panicked, or something else, but he frowned.

"Are you okay?" Concern knit his brow, and his face held kindness.

"Yeah, sure. I'm fine. Just been a long day, and with exams and the meet coming up. I'm a bit stressed." None of it was a lie. I just didn't add in anything confusing.

He studied me. Hell, he'd known me since I was much younger. He'd been the teacher who encouraged me to apply for this scholarship, when he moved to this university just before my junior high school year. I hated having so many people around me who could call me on my bullshit answers.

"Don't overdo it. You're strong, but you don't have to shoulder the weight of the world on your own." He smiled warmly and blew his whistle, heralding the end of the kid's warm up session.

Except even while I took the athletes I usually did and began to run them through the measures, I couldn't help fuming. Don't shoulder it alone? What a fucking joke. After just one day of being a bit absentminded, even my best friend had given up figuring shit out.

The Second Chance program was feeling more and more like a thinly veiled curse, and I fully intended to do something about it. I just had no idea what.

7
SECOND

Sleep wasn't my friend that night. My gourmet dinner of ramen sat heavily in my stomach, taunting me to throw up and feel worse. Orion avoided me completely, not even walking home with me. And, of course, I'd completely avoided the street where the scene of my accident was. No one had time to relive that shit.

The irritation didn't help. While a part of me was petrified that I might slip up and suddenly be dead, another part of me didn't operate well under threat of punishment. Not even punishment for committing crimes. I'd be disciplined if I didn't commit them. What sort of fucked up logic was that?

Not to mention the fact that I had a sentient thing living in my head now was really starting to sink in. I refused to dignify its existence by calling it sapient. Humans had to be better, or at least strive to be.

Waking up left me groggy, only just having fallen asleep. I washed my face, pulled on some clothes that didn't smell bad, and dragged myself into the kitchen. Laundry was the bane of my existence. There was a small container on the counter with an apple balanced on top and a sticky note stuck next to it.

Peanut butter is better.

Don't forget your apple.

See you at lunch.

Ry

Idiot. But I couldn't help smiling, even if it was a little corny. Apparently I was just being a grumpy sod. Although, what Orion had to do up at this hour, I had no idea. His scholarship was purely academic, so he didn't have to be up this early at all. Lucky bastard.

I grabbed a piece of toast, smothered some jam on it—gotta keep some variety, after all—and headed out the door. Being a bit early to practice never hurt anyone, especially since I needed to figure out how I was going to manage to do that assignment the system gave me today.

Sadly, when I wanted to get somewhere early, I tended to catch all of the red lights. I leaned against the button on the side of the streetlamp, stretching my calves. Not that the button did anything except give me the illusion of control. A tingle ran through me, followed by a shower of sparks that sent a thrumming beat through each of my limbs simultaneously. I yanked my hand away quickly, watching in dismay as the streetlights all around me began to blink yellow.

Fuck. Was that me?

Oops.

Reminder: you must discharge your excess electricity on a regular basis or else it will build up and discharge at random.

"Thanks." I muttered to no one in particular, and at least took advantage of the confusion to cross with the group of people who'd been standing on my side of the street. Two blocks later, and those lights were at least working. I didn't lean on anything remotely electrical or metal for the rest of the way to school, despite really wanting to. Looked like I needed to get some practice in with this discharging thing. And I had a feeling I could make it fun as hell.

I felt energized. Like strangely good about myself and my body. Powerful. I'd never felt that way. It always seemed like I had to drag every shred of effort out of myself by force. If discharging a little electrical power in the mornings could do this? I was going to have to do it on a more regular basis.

Not only did I feel energized, but I seemed to fly over the ground like it was nothing and I had wings. Not the sort you get from a canned energy drink. Lighter than anything.

Coach Marth's whistle caught me off guard, and I stumbled slightly, but changed direction and headed in to where he was standing.

"I'm not sure what you're doing out there." The grin on his face was wide and greedy. "But whatever it is, I hope you know how to recreate it. You've just run your best five miles ever."

I smiled, but a little voice in the back of my head reminded me that this probably wasn't natural. "Thanks, coach. I'll do my best."

Except I had no idea how to do it again. I'd been running on adrenaline since the light incident. But damned if I didn't want to. It was all I could do to stop myself shaking. Whether it was with fear or anticipation, I wasn't quite sure. Did this make me faster? Had I somehow charged myself with electricity? And how much was too much?

The one thing I knew was I had to be careful with my new skill. If this morning's totally inadvertent mess made this much of an impact, then too much would make me unbelievably fast. I couldn't afford to stand out like that. Not being in the program, not already having died. I had to be careful how I used this, because obviously it had way more applications than I'd even dreamed of.

"Dare!" Cyan greeted me outside the Intro to Cyber Security lecture. It was the one lecture I could zone into and soak it up. While we didn't go much more in depth into it in this course, it was exactly what I aimed to pursue as a career.

"Hey." I smiled, genuinely happy to see her. Right now her bubbliness could help soothe my over calculating brain. Maybe it would bring me back down to earth a bit. Since my ramped-up speed probably had a hell of a lot to do with my accidental electrical discharge, I found it difficult to concentrate, even on my favorite subject.

"You've been really quiet the last couple days." Her concerned face made her button nose twitch like a rabbit's.

I didn't correct her, because I had been quiet. But she'd only had two classes with me excluding this one. Couldn't I just be having an off day?

About to answer, I was interrupted by a hand on my shoulder, and one on hers as Levi inextricably inserted himself between us.

"Let's own this shit! Hackers beware, Dare is—" His brow furrowed, like he was trying to think of a rhyme.

"There?" Cyan supplied before biting down on her lip and giggling. Her eyelashes fluttered just that bit with the laughter, and Levi squeezed her shoulder. That or he had to hold on so he didn't faceplant. Sometimes he was rather uncoordinated. When were they ever going to admit it and just fuck already?

Although, if I thought about it, Cyan flirted with everyone, including me. I kept my grin on the inside and refused to let my thoughts wander. I had bigger things to worry about right now. And she hadn't forgotten her previous question, which she proved as she leaned in front of Levi and poked me.

"Answer me. What's up?"

I sighed, wanting to just devote my brain to figuring all this shit out. But I had great friends. Treating them like shit would be long term disaster. "I'm fine. Just got a lot on my plate."

"That's an excuse if ever I heard one." Levi looked at me this time, frowning too. "You do look a bit pale. I can drive you to the doctor if you need me to."

Levi wasn't a bad guy. I hadn't known him as long as I'd known Orion, or Cyan for that matter. I met Cyan during orientation while we were still in high school, and we'd hit it off. I can't deny the occasional fantasy about it being more than that. But those visions didn't have any place in my current predicament if I wanted to keep my train of thought going.

"I'm fine. I ran five miles, and then two mile sprints this morning. Coach is pushing me pretty hard." All of it was true, even if I was quite certain any paleness on my behalf had nothing to do with my fitness.

"Mile sprints is an oxymoron." Levi just shook his head.

"No, it's not!" My retort came out harsher than intended, and I took a breath to steady myself. "Run as fast as I can for a mile. It's exhausting. You know I can't do shorter distances well."

Levi laughed, but it wasn't unkind, and I was grateful he didn't take offence at my initial tone. "You're insane with all that sports shit."

I didn't think so. Running was helping me right now. It cleared my mind, made it easier to analyze things. And hell, it had even inadvertently showed me a variance of this power I hadn't anticipated. If I could just go back out and run, maybe I'd be able to figure out how to perform this damned next task. The clock was ticking down, and I had to get to the anthropology department. But I had to take notes, and I had to figure out just how much of my power could do what.

So much to do, not enough time.

I flopped down in my seat, eyes scanning the room for anything out of the ordinary. Did the system really exist in my head or was this all a dream? Could it seriously see everything I did or was someone constantly monitoring me? Since it had shown me the view of my accident from outside of myself, I got the feeling everyone was being monitored. I just didn't know how. Had they inserted something into my brain to communicate with me while I was in the ambulance before I woke up?

All of these made a lot more sense than the explanation given. Even if I felt it in my bones. Already having this system inside us? Maybe it only booted up on death.

I'm not sure how I managed to pay attention to the lesson and to take coherent notes, but I did. And moments before the professor dismissed us, I shoved everything into my backpack and slipped out before Cyan could attach herself to me and thus thwart my one available time window to get this task out of the way.

The anthropology department's corridors were teeming with people. I frowned as I walked through them. This was going to be a disaster. Not only was everyone everywhere, but cameras were connected at every corner of each of the passageways, even though the light didn't appear to bleed into them. Those corners were dark, filled with shadows that—oddly enough—felt like they were watching me.

Welcome to paranoia 101.

Perhaps they were like those things that I'd seen down there. In the lab. I shuddered involuntarily at the thoughts. It made every corner, every play of light feel like I was being hunted. My adrenaline spiked igniting my flight instinct.

Your assignment can be completed in these conditions. Proceed with caution.

Suppressing a groan, I focused the electricity buzzing through my veins as a distraction. I needed to touch an object in order to utilize my power, right? If the map I'd looked at toward the beginning of this section of the building was anything to go by, then around the next corner there should be steps with a railing I could balance on while I reached up to touch the back of the camera. Technically.

I wanted to grumble and complain and maybe even shout out *why me*, but in the end, I'd just been given a super power. A fucking super power. Holy shit.

Okay so, that sank in. Finally. I stood there blinking rapidly as a zillion different questions popped into my head. It gave me this power and could take it away. At least that's what it wanted me to think. Shaking my head, I cleared the thoughts. I couldn't afford to have them now, or when it might be listening in.

The thing I needed to avoid at that moment was being seen by any camera or person. I'd reach around the corner to touch the damned thing while hoping these mind shadowy things that lived in my overactive imagination and apparently in the lab didn't try to suck out my soul. Because that would be terribly awkward.

I had to keep an eye out in both directions, ostensibly rummaging in my backpack while doing so. What I wouldn't give to be a pigeon for several seconds. It was obvious I wouldn't have a lot of time to get this taken care of, so as soon as both corridors appeared clear, I moved.

Getting up onto the railing wasn't difficult. I hugged the wall and shimmied up to the tips of my toes to feel around the corner and latch onto the connection that ran into the wall. Managing to touch it with the pointer and middle finger of my left hand, I willed electricity into the system. I wished for it to only affect the cameras in this particular building, including the good Professor's.

I had no idea how accurate my thoughts would make my ability, but I had to hope. This is what I got for only half paying attention to the tutorials.

My fingers heated but didn't burn, and the sparks that leapt across felt subdued and nothing like the burst of bright enthusiastic energy that halted traffic this morning. Still, the soft smell of faint sulfur reached my nose, and I jumped down from my balance beam to land on the floor.

No twinge in my knees, and no rolled ankles. I'd live to run another day. And only two people had entered the corridors before I managed to jump down, their heads buried in their phones. Lucky me.

I had no way to check if the cameras were indeed disabled, but I was marginally confident I'd fried some sort of electrical wiring. At least, if the smell was anything to go by. Did the system even take that sort of damage into account? Destroying university property. It practically made me a vandal as well as a thief.

The office I needed was two corridors and one right hand turn over, so I set about trying to appear as if I belonged there.

I should have known it wouldn't be a problem. If you didn't know people in the vicinity, students didn't randomly notice you if you also looked like a student. Since I did, it was easy to make my way to the door.

Truth was, I hadn't been here since freshman year when I'd been torn between anthropology and psychology for my behavioral requirement. The head of department's office was right where the map said it would be: in a darker twist of the corridor with uneven ghosts lingering on the outside of the door. Those tricks of light played havoc with my brain. It took effort not to reach out and touch them, to check if they were real.

She should have been teaching a class. Professor Chapman's schedule was easy to see online, like most of the current college and university classes. I paused and knocked, pretended to hear her, and pushed into her office, relieved to see that she was, in fact, sticking to her schedule.

I closed the door behind me and leaned against it for a moment, taking in a breath. This shouldn't feel so thrilling. It had to be the nature of the electricity, because I felt far bolder than I'd ever been before. The sensation wasn't at all unwelcome.

Day Planner. Book thing. Whatever. Why would she not have taken it with her wherever she was going? Her office was tidy on the surface, but one glance at the bookshelves showed me another story. It seemed even some of the world's most respected researchers were as messy with their research as I was. She needed a tablet so she could sort shit digitally. Only I wasn't going to tell her that.

But I *was* going to steal her planner.

It sat open to this week on her desk. A pang of guilt rushed through me as I hesitated to pick it up. If she depended on a paper planner, then she needed this information. Taking it would mean her whole week, or worse, her whole month would be out of whack.

Except if I didn't take it, I'd be dead. That was the deal, wasn't it? What a stupid fucking waste if it really worked that way.

My life or her diary? Was that even a choice? Two days ago it wouldn't have been a question, because I wasn't on borrowed time back then. Guilt and I didn't have a good relationship, and I could already tell I wasn't going to get any sleep tonight either. Whether it was because of my emotions or my brain not shutting up had yet to be decided.

Steeling myself, I grabbed it and shoved it into my backpack before I could second guess myself again. I paused once I'd done so. There was no clicking of a secret door, no sliding of bookshelves, or disappearing desks. The silence crescendoed the longer I waited.

Just as I was about to heave a sigh of relief, I heard footsteps approaching the door, followed by a knock. Even almost expecting it, I practically jumped out of my skin. Fuck.

The window.

I whirled around, thankful for the first time that the voice was apparently omnipresent when it chose, and saw the single hung window.

Move. Open it. Jump out. It's a slight drop, but we are on the ground level.

I did as I was told, able to move without thinking, and execute the departure quickly. I was up on the ledge, just about to jump through the opening when the second knock sounded. It surprised me again, and I almost fell, but caught myself and rolled onto the grass, hoping against hope I hadn't shattered my tablet.

My breath came fast, and I didn't look back as I ran away from the building. Her office window backed out onto grass and closely cropped trees. The ground was cushy beneath my feet, and I fed some of that overenthusiastic energy into my body to help fuel my flight.

Finally, I pushed through onto one of the sidewalks that wove its way through and around the university. I stood, my hands on my knees, gulping in air. It wasn't that I was winded, I was exhilarated. Like a drug, all I wanted was to experience that adrenaline again. Even if it had knocked a few years off my life.

And even if I was mildly disappointed that this planner hadn't triggered a hidden opening.

Assignment halfway completed. Quick thinking on an exit strategy. Remember to deliver the item to the prescribed spot.

I know, I know. I didn't think at it, but was fairly sure it heard me anyway. While I had to attend an afternoon class, I'd be home long before the deadline. The planner weighed my backpack down, but I wasn't sure if it was my imagination or its actual weight.

I bit into my apple like a starving monkey. Hungrier than usual, I wondered if channeling my ability consumed more calories. It wouldn't surprise me, but in that case, I was going to need to eat a lot more.

Heading home tonight became my focus. After I popped this planner in my mailbox, I needed to learn more about how to control this ability, master it. And then, I needed a plan.

8

TOO SOON

Jacob was in the apartment when I bounded on upstairs. I wasn't expecting him to be home; it was already after six in the evening. Maybe he'd taken on a weekend shift for a friend. He did that sometimes, as weekends paid slightly better.

"Hey, Jacob." I half smiled at him, realizing I was starving. Underlying smells in the kitchen only increased that to ravenous, and I walked to the fridge. Pulling out ham and cheese, and some mayo and mustard, I rummaged around for the tomatoes I knew I'd bought on special.

"Perfect." Jacob's clapped the book shut that he was reading and jumped to his feet. "Just the person I wanted to talk to."

"Why?" It was out of my mouth so fast I hadn't finished the piece of ham I'd just shoved in there. Bad manners right there.

He raised an eyebrow and grinned toothily. "Davin said you didn't check in with him yesterday. Since you usually do, I thought maybe the accident the other day had more of an impact on you than we realized, than even the doctor who checked you over noticed."

I laughed it off, as much as I could with a vaguely panicked and completely fake laugh. "I am fine, but I'm also a big kid now. Checking in has become a bit of a chore, you know? Still, I'll call him and tell him so myself. I know he worried about me, big brother and all…"

I let it trail off, rolling my eyes to try and sell the lie. But then I realized it wasn't one. Why was I constantly checking in with them. I mean, calling them up was a courtesy and all, but surely I didn't have to do it all the time? Most of the concern rolled away from Jacob's stance, and he took a step closer, giving me a quick shoulder squeeze.

"Good. I assured him it was probably just that you had a lot on your plate, and that you might be getting too old for this. I had to explain I'd just seen you, and you were, in fact, still alive." He laughed good-naturedly and picked his book up again. "I'm going into my room. I just wanted to make sure I didn't miss you. Leave the bills on the table, and I'll make sure we get them taken care of."

"Thanks, J," I said, my back already turned as I built myself two ham, cheese, and tomato sandwiches. Famished wasn't even close to the growling in my stomach right then.

Orion wasn't home yet, which was odd for a Tuesday night. He was usually home before me because he didn't have classes on that afternoon.

Exhausted, yet sated, I headed into my bedroom to retrieve a packet of ramen for my dessert and decided to call my brother while I was there. Video chat, of course. He wouldn't accept any less. Otherwise someone could just be using a vocal synthesizer to pretend to be me or something. I tried to tell him once that my friends could just hire a doppelgänger to confuse him. That joke didn't go down too well. I obviously didn't get my sense of humor from my family.

Davin picked up on the first ring. "About time. Don't fucking scare me like that."

He sounded genuinely upset that I hadn't called him on Monday night. And you know something, I got fucking angry. "Why? I'm almost twenty-one. I'm perfectly capable of taking care of myself now. You never had to check in with mom when you first left."

Wow. It felt amazing to get that out. The fingers on my left hand sparked again, like they were encouraging me, lending me strength.

"Well, no, I didn't. But I'm the oldest. I promised her I'd take care of you." He sounded sort of sad, and I wondered what was on his mind, even if he'd never tell me. Sometimes he acted more like my dad than my big brother.

Our dad wasn't a bad sort. He was goofy and loved us, but he worked a lot, and traveled often. Davin took it upon himself to fill in for the old man. Sometimes, I wondered how Mom did it. But if she was strained, she never showed us. I missed my mom. I should probably call her too. Only, I promptly decided that I could call in without a regulated timetable to do so.

"Look, I promise to call in every week or so, but damn it, give me some space to grow up, please?" I said, trying to emphasize it. I really did feel bad about making him worry, but maybe it was time to cut the strangling apron strings.

"Sure." He seemed somewhat taken aback, like he didn't quite know what to say. "I'm sorry for going all big brother on you. It's just J mentioned you'd had an accident but that you were okay. I got worried, more so than usual. Want to talk about it?"

I sighed and cracked my stiff neck. Of course. That made much more sense. Davin didn't usually lose his temper. "I'm fine. There was an accident on the way home, and I went to the hospital to get checked out. It's okay. They released me, so no real harm done." This time I grinned, because he needed to see I was actually fine. And I was. I think. Better than fine. At any rate, better than I'd been before. Stronger.

He squinted at me over the stream, his eyes reflecting pure skepticism. "Fine, then. I'll talk to you … when you call, and see you in a few at your big meet?"

The track meet. How could I forget it even for an instant? Naturally I had an answer for that, but not something I could utter out loud. "You bet! Love you!"

I leaned forward before he had time to interject something else. That had to have been the shortest call we'd ever had. There were way too many thoughts swirling in my brain trying to trip me up with confusion to hold a long conversation with anyone. Not to mention electricity kept flickering around my skin, and I didn't want to blow up my phone.

My ramen was cooked, in fact a bit over cooked by the time I got to it, and I glanced at the time with a frown. It was getting late and would be dark soon. Where the hell was Orion? On the one day I wanted to sit and chat, he wasn't around. I hadn't even talked to him since yesterday when he turned his back. Though I had enjoyed my lunch.

The system was strangely silent. I hadn't heard any snarky commentary for a while now, and it felt oddly lonely in my mind. Yet, it also let me think for myself. The thoughts whirring around in my head were crazy. So many of them that plucking out just one was difficult.

Suddenly, I was so tired, I could barely keep my eyes open. The excitement of the day got to me; I needed to sleep. Setting my alarm to get me up twenty minutes earlier so I could shower quickly in the morning, I rolled over and let sleep claim me.

The bleep of an alarm had to be annoying, or else how would we ever wake up? Mine was no exception. The only difference from my usual, was that I actually felt rested.

Notification

Well, there went that peace of mind. I waited, sitting up in bed and rubbing my eyes. Static shock sparked as I ran my hand through my hair, making me grin. The message eventually continued.

Your assignment has been satisfactorily completed. Your rewards are experience, and payment. Please check your funds.

Another payday? I frowned, pushing myself up and stumbling to the door. Okay, maybe I wasn't as well rested as I thought, and I really did need a shower. And to wash my sheets, apparently. The bathroom held the night's chill still, and the tiled floor didn't help at all. These old converted townhouses didn't have things like linoleum flooring. Nope, ancient ceramic tile all the way.

I hopped from one foot to the other while turning the taps on and waiting for the hot water to kick in. It always took a while, and I chalked that up to old pipes mixed with my abundance of impatience. If I waited too long, I wasn't going to do more than jump in and out. It was still lukewarm when I stepped in. I was determined to get myself out and dressed with plenty of time to make it to the track.

Toweling off, I brushed my teeth before getting dressed, and rushed into the kitchen. There was a note on the counter, and I couldn't help the twinge of sadness that it was from J and not Orion.

Got the wrong flavor. Too lazy to return them. Enjoy. J.

It was stuck to the top of a box of toaster tarts. I frowned as I pulled it off. Cinnamon butter. Yeah, sure, that was a mistake. He'd "accidentally" bought these before. Still, that was five days' worth of yummy sugar high that could fuel my track run. I shoved a pack in the toaster while I gathered my lunch.

Routine was routine, and this Second Chance thing hadn't interrupted it much so far. Since I woke early and left even earlier than yesterday, I walked. Even though I slept for a long time, it wasn't good sleep. My brain was filled with wild dreams, some people might even call them nightmares. I grabbed my phone and pulled up my banking information.

Pending Deposit: $150

What the hell? The hundred from the first mission had cleared and made my balance a healthy over a hundred dollars for the first time in a long time. With this cleared, I'd have almost three hundred. But a nagging feeling in the back of my mind chastised me for accepting it, or for planning on using it. I'd stolen and basically fenced the goods I'd taken. But, if I analyzed that, I was technically being coerced into that behavior. I mean, either I did what I was told or I died, right? Half way to the track, I started to jog.

I arrived at school so fast, I felt like I'd teleported there. My fingers tingled with excess energy, and all I wanted to do was move faster than humanly possible. I'm not even sure how I got through practice without setting off a patrol from Area 52, but I did. However, I couldn't help but be wary about getting a shower. I hadn't discharged focused excess electricity in the last eighteen hours. All I'd done was feed it into my body. What if it went off while I was showering?

Worse, what if it went off so badly I blew the building up.

If you are having trouble managing your excess power, please refer to the tutorial on how best to expend it.

What? I cringed. My question sounded harsh even to me.

Please refer to the tutorial on how best to expend excess electricity.

Which reminded me, I'd been intent on exploring the power yesterday, but in the end I'd been so tired, I'd fallen asleep. Instead, I opted not to shower a second time today and instead lathered myself with deodorant. People would just have to put up with stinky Dare today. Tutorial...tutorial. *How do I access the tutorial?*

You request access.

I waited, and barely resisted the urge to roll my eyes since it couldn't see me anyway. *May I have access to the tutorial? Please?*

My answer was to have it boot up in front of me. I had a few minutes to spare before my first class, and that was going to have to do. Walking around like a loaded gun wasn't my idea of fun, and I was beginning to feel very static.

The menu popped up, and I realized there had been options other than the initial begin here one I'd chosen. However, in depth and helpful hints weren't much more explanatory. In depth sounded pretty straight forward.

Electricity

Type A Skill. Warning: this skill type can be dangerous. Make sure for proper storage and discharge of excess power. Which type of problem are you having?

I thought discharge at it and waited. This was fascinating. Did it mean I could store electricity to? Maybe let me store it and boost my ability when needed?

Discharging electric build up.

Please choose severity, and location.

Indoor, minimal—I wondered if I'd ever need the outdoor/explosive option.

Minimal release while indoors can be achieved by standing close to an electrical station, be it wall receptacles, or even a fuse case. Focus on the station with your mind and snap your fingers. This should allow a small excess to escape from you safely into relevant systems. Keep in mind lights may fluctuate afterward for several minutes. Do not be alarmed.

Has this been helpful? Yes or No.

Wow, it even had an exit survey. I selected yes, even though I wanted to wait until I could see the results for myself before confirming it was, but I also didn't want to walk around with words in front of my face while I searched for the perfect place to do this.

Venturing out of the locker rooms as the last to leave from the morning session, I glanced around to make sure no one else was nearby. There was a charging station on a table next to the door to the corridors. It was as good a place as any. I was either going to blow up the building, blow the grid, or else it would do what I wanted it to.

The odds weren't *that* bad.

Focusing on the wall receptacle, I took a deep breath and readied my left hand to snap my fingers right next to it. A tingling sensation ran down my arm, right to my fingers, building in a strangely euphoric way as it reached the tips. Finally, I snapped them together and the force of the power that exited was enough to make me back up a few steps. The lights above me flickered, and a brief scent of smoke reached my nostrils, but the light remained on, and I'm pretty sure only one of the charging points got fried.

I felt a little drained by the end of it, and somewhat sad. It'd be much nicer to use the power instead of wasting it. Doing things this way meant I wasted it. I threw away something uniquely mine. I had to figure out better ways to utilize it on a frequent basis that didn't end up discarding unused charge. At least my school was still standing. As always, a bonus.

Tugging my backpack up over my shoulder, I pushed open the door to head into the hall, only to run into Orion who was opening it from the other side.

He frowned at me, and tugged my hand pulling me back into the locker room. His gaze pierced like arrows and I felt my stomach flip flop with a tinge of fear. Even his voice wasn't as warm as usual when he spoke.

"We need to talk."

"Ry, what's up?" I tried to sound concerned for him, and not for myself. I wondered if he could feel my hands shaking. Then I wondered why they were shaking. Power thrummed beneath my skin, even though I'd just expended some.

He glanced around the locker room foyer. The carpet underneath our shoes was coarse, hardy. The green was a bit faded now, but I imagined it was chosen to imitate healthy grass when it was new. The walls were tiled, just like the floors in the locker rooms once you set foot in them. Pretty standard for as much as I've seen.

"Ry, what is it?"

"What's with me?" He raised an eyebrow, finally meeting my eyes. I wanted to look away but couldn't. He'd always had that effect on me. "I'm not the one getting Lichtenberg scars and saying, 'hey all I'm fine.' What's up with *you?* You've been really off since Sunday."

There were a few ways I could react, and Second Chance wasn't letting me off the hook if it's silence was anything to go by. Realistically it should flag him if I could tell him, right? Since it didn't, then I had to keep my secret from Ry. I had to admit to being relieved that he didn't die and not tell me about it. Like the secret I was keeping from him. I also hated it.

So I chose to react with indignation—which the strength coursing through me reinforced. I'd have to watch that. "Seriously? I got electrocuted, got a pretty scar to go with it that I'll never get rid of, and you're telling me I'm being odd? Tell me, dear Ry, how the fuck would you react if you got electrocuted, scarred for life, and told you were okay?"

There was silence between us, and I hated it even more than I hated that I couldn't tell him. I'd told him everything since I could remember. Best friends forever, blood oaths, mud baths, diving into waterfalls. Our friendship spanned decades even though we barely did ourselves.

Maybe Second Chance was a social experiment to see how we react to having our friendships ripped apart through secrets.

"I'd expect you to talk to me about it. I'd expect you to want to talk to me at least. Even if you can't." His tone was somber now, not irritated or frustrated like he'd been moments earlier. More like he was resigned to this outcome.

Even if I couldn't tell him? Did he know? Oh, how I wanted him to know, but at the same time then I'd be angry at him for not telling me beforehand. Besides, I knew it was just wishful thinking. The two of us ending up in the program was just too much of a coincidence, and I already thought there were too many. "You didn't talk to me about it when you almost drowned at the start of college. You, more than anyone else, should understand that I can't talk about it right now."

There. I was right, wasn't I? I wasn't allowed to talk about it, and if I was being honest with myself, I didn't want to talk about the sensations that ran through my body the day I had my accident. It felt so far away now, so long ago. Now I was different. Faster. Better. Stronger.

But Orion looked like he'd been slapped. As if throwing that scary experience in his face had made him realize people dealt with things differently. Then his expression switched to apologetic. "I'm sorry, I just thought you were shutting me out. I guess I didn't think."

I didn't realize my inability to multitask conversations in and outside of my head was going to bite me in the ass like this.

"I wouldn't do that. I've been getting kind of lost in my head, having my own existential crisis I guess. I don't mean to though." I looked at my phone, already used to being without my step counter, my fried à la electrical wiring mode step counter. "I don't want to cut this short, but if I don't get going soon, I'm going to be late, and I quite literally can't afford that."

He chuckled and brushed a hand through his hair. It was a nervous tick he rarely showed, when he felt vulnerable and sappy. I pretended not to notice. That'd just make it worse.

"Let's get you there on time, then."

SUSPICIONS

The rest of the week passed fairly uneventfully. It was difficult to quantify just how disappointed I felt. My fingers itched, sparks threatened to jump out of my skin. I spent so much time funneling it into my body that I walked around eternally buzzed.

I almost forgot that I was on borrowed time. Though I guess I could say it wasn't so much borrowed as blackmailed. I was ready for the best Friday night in forever with a few of our friends coming over to play a round or two of Carded Assholes. Best game ever. If you didn't know your friends beforehand, you might look at them in a completely different light afterward.

Except my excitement stalled when the newest system message tried to blind me.

Emergency Assignment

Location: Digsby's Diner. Two blocks due east of your location.

Objective: You must go into the diner and order one Pineapple Wake Me Up Burger. This code burger will trigger a delivery with it.

Target: You must obtain this delivery bag and shove it in your mailbox.

Time Limit: In the next three hours.

Reward: Progression experience. Monetary compensation. Speed of completion increases each exponentially.

It was four p.m. I had just over an hour before people started to arrive. They usually floated on in anywhere between five and six. We spent an age in the kitchen making all sorts of crap from whatever food people brought with them. Then we cleared the floor, threw pillows and bean bags on it, and lounged around playing cards, charades, and if it had been organized, Dungeons and Dragons.

I opened the closet to grab my coat. It was chillier today. Besides, I also didn't know how big that bag would be. Whatever I wore had to potentially hide it. The material hung loosely in folds of different lengths cut into odd triangles. Black and charcoal blended together well. If I pulled the hood up, no one would ever be able to describe me.

Considering my previous tasks, I couldn't be too careful.

"You going somewhere?" Jacob frowned. He knew I loved these nights, and Orion was in the kitchen trying to make room in our old fridge for anything the others brought with them.

"Just have to duck out quickly. Realized I didn't eat my lunch this afternoon and I'm just too hungry to wait."

I didn't eat my lunch that afternoon. I ate it just after eleven. So, I wasn't technically lying.

"Don't be too long. I have to go to work soon." He smiled at me, but it seemed a bit forced. It wasn't like me to go out and buy food. I'm miserly as fuck, constantly squirreling away money. I couldn't blame him for being suspicious.

Before I could change my mind, I called out to Orion. "Be back in a few!"

And I dashed out the door. I was quite certain he probably yelled something out to me as I left, but the whole purpose of acting fast was so I didn't have to hear it.

My body thrummed with anticipation. Flashes of blue tinged white flickered under my skin, like it was waiting for me to let it loose.

The streets tonight were bustling, as they usually were on a Friday night.

I'd been to Digsby's before, so it wasn't difficult for me to get there. Even if I couldn't help the feeling of trepidation that mixed with the excitement I couldn't shake. I'd never been there alone before.

I shoved my hands into my pockets and kept my head down. Making eye contact with the wrong people around here could lead to trouble. Not that it usually occurred until later in the night when one or more people were drunk, but it was always better to be on top of it.

The back of my mind taunted me, letting me know that no one could mess with me now. It was true, but at what cost? Shaking my head, I skirted around groups I came across. Even so I could feel the eyes on me, watching me until I was far enough down the street that I posed no threat. Little did they know. I'm skinny, wiry at best. Damn, I could run fast though. It had always been my one strength. But now, well now I could electrocute a person at twenty paces.

The human body had electricity running through it, didn't it? So if I had to, couldn't I fling my power at someone if my life was in danger?

Only in self defense.

I scowled inwardly. *If you're going to answer random thoughts in my head, try to get all of them. That's precisely what I said.*

I concurred.

It sounded almost pouty.

A thought occurred to me. *Does it just not work if it's not self-defence then?*

SC did that silence thing again, like it was mulling over what I said before it answered. *Powers should only be used for missions, or in self-defense.*

I see. I did see. That should spoke volumes.

The diner was dimly lit, nothing like the bakery or laboratory front I robbed at the start of the week. Had it really only been five days? There was grime caught in the corners of the large windows that looked out onto the street, and the glass didn't look like it had been cleaned in the last several years. But it had always looked like this, at least since we moved into our building. The smell that drifted out to the footpath was delicious, though.

As long as I turned a blind eye to the state of the actual shop, I could sit and smell that aroma for hours. Small plastic chairs and tables were scattered around the sidewalk. Far too many people hovered around, some smoking cigarettes, others swigging from a can of beer, and none of them caring that it wasn't quite five in the evening yet.

The store itself was crowded but not Heavenly Dough crowded. Taking a breath, I calmed myself and clutched my ten dollar note in my hand inside the pocket of my jacket. It wasn't the sort of place one wanted to pay with a card. The reader in here likely had a skimmer attached, and I would jealously guard the new cash flow I had.

Finally, it was my turn to order, and I tried to ignore the looks I received. It was quite obvious I didn't fit in here. I was too young to be drinking alcohol, and it wasn't like I could be mistaken for a regular. *Act.* I told myself to act. If I just acted like I belonged, I could pull this off. The sparks chased each other under the skin on my left hand, and I shoved it back into my pocket, thankful of the reminder.

Even if my heart was trying to pound out of my chest so hard it hurt. I breathed in the scent of homemade hamburgers with relish and tomatoes. I could almost taste the pineapple even though I couldn't stand it warm. Something about the inside of this place gave it a magical quality, but I couldn't quite put my finger on it. Magical in a suck-out-my-soul sort of way, anyhow.

I stepped up to the counter and cleared my throat when the words seemed to try hiding in my windpipe.

"One Pineapple Wake Me Up Burger, thanks." I couldn't believe my voice didn't shake. Nerves assailed me, that weird mixture of angst and expectation. It felt like everyone was watching me, waiting.

"That's four fifty," the woman behind the counter said without looking up as she handed me my ticket. Her dark hair was streaked with grey, and in this light I couldn't tell if it was originally dark brown or black. Her skin shone, not with sweat, but with the almost tangible oil that hung in the air like a miasma. "Be about ten minutes."

I nodded and was jostled out of the way before I could move of my own accord. I barely clamped down on the power that welled beneath my skin, trying to escape, to torch the offending person. The touch almost froze me, and it was difficult to move myself off to the side. I don't like being touched. I'm even wary about my friends. But strangers...

Right now they were lucky I had some modicum of control over this electricity.

I shook my head and moved farther away from the counter, shoving myself into a corner where I could see all avenues of approach. People in here stood in small groups, like they'd known each other forever. I couldn't tell if they were really watching me, or if it was just in my head. The need to blow off steam, to release the power I felt inside, rose.

Calming breaths didn't work too well in this environment, and closing my eyes to center myself was probably the worst idea I could have. I tried to look nonchalant. Like I came here all the time. They focused on me like I was the biggest bullshitter the world had ever seen. The power within me begged to call them all liars.

"Don't remember seeing you around here." A voice spoke from the right of me, raspy like they hadn't had water in days. I swallowed slowly before turning my head. Facing them in a hurry might be misconstrued, not facing them at all would mean I was ignoring them.

"Wanted a burger for dinner." I smiled as non-threateningly as I could. After all, it was sort of true. I'd like a burger; I just wouldn't order one with pineapple on it. Ever. In a million years. Even if pineapple became a meat substitute or was made of pure gold.

The old man who spoke up with his crackly voice eyed me out of bright grey eyes. They matched his pale hair. He leaned against one of the walls, his long, dark eyelashes a stark juxtaposition to the rest of him. An image of Beethoven with his hearing intact was the comparison that came to mind. "Make sure you enjoy that burger. That's a special one."

He turned back to the two people standing with him and melded into the conversation as if he'd never spoken to me. Did he know what that this burger was? If so, could I talk to him about Second Chance.

This man is not a member of our organization. You may not divulge any information to him. Do not violate the Terms and Conditions.

My vision cleared again, and I gulped down the lump that was suddenly in my throat. I swallowed my irritation and counted to three. Infuriated was how the system made me feel. Or was that my ability?

"Order two-three-eight," a kid about my age called out.

He waved me over and shoved a bag in my face. Inside I could see the paper bag containing the burger. And something else. I didn't even receive a second glance once I handed over my ticket to claim it. He was onto the next customer, and I knew it was up to me to just walk out of there like I needed to get home with my food.

So I did, despite the fact that I still felt like people were watching me, studying me. People were everywhere here, and it closed in on me, suffocating in its intensity. I wanted to reach out and let loose with the power that hadn't stopped building in me since I'd entered.

It was all I could do not to run down the steps and sprint all the way back home faster than humanly possible. But that would draw attention and make me stand out, and I got the feeling that for this particular task, that was a very bad thing.

The burger weighed heavily in the bag, but I didn't reach down for it. Not even when the sickly-sweet aroma wafted up to me. Pineapple mingled with meat, made me hungry and ill in the same breath. But the package was heavier than that, and with each step I took it seemed to weigh more.

Two blocks had never seemed so far to me before. How I wanted to run and have the space melt away beneath my feet. Sparks ignited at the end of my finger tips like it agreed. I hadn't known how much restraint I possessed until then.

Shadows moved like liquid oil taking shape in an art project. Eerily similar to those I'd seen in the lab, and yet somehow totally different. I wanted to reach out and touch them, to feel what they were like. And yet even the lightning in my skin seemed to recoil at their presence. They shifted with me as I walked, following me like the faceless ghosts from childhood nightmares.

I took the final turn, positive that someone was watching me, scared to I'd out the buildup of electricity practically overflowing from my fingertips. I raised my left hand to my face and noticed sparks travel along my pointer finger. It'd been too long, or else I didn't release enough during the day. Perhaps nervous energy helped fuel it.

Stress and anxiety help to build your energy reserves up. You simply need to discharge the power. As you progress, you'll learn more ways to deal with your abilities.

When? I couldn't help it, I felt vulnerable, and impatient. Apart from what would end up being a sloppy hamburger, I had no idea what was in this bag and a strong sense that maybe I shouldn't know. *When will I learn all this? You keep saying in the future, in the future, but now is technically the future from my accident. So spill it. When?*

I paused, taking a breath while the system thought about my words, about what it was I was asking. Hell, I needed to think about it myself. Most of what I could already do, I'd just winged. Frankly, it almost felt like the element was pushing me in the directions I needed to go, powering me up.

Just up the block a ways, and I'd be home. I'd always hated how dark this corner was with the streetlamp smashed out. It made the plays of dark and light turn into ghouls and monsters. The little kid in me worshipped superpowers, and grappled with the adult I wanted to become, determined to convince me those things were real.

But the answer didn't come from the system, because somebody or something grabbed at my right hand, gripping my fingers tightly where I carried the bag. I lashed out with my left fist and encountered nothing but air. I wasn't about to let that damned hand get the bag.

No matter how I twisted, I couldn't focus on whatever it was attached to me. Flashes of light flickered through the shadow, like a storm standing beside me in incorporeal thunder cloud form.

I couldn't seem to focus on anything other than the hand grabbing at my assignment target, but even that was blurring in my vision. Kicking out with my right foot, I thought of everything Davin ever tried to teach my stubborn head about Karate and manage to make a connection with what I thought was a knee.

What I didn't expect was the second culprit. An elbow looped around my throat from behind. There was no way it could be the same attacker, not without being an octopus monster, and I just wasn't letting my mind go there.

Power prickled beneath my skin, multiplying, pounding against my skull. I could feel my control slipping. It might sound funny, but I didn't think my attackers were human.

I was medium height, but lithe and fast, so my strength wasn't necessarily in my muscles. Usually agile and light on my feet, I was trapped. That damned bag was working its way out of my fingers with every heartbeat, somehow being tugged at by that stormy disembodied hand. There was nothing beyond that, despite what my foot tried to convince me of.

The air in my lungs begin to get heavy. It became difficult to breathe because that elbow was working at my trachea like no one's business. Electricity bubbled beneath the surface of my skin, jumping at my fingertips, leaking out in every breath I took.

Self defense.

It flashed across my vision, and I didn't need another hint. I reached up with my spare hand and latched onto the person, zombie, puppet master or whatever was controlling this attacker. I focused briefly on what I could see of the translucent arm and released some of my pent-up power.

Only, I'd apparently generated a lot more than I realized. It crackled as it sped along my veins like it was a hungry wolf just waiting for me to set it on my enemy. It burst through my fingers in a jolt of pain that reverberated through my body lighting all of my nerves on fire.

But it simmered down to an ache, dulled by my actions. I only had a moment to wonder why it wasn't burning me, before my would-be captor's husk began to blister and curl back as wisps of shadowed tendrils began to drift into the air. Holes of black appeared through what had seemed clear, and a foul stench began to fill the air.

The scream that echoed through my ears as they jerked their body away set my teeth on edge, and the grip on my bag with the burger lessened. It was like the second whatever was worried they might be a target next. I grinned, unable to stop myself.

Power echoed through my brain, and I focused on the original attacker. Two of their fingers, as obscure as they appeared, lingered against the bag's handles tugging more feebly now. I couldn't help but wonder what amazing type of plastic bag this was to last through so much of a kerfuffle. I didn't know how to deal with that one, and since I had no idea how many volts I shot into the other attacker, I wasn't sure how much juice I had left.

Electricity prickled along the back of my neck, making the hairs on my skin stand on end. It felt like it was telling me I still had plenty of power left. I focused all of my concentration into the right pinky finger. A sudden giggle threatened to overwhelm me. I was tired but on edge, and excited but terrified. I focused on the pale blur I could see holding onto my bag with me, and gently touched it with my pinky.

At first, I thought nothing would happen. Maybe I'd already expended all of the electricity within me after all. But then the spark hit, and a sizzle sounded through the air, followed by the stench of burning hair. A split second later, a shock of electricity that jolted my body back a few feet ripped into whatever it was that had been fighting me.

I didn't wait this time, stumbling back slightly as the bag finally came free in my hand. Without a moment to lose I sprinted toward my house, boosting each step without regard for who the hell saw me. By the time I reached the top of the stairs my breath came in gasps and my chest constricted painfully. Shorter sprints weren't my thing. I fumbled for my key, eyeing the path I just came from. I never liked to go that way, specifically because of how dark it is, because of that missing light. But now… I had a built-in bodyguard.

Finally, I jammed the key into the lock and began to throw the door to the apartments open. But then I caught sight of my face in the glass reflection. It stopped me dead.

I raised a hand to my pale cheeks and marveled at the static way my hair billowed out from my head. Like I'd just got dressed for Halloween, complete with white ghost make up and all. If I didn't know that was me, I would never have recognized it.

The face looking back at me was wild, untamed, and high on power.

And damn did it look good on me.

10
PERCEPTION

I shoved the bag inside our mailbox, not caring that the hamburger was still in it. The squelch as I closed the box sounded sickening, but I already felt nauseous from the smell, so it wasn't like it made it worse. Besides, for the scary shit I'd just encountered, they deserved all the rank drippy burger it'd be by the time someone came to collect it. Blood pumped through my veins like it was boiling and sweat beaded my brow despite the chill in the air. Taking the steps two at a time I ran up to our apartment.

It was still quiet inside. No one else was here yet. Maybe I could make it to my room and say I was sick. Not that I was. But the shaking wouldn't stop. Whether it was a result of fear, or the sheer amount of electricity I'd channeled, it wasn't dissipating as quickly as I'd like.

Your heart rate is elevated. Can you sit down?

Even Second Chance sounded concerned. It should be, shouldn't it? That much energy, all inside me. There was more of it still there, just beneath the surface, intent on breaking out. My head spun, and I barely made it into my room. The bed felt harder than I remembered, and this time the room spun too. Or maybe it was still my head, but either way, there was lots of spinning involved.

A laugh bubbled in the back of my throat and I gave into it. Burning shadows, translucent skin. Those hands hadn't been cloaked robotic appendages. Whatever it was had really wanted that awful burger.

The knock at the door brought me out of my minor hysteria. It echoed through my skull like a pounding hammer took residence inside. I ignored it. But the next knock was louder.

"Dare?" Orion's tone was filled with concern. While it wasn't fair to him right now, I was buzzed, and not quite myself. So, I came up with an excuse.

"Not feeling well. Going to bed early." I managed to squeeze the words out from between clenched teeth as I shut my eyes to avoid looking at the light beaming down at me from the ceiling. Both of which helped the nervous laughter that threatened to escape again.

I could hear the emptiness of sound on the other side as he tried to puzzle out my words. It was unusual for me to avoid a friend gathering. I never realized that hesitation had a sound. Or perhaps I was simply hyper aware right now.

"I'll bring you some dinner." He'd given up and tried to hide his worry with the excuse of food.

Once he was gone, I opened my eyes and looked up at my ceiling, daring the light to blind me. The laughter had drained as quickly as it arrived. All of the weight on my shoulders appeared to have fallen away and I sat, drinking in the silence of my room.

Your heart rate has returned to normal. It is advisable to remain lying down for the time being. You will feel tired shortly as the adrenaline ebbs.

I raised an eyebrow at the well-meaning system. *You think?*

It paused for a moment before actually replying to me. *I know.*

Very well then, it knows. Calming down fit well with me. I stretched my arms up tand looked at my hands. It was strange, but my finger tips felt numb, asleep. Like someone had placed them on a tiny pad of pins and needles. Yet, despite the tiredness I could feel starting to creep over my body, the thrill of what I'd done wouldn't abate.

Your mission has been completed. Payment has been transferred. Due to the unexpected twist of this last assignment and it's associated energy expulsion, you have ranked up.

You have moved from Junior Rank, to Novice Rank.

Successful execution of: General Electrical Pulse Control

You have gained field experience.

Successful execution of: Rudimentary Electrical Shock Application

You have gained field experience.

Unexpected twist is a good way to put it. I couldn't help the snort of laughter that escaped me. I guess I'd gained a skill too.

We could not see what attacked you, but know you were assailed. This put your most recent task up a category.

Which was very interesting information. But something else the system said finally hit me. *Wait. What now? They've already retrieved what I went to get?*

I sat up, irritation welling inside once again. My joy at discovering how powerful I could be ebbed. It couldn't have been more than fifteen, maybe twenty minutes since I put that bag in our mailbox. Who on earth could have retrieved it so quickly? Unless they had someone who was close by and received a message when I'd completed a task. Did they have a skeleton key or something?

Retrieval of items obtained is paramount to the success of Second Chance. Items will always be retrieved with as much haste as possible.

I knew it heard my thoughts, it wasn't like I tried to hide them. Just yelling them loudly in my mind so anyone could hear. So it chose not to give me more information than that. I sighed and pulled myself back up. As much as I might like to after my encounter with whatever that was earlier, I couldn't hide in here all weekend. What I could do was avoid the route I'd taken to the diner like I usually did and go out to the living room and spend time with my friends. Maybe that way I'd get distracted enough to stop noticing how quickly my charge seemed to be replenishing.

Remembering my recent reflection, I grabbed my brush and ran it through my hair quickly to tame it. I held my breath before checking the mirror to make sure I didn't look too manic. As luck would have it, I appeared to have regained some composure, even if I was still pale.

I opened the door, only to find Orion with his fist raised, ready to knock on it. He almost dropped the tray in his hands. But I manage to help him save it and rescue the PB&J he'd made from potential death. We all know the five second rule was just an excuse to see how much bacteria could jump on your food while it sat on the floor.

"You're up." He eyed me quizzically. "I thought you were too busy dying to come out and hang with us. So I thought I should bring you sustenance, just in case."

"Maybe I just wanted to see your exotic face," I quipped as I bit into the food. I'd never been able to figure it out, but Orion was like a magical sandwich maker. No matter what was in it, it always tasted like he should be in some competition. Even with a PB&J.

He raised an eyebrow at me and shook his head, a smile tugging at his lips. "More like you just want to see Cyan."

He laughed and tucked the small tray under his arm as he ushered me out of my room.

He was right, in a way, but not completely. I liked Cyan, but I liked Orion too. I just wasn't sure which one was the stronger like, or even what type. Besides, it'd be horrible to lose Orion's friendship, so it wasn't something I dwelled on.

Jacob was gone when we got to the living room, but Cyan was there dressed in an alarming shade of indigo that clashed with her hair enough to make me blink. That was probably her intention. Her smile lit up the room, and she gave me a brief hug.

"Dare! Orion said you weren't feeling well. But you look fine." She nudged me, like she was in on some huge secret. She whispered in my ear. "Though you could do with a bit of color."

Memory of the arm around my neck, of those fingers against mine wrestling with the bag made me suppress the shudder and grin back at her, hoping I managed not to snarl. At that moment, before she could look into my expression with any depth, there was a buzz at the door.

Her enthusiasm was usually contagious, but I wasn't feeling it right now, even if I wanted to. Maybe I should have stayed in the bedroom, because my brain had started to overanalyze every portion of my ill-fated trip home. I wanted to dissect it, to figure out how I'd called up that much force. Orion watched me from the kitchen, not bothering to hide the fact. The frown on his face said what I knew he was thinking. That I was keeping something from him. Oh boy, was he ever right.

Cyan buzzed the next guests through the door like she lived here too. I could hear their feet tromping up the stairs. From the sounds of it, it was the rest of the group. Sam was one of Cyan's friends. I've never been able to figure out from where. She didn't go to our school and didn't seem to go to school at all. Her finances appeared to be unlimited, because she provided us with the majority of our snacks and food for any gathering.

Sam was a good person from what I'd been able to see. Always willing to help, always there if you needed someone to go get more supplies. Her bob was always pristine, like she'd just had it styled at a salon, and the red sheen to her black-brown hair would have seemed natural if I didn't know better. Maybe her money came from Second Chance too. For all I knew everyone's everything could come from there.

Neale walked in next. Tall, athletic, on the basketball team. I'd be surprised if he didn't get scouted early. Great guy if he could get rid of that darker than acceptable sense of humor. It was like it had chosen to be the precise opposite of his almost white-blonde hair. One of these days, it was going to get him in trouble.

I heard someone trip up the stairs and cringed. That had to be Levi. It was never quite the problem at school where walls and railings were readily accessible. I sighed, unable to keep the grin off my face when he stumbled through the door. Good old Levi. If anyone was going to trip, fall, crash into the decorations that just got set up for a fundraiser? It was Levi. Luckily, we didn't own anything valuable.

Neale nudged me with his elbow. It was closer to shoulder height for me. I mean, the guy was a mini giant. I wish I had a few more inches of height. My legs would be longer. I could be so much faster, even without giving myself a push.

"Whatchya doing, Dare?"

I glanced up at his friendly grin. "I'm standing here pretending not to notice that you're using me as a resting place."

He laughed. Neale had to have the worst laugh I've ever heard. If you took a donkey, crossed it with a seal, and let it smoke for thirty years, you'd only just get in the same vicinity as Neale's laugh. "Good to see you haven't lost your sense of humor, even if it looks like you've lost a bit of weight instead of gaining. Keeping your training diet up?"

I gulped and looked away, feeling guilty. He was right, I should be eating a specific amount of calories and balancing healthy proteins with my eating habits. Making sure I had enough calories to burn was important and since last Sunday, it was something I'd been largely ignoring. Not to mention, I had a sneaking suspicion I needed to up my food game to keep my body charged enough to house my electrical abilities. Knowing my luck, I'd probably end up eating my profits.

"Been a hectic few days. I'll make sure to adjust back this coming week." I tried to put effort into the words, but even I didn't really believe myself. Sure, I meant it now…

He leaned a bit closer and studied my face, the hint of a frown evident on his own. "See that you do. I'll check in on you next week. You have an important meet coming up. Don't blow it, Dare."

I nodded. He was right. I'd just been a tad preoccupied. I did my best to grin positively. "Thanks, Neale."

"No problem." He grinned and tapped my left shoulder. "Nice tattoo though. When did you get it?"

I didn't want to explain this again. I didn't want those looks that made it feel as if everyone was trying to save me or make me feel better. They didn't know the full truth, and my brain resident had other ideas anyway. I couldn't tell them precisely how bad the accident had been, so I just went along with his perception of my scar. "Last week."

He gave me a high five. "Nicely done." And he turned to talk to Sam, leaving me alone with my thoughts.

Or at least, so I hoped. It was like my luck stopped with the whole, you're not dead yet thing.

You aren't dead. It shouldn't be so hard to grasp. It seems like you're having problems digesting this information. As mentioned in the initial tutorial, it would be best for your progress if you read the orientation guide.

I don't remember seeing the ability to open an orientation guide.

Sure, I was known for sometimes skimming important stuff, and excelling with academic experimentation as I liked to call it. Reading about how to do it, was never as much fun as actually doing it. I wasn't entirely sure, but I thought the system was getting irritated with me.

Down the right hand side, under personal information and Frequently Asked Questions. Take time and read the instructions and guidelines. It's been almost a week, and you should be far more familiar with the system than you are.

Anger welled in me, and I could feel the sparks begin to gather under my skin. Suddenly, I didn't feel like playing with my friends. I also didn't feel like playing this life or death game I suddenly found myself in the middle of.

"Hey guys, that nausea is coming back. I'm going to lie down. Don't worry about keeping the noise down, I won't hear it."

The looks on their faces as I left the room said everything. Like they were sorry for me and knew something was up. Pity, and concern, with understanding only just tempered it.

They had no idea what the whirlwind in my head was like. I didn't want to sit around listening to them laugh like everything was normal, like I hadn't died. But I couldn't tell them that, because I'd risk my life all over again. My adrenaline began to boil again, and my power prodded at my brain, begging to be let out. If this happened in a fit of anger, we'd be in for a world of hurt.

A thought struck me. Could letting my friends know about my predicament result in their demise too? For just a split second I wished I'd never been saved. I wished the electricity had just done its job and left me for dead.

Is this truly what you wish?

The question took me by surprise and for one split second, I had no idea how to answer.

11

ACCEPTANCE

The easiest way to deal with this was to avoid everyone for as long as possible, while I attempted to understand and analyze everything I was going through. With the way my ability had been bouncing around in and out of my body, I couldn't trust myself to be too close to anyone I cared about. Hell, close to anyone at all if I looked at it that way. How much irritation would it take for a strand of electricity to escape my control? No. I needed to practice with this. To feel as if I had a modicum of control. To understand my power.

Naturally that meant I had to get up even earlier and make it to the track before anyone else. It allowed for me to have a private place I could go, somewhere I could analyze the way my power sang to me, how it felt alive inside me while my feet pounded against the pavement and the track. It enabled me to practice control and release of the ability, boosting my strengths before coach got there to time me.

I loved running. It was like a mantra that constantly ran through my head. The one constant in all of this crazy shit.

As the next week passed, I began to hone my control. If I wasn't careful and didn't limit myself, I'd end up zooming in a way that would find me locked in a laboratory myself if I wasn't careful. Which made me really want to go back to that lab I'd found and figure out just what it was it contained. The system never remarked anything about it to me. Which only made it even more suspicious.

If I applied my ability subtly, I could give myself a boost that seemed like infinite energy for most of the day. I'd call it cheating, but I was only using the skills I had at my disposal.

The second advantage to this was that it allowed me to discharge excess electrical energy. I still didn't completely understand how this whole thing worked, but I did know that if I bottled it up, I'd explode and spray everyone with glass shards. Metaphorically speaking, anyway.

While that might be good if I got into trouble again, it probably wasn't best to walk around every day like a loaded gun.

By the time it rolled around to the following Friday, I'd completed three more tasks. Mundane, boring, nothing chasing me tasks. I was ready for something frightening. I hadn't even got to use my Rudimentary Electric Shock again.

Why have this power if I didn't get to use it. And I still hadn't ranked up again. I wish the interface had an experience bar so I could see where the hell I was.

I'd also been paid around nine hundred dollars so far, which went a hell of a way to reducing my schooling costs. I was curious as to how the system paid me. How did I get money from it? Did it secretly belong to a corporation or the government? All of these questions overflowed in my head and the system was stubbornly silent about it. Selective thought hearing in the flesh. Just like it hadn't mentioned anything else to do with the run-in I had with old pineapple hamburger hands.

Unsure what attacked me? Sure, they were. Either SC ignored what happened, or it didn't see it. The latter was more unsettling than I wanted to admit. They'd seen my death. How the hell had they not seen my attackers?

Managing to avoid my friends completely for the most part became exhausting, but also thrilling in its own way. Like I was a spy in a movie, except I wasn't. This was the real world, and I refused to get them all accidentally dead.

Whether that was through electrocuting them, or getting them killed because I inadvertently gave away my secret, didn't matter. Since the system refused to respond to my very loudly thought questions on the matter, it was simply something I couldn't risk.

I even managed to slink in and out of my lectures all week without Cyan being the wiser for it. Although it was obvious she did know—she just couldn't catch me in time. She was the same academic track as me, though we'd diverge when we eventually hit postgraduate. At least she was easy to spot in a crowd, thus making it simple to stay on the opposite side of her with a baseball cap on.

About two minutes before the current lesson wound down, I finished off my notes, shoved my tablet in my bag, and inched out the side door before anyone else could get up from their seat. I turned to the right to make my way out of the building, only to find Orion there blocking my way. I wasn't sure how people recognized an aura, but if I could see them, I was willing to bet that Ry's would be black right about now.

He grabbed me by the upper arm and dragged me along with him.

"What the hell, Ry? That hurts." If he wasn't careful he'd get shocked. My skin could turn into a conductor at any given moment, and I didn't quite have that under control yet after discovering it the other day.

He glowered as he locked eyes with me, and if I could have stepped back, I would have, but he held me tight. "No. I have been trying to catch you at home, and at the track, and after most of your lectures this week. You avoided me and Jacob all weekend, and you haven't even checked in with your family. So, no. You are going to stay with me because I can't trust you not to disappear if I let you follow behind."

My family? What the hell? My temper was difficult to control *before* I was pumped with electrical power. Gritting my teeth I ground out the words. "I'm not a child anymore. I don't need a babysitter. I told him I'd call him when I could."

Orion was really worried about me. His tone said it all. His grip wasn't really hurting, just uncomfortable. I just didn't like following. That whole competition thing. Plus, I didn't feel like facing anyone today, or yesterday, or even tomorrow. He raised an eyebrow at me. "That's what you focus on, in everything I said?"

He was right though. I took a deep breath, and willed the power to calm down. "Sorry. I promise I won't run away."

My voice was soft, but he heard me and immediately let go. I'd call him gullible, but I knew he wasn't. He'd known me long enough to understand that if I promised, I did it.

What I wasn't expecting was for one of the study conference rooms to hold the majority of my friends—and my brother. Orion opened the door for me, motioning for me to enter the room first, and it was too late for me to back out once I'd realized exactly what I was in for.

This looked suspiciously like an intervention. And while I attempted to backpedal, Orion blocked the door, his face a pretty convincing thundercloud. This was what I got for trying to protect them?

Warning. Watch what you say in this room. Tread Carefully.

You sound worried, I directed at it, unable to mask all of my irritation. It wouldn't do to lose control, even just a tiny bit.

I would hate to have to terminate your SC contract. Watch what you say.

Well, that sounded actually like it was pleading with me. Okay. I could do that. Still though, I wasn't in the mood to play nice with my friends. What did they think they were doing? I crossed my arms and directed my best glare their way.

My brother spoke up first, his eyebrows raised and his tone as jokingly nonchalant as it always was when he was trying to get on someone's good side. "What's with that stance, Dare? You seem hostile, and I haven't seen you for ages."

"Hostile?" I almost spat the word out and had to take a deep breath to right myself again. "How else am I supposed to react when Orion escorts me to a room full of my closest friends, and my *brother,* looking like they want to chastise me? Not to mention—stop babying me. I'll call in every now and again.

Give it a rest Dav. If I was using drugs or drinking, I'd think this was some sort of intervention."

At least Dav had the good grace to blush. I mean seriously, people. Electrical charge began to build under my skin. It prickled just underneath, like it was waiting to burst out the first chance it got. I fought against it, amazed at the calm I felt.

"We're just concerned, Dare." Orion let the door fall closed behind him as he gave me a wide berth before coming to stand in front of me. He was doing his best not to frown, but the lines on his forehead hadn't completely smoothed out. "Since this accident, you've been avoiding us, or absentminded, or just not yourself. All we want to do is let you know we're all here if you need us, no matter what."

He had a point, and I knew it. Taking a deep breath, I gave myself a three count before speaking. "Look, I get it. But it's amazing what getting electrocuted can do to your brain. I've had a lot of thoughts to deal with, a lot of realizations. I got lucky. Really lucky. But the whole experience shook me up. I didn't want to take that out on you guys. You, of all people, should know I sometimes have a quick temper."

I wasn't precisely lying. After all, it did expand my brain so to speak, and I had a lot to deal with when it came to this program. Orion was trying not to smile, because he'd witnessed my temper more than anyone else there.

Cyan frowned, and for once her sparklines was absent. Somehow that made her hair appear duller than usual. "Still, though. You haven't avoided me in the three years I've known you, until the last couple of weeks. We all love you, and we're worried about you. That's all."

She sounded genuinely upset, and I regretted hurting her feelings. But I also didn't. It had only been two weeks. Give a person some time to deal with a near death experience people. While I didn't have control, keeping them at arm's length was better for all of us. Not to mention if I let something slip they'd be terminated.

We don't kill civilians.

What?

To kill civilians would negate the purpose of the Second Chance program, which is to protect human life and the earth in their cohabitation. We only activate the program should the cause of death be useful to our goals. The only person who will suffer if you were to breach your contract is yourself. Since you should have died, it doesn't violate the don't-kill-civilians directive. Short term memories are easy to alter. That is all that would happen to these people you hold in such high regard.

That was a mind-blowing statement and a half. Was I supposed to ask specific questions? They really needed to reevaluate their orientation into the program. Because the amount of shit it hadn't told me was ridiculous. It should be easier to protect them this way. Watch my tongue. Don't let them see anything odd.

It was so easy to forget that time didn't stop and let me discuss shit with my newly-acquired inner voice. No, while I was conversing with SC, my friends had been talking to me and I'd failed to respond.

"Sorry. Could you say that again?" I tried my best to appear contrite, and I wasn't sure how successful I was. It made me wish Cyan's friend Sam was here. I'd never met anyone who could diffuse situations so easily. Neale, Levi, Cyan, Dav, and Orion were, and they all appeared concerned by my inattention.

Neale sighed and crossed his arms. Even in lecturing mode his eyes never lost that twinkle of kindness. "We want you to talk to us, tell us what's going on in that head of yours. I know how much the pressure of winning in sports can pile up until you feel like you're going to explode. I'm always willing to listen unless I'm actively playing. You should know that."

And I did. Although his choice of words made me have to bite my tongue. "I know. I'm sorry." My left arm began to pulse, like it was reminding me how much had been left behind, how much had really changed. That as much as I might wish it to, nothing could ever go back to what it was.

I barreled on before anyone could choose to interrupt, clutching at my left arm to try and get the throbbing to abate. "I'm okay, seriously, and I don't plan on staying just ok. This whole scar deal is not what it's cracked up to be. And how I got it, I'm still dealing with that, and you have to let me. You need to understand that it's not something you can assist with."

I could see relief in all of their faces at my finally speaking to them. Every one of them except Orion. He side-eyed me from where he stood, his entire body rigid with disbelief. Had I slipped up somehow?

It was working on the others though. I did need more time, and more space to think. Only it was about how to exert control, and just what SC did, and how everything really fit together. They were right in that I'd become withdrawn, but I really hoped they could understand why.

Dav rolled his shoulders and pushed his brown hair out of his eyes. "You know mom worries. You're the youngest, it's a burden, but she just needs to hear from you."

I held up my hand. I still wasn't even sure why he was here. "But I'll check in as time allows. I'll even text her more frequently. But stop tracking me, that's not okay."

"I get it." Dev appeared a bit sheepish, but concern still peered out from under his shaggy eyebrows. I didn't think my big brother would ever stop trying to protect me. "Sorry. I didn't mean to be heavy handed. The accident worried us, especially since you didn't really tell anyone."

That's what I got for being the responsible one. Always on time, always organized, organizing everyone else, not to mention my grades and track history. But that was just it. I worked for everything. It didn't come easy. I trained until I could run like the wind all day and night. My grades came from studying. It was going to take so much effort to maintain the latter with these stupid assignments.

But now, everything was different. Maybe not for him, but it was for me. I was stronger, faster, more capable of taking care of myself than ever before. They just had to let me.

"I mean it, Dav. I just...it's been a lot to take on my plate, and I need some space." I deliberately met his eyes, and he flinched. I'd never made him flinch in my life.

This is necessary to maintain your cover.

Thank you, Sherlock.

A slight shiver of resentment spiraled down my spine, and now I'd probably pissed off the SC system. Because that was exactly how great my life was going today. The pins and needles under my skin began to ache.

Cyan walked around the table and placed a hand on my shoulder, locking her bright eyes onto mine. Some of her sparkle had returned. "Just because you're the responsible one doesn't mean you can't ask for help sometimes."

Which was precisely why sometimes I just didn't want to be around Cyan. Her ability to look into people and see what was up with them was close to scary. Empath was what she called herself. I secretly thought she might be half-witch. "Thanks. I'll remember that. It's nice to hear you say you're there, even though I kind of knew it. I just need some time for me."

Even Levi smiled this time, not that he'd said anything anyway. Excellent. I was finally getting through to people.

"Thanks, guys. Really, there's no need to worry."

Neale jumped the table and slung an arm around my shoulder, giving me a brief hug mostly disguised as using me as a resting stop. "Stop worrying us, Dare. We worry about our friends."

"Yeah, yeah. I've got it." I disentangled myself from his grip and gave him a smile and fist bump, ignoring the sparks fighting for attention in my mind. "Thanks."

Levi appeared to have chosen to walk around the table before saying goodbye. Probably the best idea since jumping the table like Neale had done would only result in dear Levi faceplanting the floor in a spectacular fashion. Hell, he almost tripped over his own feet on the way around the table anyway.

"Trust me, I know how irritating it can be to think no one understands you. But even if we don't understand, we're still here for you." Levi smiled and gave me a quick hug.

He'd been a hugger as long as I'd known him, and they were never intrusive, just a sharing of gesture that, when used correctly, could replenish and not steal. I'd not expected his words to be so wise, though.

Dav stopped in front of me before leaving. "Look. I'm here when you do want to come and see someone. I'm always here for you. Hell, I drove two hours for this. I always will. You know that, right?"

"Yeah, I know. And ditto." I smiled and gave him a real hug. Family was an exception, and Dav had one of the best hugs I'd ever experienced. But I pulled away and looked him straight in the eye. "Just let me grow up now."

I watched them file out of the room, my heart slightly bitter. They'd meant well, but damn, it had only been like twelve days. My friends cared. Seriously cared. As long as I watched my mouth, they'd be fine. Unless they saw something they weren't supposed to. Like if they kept spying on me.

Irrational anger went away with a few deep breaths. I knew instantly I had to be better about dealing with it immediately, because otherwise it fed my ability, which gobbled it greedily, expanding it for later consumption.

I let the pent-up breath whoosh out of me in a sigh, only to realize that someone still stood behind me, and they were tapping their foot impatiently. Slowly, I turned around to find Orion standing there, leaning against the huge table with his arms crossed. His face told me not to dare lie to him because he'd know that I was.

"You've got them fooled, you know," he said to me in that deeper version of his voice that told me just how pissed off he was. His feet were planted firmly on the ground letting me know he wasn't going anywhere until we sorted this out. I resisted rolling my eyes.

"Fooled about what?" I fished, to see what it was that he actually knew.

He raised an eyebrow. "Fooled them into believing that the accident wasn't really a big deal. You're secretive now. You come and go at odd hours, and lately you've eaten out a few times. If I didn't know better, I'd say you started selling drugs, because you've changed, and your lifestyle has changed, and I need you to trust me."

"Drugs? I didn't realize you thought so little of me." Anger stirred in my stomach and began to climb up like it wanted to exit through my mouth, pulsing and crackling the whole time. "I'm not doing drugs, nor am I selling drugs. You should know me better than that."

"But do I?" His answer was so fast on the heel of what I'd said that I wondered how he timed it so well. What hurt the most was that he said it at all. "You used to tell me everything. We've always been super close. But now? You don't even eat with me, you don't have lunch with us, and I haven't seen you at any of our study sessions since you had that damned accident."

"It's been twelve fucking days, Orion. It might take me a tad longer to get over, oh, I don't know, being electrocuted?" The words were out of my mouth so fast, I didn't have time to bite them back. And it felt so much better with them out there. Frustration partially expelled without blowing up anything. Win for me.

He eyed me, like he was processing my words because he hadn't thought of that aspect. "No. There's something you're not telling me. And even if you share it with no one else, I don't understand why you won't tell me."

He was genuinely upset, and I hated that I was the cause of it. But I couldn't tell him. Even if I wanted to, the system would literally shut me down. I just wanted to live, and it was going to take me more than two weeks to figure out how I was meant to juggle SC and a super power, while maintaining my life.

"I'm sorry," was all I could think of to say, and it didn't seem to placate him even slightly.

"Fine. It's fine." He wouldn't meet my eyes, his hands shoved in his pockets. "I get it in ways you couldn't possibly understand. I'm still here, and I always will be. But I won't forget that you don't trust me enough to tell me whatever is on your mind. Shutting me out like this isn't good—for either of us."

The scowl on his face was unfamiliar to me, and he pushed himself away from where he stood, heading for the door. He didn't even give me a hug, and I could feel the waves of anger rolling off him—directed at me, for the first time in my life, and I found it fearsome.

12
ROCKY ROAD

Orion and I had never fought. Not in as long as I could remember. We'd known each other since we were three, if I believed what our mothers said. Two months apart, we'd basically been thrown together as soon as the Majors moved in next door. Orion was a middle child of five, while I was the youngest in our family, but we didn't care what our siblings thought of one another. All we cared about was having someone who was always on our side, because in big families, you needed to have someone on your side. Even in my earliest memories, Orion was always there. We studied together, we played together, we joined sports teams together. At least until we hit middle school, anyway. Orion wasn't the most athletically-inclined person. In middle school he joined the science club and set himself on the road to academic greatness. Me? I joined the athletics club—running, to be specific—and never looked back.

My grades were a result of determination on both mine and Orion's parts. We'd been talking about going to college together, about pursuing dreams. I wanted to compete in the Olympics as a long-distance runner and work my way toward a Cyber Security masters so when I retired from competition, I could do the other thing I loved. Computers were my entire life.

Building them, learning how to code, how to create our own virtual worlds—it was expression at its finest and allowed a measure of freedom my brain only seemed to find in running otherwise.

Orion entered medicine. Cancer stole his father when he was twelve, and he'd decided on his career choice three days afterward. Medical research and the cure for cancer. Noble, but sad at the same time. That it took losing someone to cement the idea only hurt more.

I never thought he'd give up on me so easily. After such a history, what was two fucking weeks? Was I right to be so angry at him? I wouldn't give up on him after two weeks of weird behavior. Sure, I'd be worried, but not angry. Our friendship meant a hell of a lot more to me than that. But apparently, I'd read him wrong.

Trembling, I lowered myself to the floor, not caring that no one was in there with me anymore, only caring about the tenuous thread my friendship seemed to be dangling from. Only aware of the way my blood seemed to boil, the way anger began to seep into my skin.

I attempted to take steadying breaths, focusing on the memory of my mother's voice. The force inside me ebbed a bit and I allowed my mind to rest for a moment. If I'd died, none of this would be a problem right now. My friends would be mourning me instead of overly protective of me And I'd be oblivious, being dead and all.

I let myself fall back onto the carpeted floor, trying not to think about what had been on this carpet, how clean it was or wasn't. Fine. My body zinged as I sat back up and stretched. I couldn't let this fuck up my own track record. But my hands itched like I had ants crawling beneath my skin and I shuddered, releasing a small amount into my body. The pick me up leant me a bang of energy, but there was still more waiting to overflow. I looked around the room frantically to try and find a power outlet.

Spying one over by the entrance I took the few steps to it, listened for a moment to make sure no one was walking outside, and placed my fingers against the sockets. I could still vaguely remember my mother telling me not to play with the plug-ins as a child, using her typically Australian expression for the device. My defiance, even as an adult, brought a smile to my face. I did so hate wasting this energy, but I didn't have anywhere else to send it right now.

Focusing on the tips of my fingers, I willed the electricity that was flitting around in my body, trying to overflow, to gather at that point. When I thought most of it had, I released the pent-up energy.

The lights in the room flickered more severely than they'd done last time, down to a point they almost turned off multiple times. It took several seconds for everything to settle. But I didn't care because the release it gave me was worth it. It allowed me to clear my head, to usher in reason over my obstinance. My skin buzzed this time, feeling alive, and for just a moment I was invincible. It was all I needed to kick myself out of that funk.

Screw this shit.

I shook myself off before exiting the room and heading to my lecture. I had bills to pay and shit to do, and I was so over all of this guilt I felt at being alive, at being different and not being able to tell anyone. Not to mention the amount of practice I was putting in to get this ability crap under control.

Friday, bloody Friday. Not exactly how I was looking to ride out this week. I threw my backpack onto my bed and let myself fall next to it with a resounding creak as the bed springs strained against my insistence on bouncing. I wanted to scowl at it, but today had sapped my emotional energy and left the electricity bouncing around inside me less controllable than usual.

I rolled over and buried my head in the pillows. Despite my best efforts, my power fed off my mood. And my stupid brain dragged me back to my aggravation multiple times since that friendly intervention despite my explicit efforts to do the opposite. I'd have to avoid the living room and act like I wasn't in my room when people got here for the weekly Friday gathering crap.

State Championships were only two more weeks away, and my mental state had stagnated. I really needed to let some more of my overflow out. My hair wouldn't even sit flat against my head at the moment. I just kept generating more and more.

There was a fraction of time before they arrived. I sat back up and accessed my interface. Pulling up the tutorial, I frowned. Grounding elements. I was sure that hadn't been there initially. What, did it just add shit willy nilly? Sighing, I threw my reservations out the window and dove into the words that burned themselves into my eyes. Grounding sure sounded like a way to gain strength and not be overpowered. Perfect skill to master.

In order to ground myself fully, I'd eventually need to add some form of earth magic to my routine. Which didn't help me at this moment, because I didn't have any bloody earth magic. However, knowing that wood and rubber were ways I could release electricity without frying anything helped. Though wood might actually splinter. The more I delved into it, the more it made sense.

Being that my electricity couldn't actually affect me personally as far as I'd experienced, other than the shocking sensation without the damage, channeling it into something that could deaden electricity made the most sense. Rubber was an insulator, as were glass and plastic surprisingly enough. Perhaps I could carry some sort of insulation around with me, for emergencies when I didn't have other outlets.

Jumping off my bed, I scanned around the room. I knew it was somewhere. Mom thought they were stress balls when she bought them for me last Christmas, but they weren't. Just squash balls. I just didn't have the heart to tell her. But now it seemed like she'd been clairvoyant, because they were made out of rubber.

Finally, I found the small black ball. Roughly four centimeters in diameter, just over an inch and a half, it felt comfortable in the palm of my hand. Closing my eyes, I clutched it tightly in my left hand and focused. My electricity today was wild and not easy to direct. Like it was impatient for me, wanting to avenge or defend me. But I managed to expel some of it through my fingertips right into the heart of the ball.

A shock reverberated up my arm, but apart from mild discomfort, there was nothing else that directly affected me. The ball grew warm for a split second yet remained intact in my hand. While it wasn't the best solution, I could keep a tiny squash ball in a backpack or pocket. For now, at least I had a way not to accidentally kill someone if they surprised me all the while letting the edge off my bottled-up power.

Skill acquired: Rudimentary Grounding

Excellent. I could only wish that these skills came a little faster. My upgrade made me think about all my previous missions, which brought me back to a more immediate problem.

Like, what had they been doing in that lab?

Damn my brain. Dilemmas sucked. Especially since I didn't feel like going out into the living area and talking to my interventionist friends. It was the first time I wished I had a valid reason to get away from the apartment on a Friday night.

Assignment type: Recon.

Time: Before 5:30 p.m.

Location: Fountain gathering area on campus.

Task: Observation only. Do not be discovered. Consequences will follow if you are. Identities and subject matter of paramount importance.

Due: Midnight. Report directly to your Second Chance interface.

Compensation: To be determined.

Seriously? I phrased the question very loud in my head, specifically directing it to the damned interface that was so opportune with its demands.

You said you wished you had a valid reason to get away.

Valid for others to hear, not just for me. Still, I shouldn't be so nasty, so I sighed and begrudgingly sent a mental thank you.

I could almost hear it grinning. I still wished I could tell when it was listening in. The lack of privacy was an annoyance.

Any excuse was good excuse. I grabbed my backpack and headed out my door, pausing in the kitchen to grab an apple. If I had to, I'd be extravagant for once and spend some of my black-market money to buy a burger or something on the way home. Rebellion never felt so good.

Orion stopped at the edge of the hallway when he saw me biting into the apple. I winked at him, feeling mischievous in the moment.

"You're not staying for the game night?" There was a tinge of sadness to his voice, and for a moment I felt a pinch of guilt, but it didn't last long.

"Have to duck to campus, left one of my favorite socks in my stupid locker." I shrugged and slipped out the door, trying not to worry at the sinking feeling in my stomach. We'd been friends for so long it felt odd trying not to care. But after the way we parted that afternoon, how could he act so normal? Was this system making me care less about the things I'd loved my entire life?

I don't have the power over your free will.

So I can refuse to do these assignments?

It paused. *Well, no.*

Then you do have power over my free will.

But not in the way you're implying.

It sounded defensive. I'd take that as a victory for now. Technicalities, eh? Was nice to know the thing in my head could be pedantic. It had been cutting it close though. What was this task that I had to be there in forty-five minutes? Who would they have sent otherwise?

The apple tasted sourer the more questions I asked myself. There were no answers forthcoming, so SC was in off mode right now. Or at least pretending to ignore me and my inquisitive mind.

Still, eerily quiet. Oddly enough.

The traipse to the campus felt much longer than it usually did in the mornings when I'd woken fresh, when I felt like I was on top of the world. Right then I was tired, with a full day already behind me and heaps of friendly emotional baggage as well. Nothing that a little surge of energy wouldn't fix. It was becoming second nature to use my ability. I could get used to it. How did one inform their friends they lived on borrowed time?

You don't.

I didn't ask you. It was rhetorical.

I've never understood that concept. Don't ask a question if you don't want an answer.

Then don't choose to answer only what you want to answer.

Today was going great. Not only had my friends staged their bloody intervention, but now the computer voice living in my head was deciding to give me hard time too.

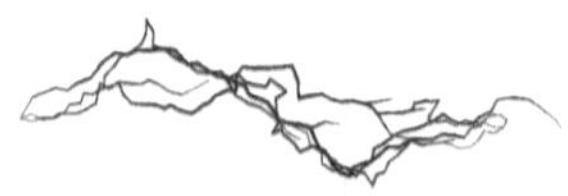

Setting foot onto the campus this late in the afternoon, especially a Friday, was an eerie experience. Sure, sometimes I was here in the mornings when it was still dark, but that wasn't nearly the same thing. Shadows fell differently at this time of day. With the sun setting, it stretched fingers of warm light through the buildings like bleeding hands trying to keep a hold on life that was slipping away from it.

I shuddered and eyed the fountain in the middle of the quad. Not many people lingered around it. Most of them were busy going to or from places, things to do, tests to take, teachers to fuck.

There was that cynical part of me again. I specifically knew of people who went about their education that way. Using charms instead of brains, using their bodies in other ways. It was their choice, and I thought that was okay. If whatever they wanted was worth a different effort to them, wasn't it still effort?

Me? I exerted myself physically all the time. It made my brain work better, and allowed me to afford to come here in the first place. There really wasn't a difference.

I realized I'd stopped and stood gazing at the fountain. For the first time all day, I didn't feel the electrical charge in me churning to get out. The scene in front of me was idyllic. They'd only turned the fountain back on last week after the ridiculously cold winter. Dolphins balanced on stone waves tossing a ball to each other. Art and I have never really gotten on well, but this fountain always made me feel at ease. Blinking as a few water droplets landed on my face, I backed away and then set off to sit under one of the trees.

For as long as there was still sunlight in the sky, anyway. I frowned looking up. It was almost five-thirty in the afternoon. How long was this going to go on? I couldn't sit beneath a tree and read once it was pitch black outside. That cover wasn't going to work.

We think it'll take maybe two hours.

Do I need to stay the entire time?

Not necessarily. We require names and general conversation topics. It's recon, nothing more.

Okay.

Tree it was then. Sadly, it wouldn't keep me out of the house as long as

I thought it would, but I could always stop for that generously-donated dinner on the way home. I settled myself at the base of a tree and pulled out my tablet. If nothing else I could use this to figure out who it was gathering in this place, and if I needed to, I might be able to record what they were saying. Doubted it though, I didn't have good audio equipment, and the wind would probably interfere in anything I could record anyway.

The pulse in my fingers beat heavier than ever as I activated the tablet. Like the electricity inside me resonated with the tech.

As five o'clock neared, people began to linger around the fountain. Some of them sat on the lip of the edge, trailing their fingers through the cold, clear liquid. Others stood in groups, clutching their books to their chests, talking and laughing like this was a regular thing. Others slunk up close to the fountain, staying in the shadows where I couldn't see their faces, but I could feel their eyes on me, watching, waiting. None of the others did that. None of them even noticed me. I wanted to keep it that way.

But even as I began to identify and note down each individual in attendance as the gathering turned less casual and more like a larger group event, I could feel those eyes on me. No one I'd identified yet even looked my way. I wasn't the only student out in the quad, leaning against a tree. The eyes I could feel watching me belonged to shadows and specters. Like they were waiting for me to move into their domain, and as the sun continued to dip down, I could feel their reach spreading more and more.

Just as slowly as the sun dropped, the anticipation in my power rose to the surface. Surely if those shadows were those robots, I could fry them. I had power, loads of it. Hell, I could probably overload the citywide electric grid if I felt like it.

Sparks erupted from my left hand as if agreeing, and for a moment all I wanted to do was find them and confront those damned things. Whatever they were.

I stuck it out though, sitting there, my back against the tree, slowly starting to itch. Touching nature wasn't really my forte, because a lot of it made me sneeze. As I catalogued the twenty-ninth person and attempted yet again to tune into what those gathered were saying, a cloud covered what was left of the sun and plunged the area into almost complete darkness.

Those figures slithered through the throng of people fast, their elongated fingers stretching, touching human flesh. I watched in horror as their faint red eyes fixated on me and could almost sense the grin of glee that had to be on the faces I couldn't see. Each person they touched shivered for a split second before turning back to their conversation, oblivious to how they'd become half a shade paler.

What were they doing? Were they feeding?

I had no idea what this meant, none at all, but I backed up quickly to standing, shoving my tablet back into my bag. My head buzzed with sudden energy, giving me a splitting headache for a few seconds. I didn't know what those things were, but I didn't want them coming closer to me, and they kept inching their way toward me. Frantically, I glanced around, but again no one near the fountain had noticed me.

Even though I noticed them, even though I noticed what those—whatever they were—were doing to them. Leeching energy perhaps? Stealing thoughts? My brain couldn't quite comprehend the change that came over them. All they appeared to be discussing was standing up for better school cafeteria lunches. Was that something worth spying on? Were these potential new recruits or something and if so, were these dark shadows something that foretold death? Because right now, I wouldn't be surprised if they were playing tag, you're it.

Could I only see them because I'd died once already?

And why was I utterly certain that these particular shadows had everything and nothing to do with that lab I'd found? Something about them called to me. Maybe that was part of their danger. So close now, just six or seven feet away from me. Clawing at the grass, pulling their smoky bodies along. Their features were obscured, but not by material or any sort of hood. They were hidden by the same smoky substance that made up their bodies. The claws could still rake massive holes in the ground, gouging out earth and grass, leaving definite traces behind. Still, I was the only one who apparently saw them.

And they knew it. Even as they converged on me, the whispers began to hit my mind. Sibilant, suggestive, and just beyond my reach of comprehension.

The cloud blew past the sun, and the last of its rays reached through to me, expelling the claws that reached toward me for the few moments of light left. Not even one blew away to reveal metal appendages. Not one of them appeared truly corporeal.

This was getting a bit too surreal. Not caring about the damned assignment, I pushed myself away from the tree, ignited my energy with a burst of power, and ran through their almost invisible forms and through the group of gathered students at a dead run.

Warning. Assignment is incomplete.

I didn't answer it. I didn't direct anything at it. It didn't sound the same as the buddy voice I talked to all the time, and it didn't matter. I wasn't staying around to find out what the hell those creatures were, whether I was alive, dead, or somewhere in-between. Not now, not until I had more comprehension of this new life, of my new abilities, and where I stood in this whole mess.

Injecting shots of electricity into my body, I fled as fast as I could. My feet flew over the ground, barely touching it, and still I could hear those voices, speaking to me, pleading with me, trying to lure me closer—the meaning of their words just out of reach.

I ran blindly, attempting to shut the noise out and just get to somewhere with more people. Campus was far too deserted at this time of night.

Warning. Return to your assignment.

Ignoring it became easier. Finally, I hit Walnut and the buzz of evening traffic. People and cars were everywhere. Almost seven at night on a Friday, in the cool breeze of spring. Perfect weather for everyone to breathe and let loose after such a harsh winter. I stopped at a halal kebab stand and pulled out some bills with trembling hands. They were crumpled and cold, old and smelled like they'd been in a pile of dirty laundry. But they were tangible and so was the lamb kebab I devoured, and the tahini that dripped down my chin.

I gulped in breaths afterward, downing the spare water bottle I always kept in my backpack. My adrenaline was still going strong, still pushing me farther, wanting me to run. I was closer to home than I realized, and while my legs felt weary, I let my sense of neighborhood knowledge drag me toward home. Almost trancelike, I watched the city pass me by. No weird shadow monsters, no strange whisperings that I couldn't quite grasp. Just the bustle of traffic, lights, and people enjoying a Friday night.

Sure, it was earlier than I wanted to come home, but hey. Maybe I'd take this time to sit down with my friends and actually appreciate the new lease on life I'd received. A new sense of relief ran through my system and I smiled as I opened the glass door downstairs. My key stuck slightly as I pulled it out, and I laughed, releasing a tiny bit of that pent-up energy. The lamb kebab in my stomach made me feel warm and cozy and more inclined to understand how worried my friends had been. My head was still on my electric high, powered to the max, feeling invincible.

I staggered up the stairs, only just beginning to realize how tired I was, and pushed my key into the lock at the top of the landing. Except as I pushed it open, I felt a wave of nausea sweep over me. It was so huge, so all-encompassing that I fell into the room. My stomach cramped in ways I couldn't even imagine existed, and my entire body felt as though I was being shocked with my own power. I shook against the ground, smashing my head into the wood over and over again.

I tried to grab onto my power, but I couldn't reach it, couldn't catch it. I tasted blood on my lips, down my throat, and ultimately the room began to spin with tinges of red interspersing it. It wasn't the room I wanted to see, it wasn't even the room I'd lived in for the last few years, but a cave with shadows bleeding in from every edge of it.

Voices peppered around my awareness like they were light years away, and my head grew heavy. I think I was still shaking, convulsing, but I couldn't even tell where the floor ended and I began anymore. I coughed, tasting blood again, mixed with bile. And finally, with one last heavy spasm, I smashed my head so hard, the pain knocked me out.

13
PUNISHMENT

I woke to the feeling of dried blood on my lips, the taste of it lingered in the back of my throat no matter how much I tried to swallow. My body ached in ways I didn't understand, in areas I didn't realize could ache.

Something cold sat on my forehead, lulling me into a sense of peace. But the sparks didn't let it last long as they sizzled and pinched against the insides of my body, boiling the bile where it sat in my stomach, tempting it to rise up.

Trying to control its uprising by calming myself didn't work. The electricity was angry, wild, and I couldn't do a damned thing.

I sat up so quickly that the room spun, and the pain shot through my head, my arms, my legs. Moving hadn't been the best idea, but I didn't want to remain lying down. Yet I couldn't physically control my limbs. I fell back down, frustrated as the pain sizzled throughout my body. Hot, yet cold, with an ache I probably couldn't medicate. What the fuck was this?

I did try to warn you.

Come again? What the hell did you warn me about? My body suddenly felt cold, like I should know what SC was talking about. It sat at the tip of my brain, mocking me, calling out to me, teasing me.

The pause was infuriating, and it was only then that I realized the background noise around me. People moved in and out, trying their best to be quiet. Then I remembered entering the apartment. If you could call it that. Perhaps nosediving into the living area as my limbs decided to stop obeying my commands.

Yeah, that about summed it up.

I did warn you. I told you to turn back.

Wait. You mean turn back and go where those weird things wanted to claw my guts to bits?

Claw?

Their hands. They had hooked nails that dissolved when the sun hit them and blood red eyes, and smoky bodies that screamed at me with no noise. Those fuckers. My head hurt just trying to think about this. But I had to, for the sake of my little friend who apparently only chose to see what it wanted to when chastising me.

Those students were completely normal. Why are you making things up?

There was no hint of teasing, no hidden joke. It was impatient under the strained tone, irritated with me.

I'm not making things up.

You left your post on campus only having gathered twenty-nine of the necessary forty-seven identities. Your notes on their topics of conversation lacked detail and demonstrated wavering attention. You did not complete your mission. You were given the chance to return and chose not to. This is your punishment.

I didn't quite grasp what it was saying at first. But the spasms in my limbs, the pain in my head, all of it slowly came together. This was punishment for not completing a mission. It was my first transgression and, as such, not death? I couldn't help but feel shell-shocked. Questions ran rampant through my mind, hounding me to ask them.

Why was this my punishment, and what was it supposed to entail? How long was this going to last? Was it more of a warning than anything else? Last but not trivial at all, how had it done this to me?

But all of those words fell away when my eyes finally gave into my cajoling and opened to reveal Dr. Leigh Caroline checking my pulse. White curtains hung around me, denoting that I had probably been taken to the emergency room. That was going to put a hole in my meager savings. I might have been on Mom and Dad's insurance, but I still had a deductible. Ambulances were rarely covered.

"You really should listen when it warns you," she said, her voice low and her eyes on the chart in front of her.

I wanted her to say more. Her silence weighed heavily on my already pounding skull. The spasms wouldn't let me speak out loud yet.

Finally, after what seemed like an age, she stood up and peered over her glasses at me. "That was foolish. You can't just leave an assignment like that. You're lucky your friends thought to bring you here."

Very lucky. Although UPenn's hospital was close to our place, Mercy Hospital was too. My ending up here was probably entirely coincidence. I'd be happier about it if I could get my thoughts straight. If I could manage to think for longer than the pain allowed me to.

I wanted to speak, but my body spasmed again, and my teeth clenched forcing me to swallow the words I'd have preferred to yell.

She scribbled down a few things on the chart and finally looked at me, her lips pressed into a firm line as she pulled out a device from her pocket. This one was slim, and appeared to be made of seamless silver metal. She ran it across my forehead, and then down my arms. It emitted a low rumble as it dragged its blue light across my skin. "There's no arguing against it. If it tells you to do something. Do it. Don't argue. No matter what."

I wasn't sure, but it felt like she was trying to get a point across to me, one that she didn't want to say out loud. I tried to study her face, but the spasms kept making my vision swim. She appeared to be studying the results her scan thing gave her. Had she told me to keep on even if something was threatening me? Did the system just not care that something had been about to attack me?

Considering I should have been dead, and it didn't yet have much invested in me, I could see why I'd be a necessary sacrifice, but I didn't understand why it acted like it hadn't seen them. Dr. Caroline was still looking at me, her green eyes laser sharp.

"I'm not telling you this to berate you. I'm trying to help you understand the situation you're in. I've been there, even if it was a while ago. You're here for a reason. That reason is to assist the program in every way you can. With everything it asks of you despite what your personal convictions might be." She patted me on the shoulder, hope that I understood her, that I wasn't going to be difficult reflected in her eyes. "I've adjusted your severity to coincide with the type of infraction. Your power is…"

She paused, pursing her lips and glanced at the silver thing again. "It fluctuates severely."

No shit, I thought, but did my best to nod. I wasn't sure I managed to get the sentiment across.

The doctor smiled. "Sorry. It takes a bit to get the hang of it, but once you're used to it, it's not such a bad thing."

I tried to nod again, ignoring the stabs of pain that made their way down my spine with the effort. "How long?"

The words came out of my mouth mostly garbled, but from the frown on her face she tried her best to figure them out. A brief smile tugged at her lips and she answered. "Just a couple of days. Now rest up. You're in good hands here."

She left my cubicle, and I tried not to let the shock wash over me. For a minor screw up because I didn't want to be eaten alive by ghouls, I'd be in pain for the next two days. I didn't want to be dead, but right then, I wasn't so sure I wanted to be alive either.

The beeping of machines surrounded me, but none of them looked anything like I'd seen in hospitals before. I wasn't sure if I was even in a real hospital room. What if they'd put me in the basement, left me to rot down there in my own pain and self-inflicted electrical shock?

"What the fuck is this supposed to achieve?" I yelled out the words as loud as I could, or at least I tried to. My teeth rarely stopped clenching from the shocks that ran through my body, and the pain had receded to a dull rhythm in the back of my mind.

It's supposed to remind you that while you are alive, you are subject to the assignments given to you by the Second Chance system.

Gee. Thanks.

You sound disgruntled.

Really? I tried counting to ten, but in the end didn't care and just let loose a tirade of thoughts that had been plaguing me since I ended up in here.

SC brought me back to life, for their purposes. I didn't ask to be brought back to life. SC chose to, that's not on me. So acting as if I should be grateful for something I didn't ask for is obnoxious. Especially knowing then what I know now, I would never have chosen a second lifetime if it was one of servitude.

SC was quiet. I imagined that I'd hurt its robotic feelings or whatever it was, but I couldn't even convince myself of that. This whole debacle made me want to scream. And my yelled question earlier should have at least brought someone in, if indeed they had anyone in this ward. It led me to believe that I wasn't in a ward, that I was in some out of the way place where only Doctor Caroline and her staff had access to me.

How many hours had passed? I didn't even want to contemplate the couple of days that I had ahead of me.

We did not realize the point you just brought up. Giving people a Second Chance at life was something we assumed would be welcomed by the individual.

Yeah? Well, assumptions are the mother of all fuck ups.

It was one of my favorite sayings, and the system didn't seem to know how to deal with it. I let it stew in its lonely algorithms while I tried to concentrate on sourcing the origin of the pain firing through all of my nerve endings. Maybe if I found it, I could somehow stop it? If someone touched me right then, I thought I'd scream.

You have given us a lot to think about. As appreciation for this, your punishment has been reduced.

What? A glimmer of hope lingered in the back of my mind.

We will reduce your disciplinary lesson by twenty-four hours. Thank you for your feedback.

Its presence vanished. As much as I knew it was still there, I also knew that talking to it right now would be entirely counter-productive. It'd been almost two weeks and I still knew relatively nothing about the program.

Has it really only been two weeks? I wasn't sure I could imagine life without my ability anymore. Would I even want to?

Idly, I activated the visual information behind my eyelids. Except every time I spasmed, the damn thing flickered. Turning my power against me seemed an inordinately cruel form of punishment. Yet I understood it. I even— sort of—admired it.

Though my power simply seemed to want to escape the confines of my body. It was angry, if that was even possible.

Sleep beckoned me in the moments between convulsions, but each time another shock shook me, my brain woke up. Why had it not seen those shadows? Maybe it was because even though it knew they were there, it didn't consider them a threat. That meant the system, again, knew a lot more than I knew about these things. If it did, why wouldn't it share them with me?

It could have told me not to worry, that they were remnants of my death and unable to hurt me. Yet, I doubted that, because two of them had attacked me previously.

In the interests of keeping their protégés alive, I'd have thought they would help us survive by arming us with knowledge. I didn't feel like I knew more, or that I absorbed the order of the world any faster than I used to.

Eventually exhaustion overtook me, and I dreamed of electric beetles stinging me half to death while I ran from them. Their leader bug lorded over all of us, laughing as it reached out its pincers to grip me by the arm.

Only I woke up to find Dr. Caroline there, taking yet more blood, to perform more tests.

"Hey," she said as I leaned back down into the pillows as if I'd never sat up in the first place.

"Hey." I responded through my clenched teeth that were probably locked that way for eternity now.

"I've been informed that you gave the system unexpected feedback, and it has thus decided to cut your sentence down a little. There's a first time for everything. Congrats." She smiled while she checked my vitals.

"Yeah." Congrats to me on a whole twenty-four-hour respite. It couldn't come soon enough, but damned if I didn't want it to come right now.

She frowned as she examined the rest of me. Her light brown hair was streaked with grey, and a strand of it kept falling down in front of her eyes. She flicked it away, irritably, before whipping out her little scannydo. I had a sneaking suspicion that it was what controlled my ability. Not the SC system, but that thing in her hands. If I'd had any decent control over my body, I would have snatched it off her.

"It's a good thing you got it commuted. I'm not sure why, but the spasms aren't agreeing with your system, and your ability is almost…" She checked the chart in her hands and adjusted a few dials on the machine that was monitoring me. "Honestly, it's sort of feral."

"Good thing," I ground out, having managed a little more finesse when speaking now. "Because…e-electric sh-shocks u-u-sually w-work so w-well."

Damn. It took forever to stutter out the words and express what I was trying to say. I was so tired from attempting to speak. Relief washed over me when she smiled.

"Good, you're fine. If you can be sarcastic while undergoing this, I don't think they broke you." Notating another few things down on her clipboard, she flashed me a smile. "I'll be back in a few hours. Try to rest."

Another shock made me clench up. Didn't break me? She spoke of it so casually before ducking out of the room. How many people had it broken before? Not to mention that I wanted to know what the hell they'd done to disable my resistance to electrical shock. I knew I'd had it. With the amount of power I'd exuded several times over the last weeks, I should have fried.

Of course I'd try to rest—and fail abysmally at doing so. Power zinged through me with nowhere to go. Maybe some of the stuff she'd been doing drained some of the excess, but not enough. Right now, I could probably power Times Square in New York City. I didn't want to risk touching anything lest it burst into flames with the static.

It took a while, but finally I fell into a troubled sleep. In it, dark, shadow filled monsters chased me around. Electrical storms raged inside of the clouds that made them whole, red eyes gazed at me while their claws reached out toward my face.

And when they opened their mouths to devour me, strikes of lightning shot out, trying to sizzle me alive.

Punishment made me angry. Maybe angrier was more accurate. I was in the worst mood ever when I finally got home on Sunday afternoon. The house was empty, which suited me just fine. The doctor had let me sleep after the shocks stopped because of how little I'd had while undergoing what I'd like to refer to as torture. Yep. Angry had become my new way of life. I wasn't sure if I was okay with that.

With little more than two weeks left until the State Championships, I hoped I could recover in time.

I wasn't hungry, not even a little bit, but I remembered promising Neale that I'd eat properly and maintain mass. Calories were important for a long-distance runner. I grabbed two apples and made a couple of ham and cheese sandwiches to take into my room. My stock was running low. I'd have to duck to the shops this week. But I wanted to delay that, because it meant talking to Orion, for which I was not yet ready.

The bread was just this side of its used by date, and definitely not fresh. I ripped it apart with my teeth anyway, pretending it was the Second Chance system's punishment module.

You agreed to and accepted that punishment could occur when you agreed to the ToS.

I wasn't sure if I was imagining it, but I think it sounded slightly offended. *Of course, I never imagined that I'd be forced to endure electric fucking shock therapy.*

What else would it entail? Electricity is your skill. Punishment must fit the method.

I don't know. Maybe not get paid? Get fined? Move up in ranks slower? Something not torturous?

I gave up trying to reason with it. Whatever it was, that voice in my head wasn't human. It probably wasn't even a machine. Could be an alien from a different dimension totally screwing with me for all I knew.

We are not an alien.

That was definitely indignation. I couldn't help the smile. Maybe it was taking on human characteristics after all. *Could have fooled me.*

You are…teasing us?

Maybe.

I took another bite out of my sandwich, proceeding to gobble it up faster than before while the system contemplated my comments.

We are not alien. We are not human. We were created to keep you safe from yourselves.

That was a hell of a lot more information than I'd received before, and I buried my thoughts as actively as I could while outwardly chewing just as slowly as I had before.

So you're sort of protectors of the human race?

Of earth and the human race. We intervene with the sole purpose to keep human beings safe.

How?

How?

I paused, trying to think of a way to phrase it that it might actually give me a legitimate answer. *How do you determine what events or items require intervention?*

Simple calculations. We extrapolate from data, seismic shifts, and dimensional tears what the future will bring and take steps to prevent catastrophes.

So the items we filch, the meeting I bungled, those all were check points?

That is information I'm unable to divulge. I might have pushed my parameters already.

And the deathly silence that followed meant it really had taken leave of the conversation. By now I could tell when it did that. Still, it was a hell of a lot more information than I'd been able to glean from the very unhelpful interface and tutorial.

I was beginning to suspect that SC leaned more toward the chaotic neutral.

14
THIS TIME

SC went quiet after that conversation. Its penchant for swapping between I and we indicated that it might have an overarching hierarchy or something. Sort of like a command center. Maybe each individual section could act independently to a certain extent and within guided parameters. If mine's reactions were anything to go by, it had said too much.

Despite everything, I hoped it didn't get into too much trouble for doing so. It was my fault it had risen to the bait. Sort of anyway. I couldn't talk to anyone else about it except for Dr. Caroline, so it was nice to have the voice in my head to confide in. And wow, was I glad that people couldn't hear my train of thought, because that was some questionable processing right there.

Still. It felt lonely. Powerful, but lonely. Which, of course, I combated by running. Running to school. Running at school. Running home.

There were no more assignments, and my lectures were routinely informative. One of the results of this whole debacle was that I avoided the hell out of the quad. It didn't matter if I had to take a path that led me two buildings past where I needed to be, I wasn't going through there anymore. Strong or weak didn't matter when you couldn't put a finger on your attackers.

The fact that SC didn't acknowledge the scary demon shits I'd seen creeping around those people and the fountain, didn't help.

Were they what had grabbed me during the pineapple burger incident? I shuddered at the memory. Their fingers definitely hadn't felt smoky, but everything about them had been.

"You okay, Dare?"

I didn't realize I'd stopped and leaned against the wall while flash backing to all that crazy shit. Cyan's eyes crinkled with concern, and her usual bubbly smile was absent. She didn't look herself with a downturn to her lips. It wasn't an expression I recalled ever seeing her with.

"Just a little winded." Which wasn't a lie. Avoiding the quad often meant running to make it to my next class on time.

"I was worried about you. Friday was a bit crazy." This time she smiled, but it was one of those uneasy expressions where she wasn't quite sure if she should.

I'd forgotten she was there. Hell, all my friends were. Or should have been. I hadn't been in any state to notice them once I pretty much collapsed through the door. "Yeah. I can't remember most of it."

"Did they find out what happened? Were there," she paused, looking away from me while she bit her lip, "drugs in your system?"

I thought for a moment. Taking that route, letting them assume I'd been drugged and not that I was being tortured by my own electrical ability in some fake hospital wing. Except that wasn't the way to go. I knew them too well, and they'd only hone right in on that.

So, I shook my head, and pushed down at the annoyance my ability was already thirsting to feed off. "Haven't been taking care of myself. With the accident, my not resting, and forgetting to eat and drink fluids, I overworked myself and added severe dehydration to the list."

I watched her face as she digested my words, keeping up as easy a smile as I could. At least I think it was. Cyan's eyes didn't leave mine this time. It was like she stared into me, trying to pull out the truth by sheer force of will.

"You know we're worried about you, right?" She put a hand on my bicep and drew it back like she'd been bitten as a spark of electricity struck her. Great.

Hopefully she'd write it off as static.

"I know. Frankly, so am I." I laughed self-depreciatingly to make light of the situation, but she didn't seem to be buying it. "Look. The doctor cleared me, but only after making me take mandated rest, so I'm okay now. Just been a bit more tired than usual, and now I'll make sure to take care of myself."

Mandated rest wasn't precisely accurate. But they had let me lie down while my body attacked me from the inside. So kind of them.

She eyed me, her arms crossed now, and the blue tracksuit she wore crinkled in all the right places. Sometimes I wondered if she arranged her clothes specifically to do that. "As long as you stop trying to avoid us. And by us I mean Orion. He might be a bit of a dick right now, but you know how he gets when emotions are involved. He's not the best at dealing with them."

I knew that. She knew that. Hell, Orion knew that. But what I had wasn't something I could tell them. So I lied to her face. "I know. We'll figure it out."

"Good." Her real smile was back and it turned into an impish grin as she looped her arm through mine, apparently undeterred from the shock earlier. "Let's not be late for class!"

I let her drag me along. After all, I couldn't ignore her forever. At some point, I was going to have to give over. The ToS did state that I had to keep up appearances, and now that I knew what punishment was, I'd do anything I could to avoid it. If I couldn't figure out a way to override it first.

When SC still hadn't spoken to me by Friday, I started to get worried. No comments to my thoughts, no random assignments. The morning rolled around, and I made my way to training. Early as usual, I put myself through the paces, adding in some sprints to try and get a handle on improving my endurance through electrical enhancement. It was difficult to resist the tug of power as it played along my nerves.

Instead of a chill, the sensations it caused left me feeling heady and energized. Ready for anything the world threw at me. Indomitable. I didn't intend to use it in competition, but I had no idea what my next assignments might be like. If I needed to use my ability in ways the tutorial didn't cover yet, then I wanted to be able to. I wanted that control, to feel the power respond to me in the precise way I directed it to.

All the tutorials did was provide guidance with releasing power beyond myself. Focus through the fingers. Touch to release. Practicing control. It was like it hadn't realized how much I could fortify myself with abilities like these. SC made me heal faster, but with this, I could reinforce myself to avoid injury. In theory anyway. I wasn't quite ready for a physical trial yet. I wondered if SC would come back if I started criticizing their training methods.

Coach Marth approached me after he'd dismissed the other runners. I trained alone, worked better alone, and he knew I preferred the locker rooms to myself, so I usually waited.

"Something on your mind, Dare?" he asked, peering at me from under the rim of his sports cap.

I shrugged. He'd never been the sort to accept bullshit answers, but right now I felt like anything even close to the truth would be classified that way. "I'm okay. Had a bit of a fall over the weekend, so I'm trying to up my endurance."

There, it wasn't a complete lie, and I didn't divulge any SC information.

"Take care of those legs. But most importantly, take care of yourself." He sounded so serious and sincere that I wondered if he knew something I didn't. SC remained silent though, and had never identified him, so it stood to reason he wasn't a part of the whole shebang.

"Will do, coach. I promise." I only hoped that promise wouldn't come back to bite me in the Achilles. "Thanks."

"Don't mention it. Just do it." And he waved my thanks away as he headed into the locker room before me.

Orion was waiting for me when I got out. I tried not to let the complete and utter surprise show on my face. He'd been avoiding me for almost a full week. There were names I wanted to call him, but I pushed down the initial reaction.

"Hey. Can we talk?" He shoved his hands in his jeans pockets and looked down at the toes of his shoes. Sometimes, he could be shy. Not often, but when he had something important to say.

I nodded and fell into step beside him. He walked slower than I did, so I had to adjust my pace. It felt like the whole world was passing me by.

"Listen. I'm worried. I think there's something going on, and you won't tell me, but if you can't, there's got to be a reason. And knowing you, the reason is probably not too bad." There was a light chuckle in his tone, and I echoed it. "So, what I'm trying to say, is that I'm sorry for being a douchebag lately. But as soon as you can, share it with me, do, okay?"

He stopped and focused his gaze on me. I wondered if he knew how impossible it was for me to resist that beseeching look on his face. I swear he learned it from a puppy dog.

"Promise."

He grinned. "Excellent. Then you're on snack duty tonight."

"Shithead," I mumbled, but it was nice to have our familiarity back. I'd missed it even more than I thought.

In charge of snacks, eh? I grabbed some chips and dip on the way home. After giving it a few minutes thought, I grabbed some summer sausage, cheese, and crackers. Because damned if I wasn't going to do this right. My good mood began with Orion coming to see me after practice. And I wasn't of the mind to let it go any time soon. This whole SC debacle was a lot to take on. I needed to put in more of an effort to maintain my real life. Besides, it wasn't like I lacked energy now.

SC was a component of my life now. A part that I questioned, but a part nevertheless. Maybe I'd only end up with tasks every week or so. I could handle that. It would give me time to perfect my control, and to figure out other ways to use my abilities that could benefit myself, and others. Electricity was everywhere. The possibilities sent a fresh surge of excitement running through me as I leapt up the stairs.

It was difficult to juggle opening the apartment door with the bags I held, but I managed it. Orion relieved me of a couple of items as I entered and laughed at my triumphant grin.

"Ooh." He ogled the contents. "You went all out! Been saving?"

"Ramen for life allows me a multitude of savings. Sometimes. Every month or so." I cringed for effect. "Besides. How many nights a year do we get to let loose and game?"

Orion laughed as he set the bags down on the table. "Like fifty of them. Still. Sam isn't coming tonight, so we didn't have our usual source of all things amazing."

"Glad to be a substitute, then." A small tingle ran down my left side, and I forced a smile onto my face. "I'm going to lie down for a bit before they come, if that's okay? I might have overdone it this morning."

"Sure. Leave all the hard work to me. Making me cut up snacks. Typical." But his lips twitched while he spoke, and I knew things were okay again.

What wasn't okay was that in all my jubilation, I'd managed to accrue a surplus again. While fantastic that I could recharge so often, I needed to figure out other ways to rid myself of the excess.

I didn't unwrap my other purchase until I got into my room. I'd bought two 20100 mAh charging bricks. I figured if I could channel a small enough strand of power into it, this was a way I could store power to drain and use in a pinch. Or else I could plug my tablet into it and never worry about battery life.

I'd figure out the logistics of using the stored energy later. The important part was to develop some finesse with my ability, and to expend some of the excess build up. I settled myself comfortably and held the first brick in my hands. Turning it around I made sure to touch the charging port for the brick with my right pointer finger.

I took a deep breath and let myself relax. Thinking of clouds and stuff that floated. Which led me to thinking about feathers and why were they so light when they could be so strong. I sighed and brought my focus back to the brick.

Forming the thought of a trickle of power in my mind, I envisioned it traveling through my body to gather at my finger and allowed the stream of power to begin charging the block up. Only it felt like it was minimal, yet within seconds, the brick in my hand began to smoke, and I dropped it onto my bed where it bounced and hit the floor with a solid, smoking thud.

"Shit." I muttered and glared at my hand. A ripple of energy passed through my body, like the electricity was laughing at me.

Trickling wasn't working. Not to mention it barely made a dent in what I knew I had to expend. I hadn't counted on the fact that while amazing for charging phones, these batteries were way too small for my excess.

I threw myself back onto the bed and stared up at the ceiling. As long as I watched myself, tonight should be fun. It had been far too long since I last allowed myself to let loose.

Notice: Urgent attention required. Your skillset is required immediately. This mission may be more difficult than your previous encounters.

Emergency Assignment.

Location: Treknor compound. Outer gate, Corner Torresdale and Tyson.

Objective: You will meet up with two other Second Chance Operatives. Intermediate Cleaner. Associate Blocker. Your Blocker outranks you and thus leads the task.

Further directions will be provided once you meet up.

Target: Enter the Treknor compound office facility and remove the required file.

Time Limit: Meet at seven o'clock once it's dark. Do not move before directed by your Blocker.

Reward: Progression experience. Monetary compensation.

Caution: You must wear black.

Well. If that wasn't just the cherry on the sundae. How was I going to weasel out of tonight's activities? I'd promised Orion I'd be here. This was a disaster. I could hear voices in the living area, but they weren't loud enough to decipher. Had I misjudged the time and they were already here?

I pushed myself up, glancing at my phone as I did so. Sparks danced across my fingers, making the screen flicker briefly. *Stop it.* I growled in my mind. The last thing I wanted was for my phone to break. It had already been through so much. Even if I really wanted to spend the night in, there was a part of me that wanted a chance to see what I could do. To take on monsters in the dark, or robots overhead, or super smart computers that were secretly running the world.

If I headed out now, I might still be able to avoid the guests, but Orion was going to be so pissed off at me. Staying in here wasn't going to get me prepped anytime soon.

I tugged on the shoes I'd kicked off before I collapsed onto the bed and headed out into the hallway before I could change my mind. I hadn't taken more than a few steps when it became clear that the talking was Orion, and he was on the phone.

"Nah, not going to work tonight. I'm not feeling the best. Sorry. Can you let the rest of them know?" He sounded tired.

The guilt hit me only a moment later, as he said thanks and bye. He was probably getting less sleep because he was worried about me. Even though he put on a really brave face. Regardless of how old I got. I was the younger one, so he always joked that he had to take good care of me.

Idiot.

Steeling myself, I walked out into the living area, but he wasn't there anymore. I frowned as I heard the front door fall closed. He'd left? If he was feeling sick, why did he leave? Oh no. Maybe he was feeling really ill. Like go to the emergency room sick. I wanted to run after him, but I didn't have time because I wasn't sure how long it would take me to get to the meeting spot.

No explanation, just a cryptic message. Yet, I'd heard him. He said he was sick. It wasn't like him to lie. Resigned, I walked into the kitchen and began to slather some peanut butter between two slices of bread. I was hungry and emotionally exhausted. First up I had to put on my spying gear. I grinned at the thought. It was a good thing I liked wearing darker colors, or I'd have had to buy new clothes. I could plod forlornly in the direction of the meetup location. As I closed the fridge, I found a note attached: Have to duck out tonight. Sorry. Raincheck. Orion.

Something is troubling you.

Well observed, Sherlock. I quipped as I bit viciously into my sandwich and pocketed an apple for dessert. Why did it always come out when I least wanted or expected it to?

I am not Sherlock.

You are to me.

There was a pause, and then a completely unexpected answer. *Thank you.*

I blinked. It seemed that the system didn't quite understand my brand of sarcasm, and now assumed I'd given it a name. It was my own fault of course, but I couldn't bring myself to tell it. All things considered, this voice in my head wasn't that bad. Even if it could kill me for blinking in the wrong way.

It had to be all the way over the other side of town. Even the GPS on my phone mocked me with the distance. While I could run it, I'd be useless by the time I got there. It'd be pretty much flat out pace for the ninety minutes I had to get there in time. Pulling my favored hoodie tighter around me, I shoved my hands into my pockets. These pants were newer and sort of clung to my calves, but were freer farther up. It allowed me to run if I needed to without discomfort. Let's face it. I always needed to run.

I made my way to Market so I could grab the bus, which would take me to 30th Street's train station. If I was lucky and the connection timed out right, which the app said it should, then I could jump on the train and let it take me out to Tacony near the compound. Didn't they know how long it would take me to get there?

Even after I got off the train, I was going to have to run about five blocks to make it to my destination. What would they have done if I wasn't a track athlete? Questioning things was the best distraction for me to avoid thinking about the fact that I was about to get in an electronically controlled silver tube.

The bus stop on Market Street was crowded at this time of a Friday night. I didn't have the time nor patience to wait for the second one, so I pushed my way into the front of the crowd, receiving several death stares in response. While I'd like to think they stemmed purely from my pushing past, I was pretty certain I statically shocked every single person I came into contact with.

Damn it.

I hunkered down and shoved my hands in my hoodie's pockets. Necessary evils would be how I got this done.

Finally, the bus arrived, and there was some jostling and swearing as people tried to force their way onto the almost full bus. I managed to snag a standing spot close to the back doors, but damned if I wasn't feeling claustrophobic. Didn't help that the whole vehicle was made out of metal. I'd forgotten that busses might not run on electricity, but they certainly used it. Fantastic, let's just put an electric eel into a metal box. That boded well.

Electricity danced through my veins, like a giggle under my skin. Awesome. My ability had a freaking sense of humor. I could feel it wanting to reach out and jump onto the pole I held. Fighting it back under control became exhausting.

I sighed and tried to turn off my senses. There was a faint smell of urine coming from the back of the bus, and the guy next to me was sweating profusely. Either he'd run for the bus or he was sick. Personally, I thought it was a bit of both. 30th Street couldn't come soon enough.

I fled as soon as the doors opened, breathing in the scents of the street instead of the enclosed bus. This area of town was peaceful, and apart from the regular old smell of exhaust fumes and chill on the air, it was a welcome change from the bus.

Sandstone buildings cast different shadows in the evening. Even so, the smooth surface lent an oddly serene sensation to an otherwise nerve racking experience. I made my way along the street with its endless construction. Steel scaffolding obscured the usually attractive area, hiding the potential within.

Entering the terminal, the sheer majesty tried to overwhelm me as usual. Ceilings so high it made me feel short. Sunset had begun, casting a different mood through the building. Reflections cascaded through the windows as I walked, leaving an orange hue behind it. Lights dangled down from the ceiling like thinly attached stalagtites making me wonder if any of them had ever fallen and smashed on the marble floors below.

What if one fell, could I outrun it? Electricity coarsed through my body with an eagerness that threatened to overwhelm me for a moment. Like it was asking me if we could, just once, run without giving appearance a second thought.

No pressure, though.

And no paying attention to the whisperings in the back of my head that told me to go on: try it.

I had to calm myself, so I squeezed the balls in my pockets and hoped for the best. Acting as normal as I could, I bought a ticket from one of the shiny machines. So much was mechanized these days, and I had to willfully hold back the power that wanted to short out the machine. Maybe I wanted to short it out, but I'd blame my ability for now. I was so proud of the fact that I didn't short-circuit the ticket machine that I almost forgot my existential dread about riding in the train.

Ticket in hand, I stood at the top of the stairs wondering what would really happen if I didn't go. But if I didn't force myself to go down those stairs, I'd have to take the escalator, which ran on electricity. Without even trying, I knew doing that right now was a bad idea.

Steadying myself, I took the first step. Nothing exploded. Everything as normal, I continued down, and waited all of five minutes for the next train to come along and take me to my destination.

Plastic seats were my savior. As long as I made sure none of my body came into contact with the metal parts of the train, I should be fine. By now my power was running rampant inside, begging to be let out. I fueled as much of it back into my body as I could, replenishing reserves. I hadn't yet experimented much with the brain. Considering its complexity and my lack of neurological knowledge, I'd been waiting. But it was tempting. Maybe I could free up more of my mind, or improve its function.

Or fry it.

Hi there overthinking my old friend. I liked the beat of a train car and the way it ran over the joins. It was enough to lull me into a relaxed state and forget, even momentarily, about how badly I could sizzle everything in here if I wasn't careful.

The tin can hurtled through toward the impending twilight with all the trappings of doom. I massaged my temples in an effort to distract myself more, keeping up a smooth rhythm to replace what I couldn't get from running at the moment. It'd all be fine, I just had to sit on this plastic seat until we came to my stop. That's all. Sitting wasn't difficult. The mantra helped me.

It took thirty minutes to get to my stop. I'd be a few minutes early, but that was better than being late. It wasn't dark yet, but the sun was setting, bathing the entire city in blood red rays. I really hoped that wasn't an omen.

Shrugging my hoodie up over my head, I shoved my hands into my pockets as I began the jog to the compound. I loved the soft material of this hoodie and how none of the cuts were even. Its stitching appeared haphazard and careless, but the inside was warm and right now I was grateful for that. It felt like a representation of myself, all different angles that came together nicely.

Treknor compound was owned by one of the richest men in the world. A tech genius with so much money he probably bathed in it and used it as kindling for his fireplace. Maybe if he put that blasted money toward, I don't know, curing cancer, Orion would be less grumpy. This was one of his lesser known holdings, if I had my facts correct. From where I was headed through the city, it seemed rather sketchy if indeed it was his.

Breaking into one of Treknor's compounds didn't seem like the wisest of decisions to me. But I was just the messenger.

Finally, I arrived at the spot my GPS indicated.

Wait here.

I was going to. I shot back at it. I'd already stopped, so I had no idea why it thought I should be told to do something I was already doing.

Your contacts will arrive shortly. They are en route. Make sure your clothing disguises as much of you as possible.

I grunted in response, pulling the strings of my hoodie tighter so that only my eyes and nose peered out. Leaning up against the brick fence I could see why this was the meeting point. The trees hung over the top of the wall, obscuring the area below in shadows and fresh spring leaves. My black clothing allowed me to blend in and hid me from view. Waiting wasn't my strong point, but I went over the information from the week's lectures in my mind getting ready for the midterms that were coming up. It was lucky I'd learned tricks to retain knowledge well, or I'd be screwed.

Maybe, when I had some actual free time, I could go back to the bakery. Why couldn't one of my abilities have been invisibility?

Invisibility as you imagine it, doesn't exist.

Thanks for bursting that bubble.

SC went silent again. The time drew out longer than I expected, so I activated the frequently asked questions section of my interface and tried to look up Cleaner and Blocker. The former was related to cleaning up mess left by the execution of tasks. It involved the use of fire, air, and water affinities. And a Blocker could basically protect the team, using earth skills as a basis.

I raised my fingers examining them. Tiny sparks of electricity ran down them jumping around like a bean. Guess it was good to have someone who could disrupt electronics when working on breaking into a compound such as this.

Sighing, I leaned against the brick wall and looked up through the tree leaves, trying to see if I could see the stars in the almost black sky.

"Dare?" Orion's voice pulled me out of my astrological search and I started, focusing on the person next to me dressed in a black hoodie and running pants. "What the fuck are you doing here?"

15
WAIT, WHAT?

My brain wasn't doing the best job at comprehending. My electricity on the other hand, sped along my veins, just under my skin, screaming at me to let it out. Orion stood there, hands on hips in front of me, his face partially obscured by a mask that covered his nose and mouth. I think he had those for cleaning at home. Black, charcoal, to filter the dust or something. I shook my head trying to clear the weird thoughts.

I swear there was no one else who could look that thoroughly disappointed and annoyed with me at the same time. The shadows around us leaked in and out of sync with the wall, giving me an odd sense of headiness as I opened my mouth to speak.

"Did you follow me?" I asked, oddly enough, at the exact same time he did and I frowned, barreling on before he could tell me to be quiet. "No, I'm meant to be here. Are you?"

How much was too much to say without getting myself killed? Or his mind wiped?

Orion is a part of the SC program. You are within rights to speak to him about anything. I thought you knew that.

No, I didn't fucking know that! I mentally yelled at the stupid thing in my head. *You never told me.*

Orion pulled his mask down so that his lips and nose were visible. Something in his eyes told me he'd been expecting this but had been hoping it wasn't true. "I'm the Cleaner. And I assume you're the Runner."

Several dots connected themselves in my brain. Times when Orion had seemed preoccupied, but I put it down to his furious brain working overtime. There were times when he suddenly had to go, but I just assumed it either had something to do with his family, or else with his part-time job.

"They were never family emergencies, were they?" I asked, my voice trembling slightly as I realized how long this had been going on. Little images fit together in my mind faster and faster. Clicking into place, beginning to make sense. "When did you—"

But he cut me off. "Not now. We have a job to do, and getting sidetracked with questions like this is only going to put us in danger. Focus on what it is you'll be doing. We can talk later. At home."

The twinkle in his eyes was back, and I couldn't deny the relief I felt at seeing it. He'd been so angry with me last week, and so distant with me in the conference room. Today started to feel normal, except now I knew he must have died, and I felt like total shit for not knowing how. What sort of friend didn't even notice when their best friend had a rough patch that could be indicative of trauma or death?

"The Blocker will be here shortly. Don't ask too many questions. Just do what he tells you to do. If I'm right, we won't have a big window to do this in." He pulled his mask back up and reached into a pocket to grab me one of them. He handed it to me without making eye contact. "I didn't think they'd send you on this. You're too fresh."

"Fresh?" I asked, knowing he didn't mean anything by it, but taking the mask anyway. It was a struggle to hold down the bubbling power at my fingertips. It seemed to want to pick a fight. "Wait. How did you even know?"

Orion shook his head. "I didn't. Not really. I surmised. But I can't talk to you about your incident unless you approach me because you've been informed that you can. I'm guessing you weren't informed."

"Got it in one." I tried to glare inwardly at the visitor in my head and only managed to end up looking cross eyed.

I think Orion was about to say something else, but footsteps approached. Soft, barely audible underneath the rustling of fresh leaves above us, but definitely there. I paused, watching as Orion did the same. It felt like we were blending with the shadows against the red brick wall. The moon was partially obscured by clouds lending us little light to see by.

"Introduce me to the newbie, Cleaner." The voice held boredom as our Blocker ducked under the leaves. He actually wore a ski mask, so all I could tell was that he had pale skin and eyes that were so dark I couldn't identify the color.

"This is the Runner." Orion shrugged, as if my existence meant nothing to him. Perhaps it was best, but surely the system already knew we were best friends. It had to. It had been everywhere with both myself and apparently him. I didn't quite understand, but I got the feeling operatives, agents, or whatever we were, weren't supposed to be on friendly or personable terms?

There is no written rule against the fraternization of agents. However, sometimes the tasks can be difficult, and having to sacrifice a friend is far more difficult than having to sacrifice someone you barely know.

Thanks, I internally muttered. So much to go over, so much to consider. I tried not to let the potential of death SC hinted at bother me.

"Good to meet you, Runner. I'll do my best to explain this so it's easy to follow. It's sort of difficult considering it's your first big assignment, if I've got it correctly. You're only a Novice. They're throwing you in the deep end." His smile was slightly disarming, but I wasn't about to let that distract me from those words.

"Why?" I blurted out. Getting thrown in the deep end didn't sound like something I, or anyone else, wanted to do.

"Runners are hard to keep." He took a breath and looked at something on his phone, like an app or something.

"To keep?" Did he mean keep alive? Or else, we were like expensive or something. The exotic pet of SC. Excellent.

The Blocker shrugged, and I thought I'd made him uncomfortable because he cracked his neck from side to side looking anywhere but at me. "Runners are often purely electricity-based, while most other designations have alternate elements that can be used. For some reason, our Runners don't seem to last long."

Okay, I could appreciate that. Or not. It felt difficult to breathe. I tried to turn my attention fully to the task at hand, but even my nod of understanding felt half-hearted. The Blocker didn't seem to notice. The parking lot beyond this tree line suddenly seemed vast, and I no longer had the confidence that suffused me when I'd realized Orion would be by my side.

"This is the best place for us to cross over and onto the grounds. Once we're on the other side, we need to stay in those shadows and disable the security. We will have four minutes to make it to and into the house before the backup generator boots up and switches over. We set out in T minus seven minutes. Any questions?" His voice was full of business, confident and sure about how this would go down.

"Am I the one who disables the security?" I asked, hoping my voice didn't betray my annoyance. Apparently it had taken all of sixty seconds for him to forget I'd never done this before.

"Affirmative. Just a light discharge of power at the box as we approach it, and then get ready to run. We'll need you for the second step of the plan inside as well." He smiled, and the balaclava stretched in an odd way that gave him a macabre look.

This wasn't as scary as I thought it'd be. I'd keep trying to tell myself that. The fact that my power seemed to agree, lent me confidence. Running was one thing I could do. That would be the easy part.

A small countdown flickered at the edge of my vision on my left side. Just under five minutes left.

"Do we have anything to climb over with, or do we vault it?" I asked nervously, not wanting to fall over the other side and damage any of my running muscles. I wasn't even warmed up for this. I started stretching while I waited for an answer.

"Jump up and pull yourself over. It shouldn't take too much. You look pretty fit." He eyed me thoughtfully. "You'll be faster than us on the run to the house, but try not to outpace us too badly. We don't want to be split up. It could be the difference between success and failure."

"We can fail tasks?" I asked quite surprised by the fact.

The grin on the Blocker's face seemed strained. "Well, you *can* fail tasks. As to whether or not that's a good idea? I'll let you decide that."

"No." Orion offered. "It's best not to decide that at all. Just get the job done and reap the rewards. Aiming for anything less is foolish."

The Blocker shrugged. "That's why you're the Cleaner and I'm not. Once we're in there, we'll go over the next step of the plan. You should have all the info about the layout and the staffing the compound has."

"Where?" I asked, starting to feel the panic rising in my gut. I put all my effort into containing my nervous energy. This was nothing like the other tasks I'd performed. Filching files and accidentally opening underground laboratories where I had to escape robotic monsters, grabbing planners… This was absolutely nothing compared to breaking into a heavily-secured compound and obtaining god knows what we were here to obtain.

"System, show relevant information for GQXFminor." He smiled again. "Forgot you're just a Novice. You won't have access to this yet."

Information flooded in front of my eyes, overwhelming me momentarily. I only had enough time to make sure I memorized a safe path across the compound before Blocker was speaking. "Go in three, two, one…now!"

And then I didn't have time to think anymore—it was all I could do to keep up.

We made it over the wall with less fuss than I'd anticipated. I didn't remember Orion being so agile, and it took me by surprise. That was where the easy part ended.

About twenty feet from where we landed was a small power station. Its hum reached my ears easily, like a soothing melody resonating with the electricity that flowed inside me. I could feel my own power gravitating toward it, tugging me with it, giving me no option to go another way. If I listened to it for too long, I didn't think I'd be able to contain things.

My power itched to escape my fingers. Keeping in line with the wall wasn't difficult. It was dark here, shadows abundant, lending us their camouflage. I belatedly realized that the station was covered in plastic housing. Most of it might have consisted of metal sections, but with the plastic covering positioned the way it was, I wasn't confident I wouldn't start a smoldering stinky fire. Not with the way my own electricity writhed against my skin, cursing its confines.

I'd thought all I'd have to do was touch one spot and let a surge escape me, thus shorting out the system until the backup could ignite. But this? It was beyond me. I wasn't entirely sure how I was going to go about this.

"Um. I can't focus it through plastic." There, I'd spoken up and not kept it to myself. As absurd as speaking the process out loud sounded, it ushered in a wave of relief.

Blocker turned to me with a frown. "Then open the door. Open it, short circuit it, and let's go."

When I got home—hell, if I got home at this rate—I was going to take the time to research and figure out all the different types of electrical stations. The plastic door to the main fuses for the fence and outer security was locked. I struggled trying to open it so much that I slipped, flew onto my back, and landed with a rather loud *uff* on the ground. Orion rolled his eyes and stepped over me, igniting a frozen shard from his finger as he aimed it directly at the lock. It extended into the lock and a sharp click sounded, opening the door. He bowed theatrically, mocking my ineptitude. After all these years, you'd think I'd be used to it by now.

I breathed a sigh of relief as I reached forward with my left hand. But just as I exerted that tiny bit of effort to allow a trickle of my power to run through the system—thus shorting it out and plummeting us all into total darkness because the lights in the compound also lost their power—I heard what I'd never wanted to hear in my entire life.

"Don't move or I'll shoot."

The voice was made of steel and very compelling. But power surged inside me, rising up, trying to escape anyway it could. It was like the indignant kid who'd been called a chicken. Fight me was its motto and oh how I wanted to be swept along with it.

The four minutes were ticking down, and it was difficult to remain still. The amount of effort it took to resist the temptation to just go for it made my body shake. Lucky for me, the tremors that wracked my body didn't seem to account for movement or I'd be dead.

But the Blocker was on the ground, crouched with one hand touching the dirt. I wasn't sure why I could see it, given the darkness surrounding us. Food for experimentation later. It could have been my imagination, but I was certain his hand glowed for a split second before a massive pillar of earth shot up beneath our would-be attacker and caught him in the chin. It happened so fast I could barely track it despite my better than expected vision, and it knocked him flying, like the perfect upper-cut.

"Go. Now," the Blocker called out, no hint of desperation in his voice.

He didn't have to tell me twice. I pulled up the map in my mind, overlaying it on the terrain in front of us so I could navigate through the maze of guard points. I ran so fast, I swear even Coach Marth would be impressed with my sprinting speed. Though I admit I fueled my speed with a lot of added electricity. It was practically bursting out of me, and I had to expend it somehow. I stopped when I reached the house, waiting for the other two. In my haste I'd forgotten that I shouldn't go too fast. Fear and adrenaline pumped me full to capacity again, making it feel like my skin strained to contain it. The others were nowhere near as fast, so I had time to wait and to think.

Wait and practice calming myself down was probably more accurate. The need to just let loose kept whispering in the back of my mind. Power like tendrils tickled at my brain, under the skin, inside the skull, as if it were haunting me. I resisted it with childlike petulance, refusing to admit I might be tempted at all.

Still though, in the darkness around me, I felt like my eyes didn't need help to see. And even then, even hiding in the dark if I looked through the window, I could see shapes moving around. Only, if I listened closely, these made a noise. A click here and there, a buzz so high pitched I almost missed it. Shadows clung to the walls, and dripped like molasses from the ceiling to the floor making me feel decidedly uncomfortable. I wanted to quantify them. To reach out and touch them. See if they were the real sort from the lab, or the ones that assailed my mind constantly.

It seemed like hours before the other two joined me. Enough time for me to question everything, and need to solve it all.

"Door is this way." Our Blocker motioned for us to follow him, and even through the dire situation I found myself wondering what his name was. What had his life been like before this? How many of us were there in this completely twisted situation?

Orion was light on his feet, moving with practiced ease that bespoke of him being at this a hell of a lot longer than I had. It meant he had to have died a good while ago. What if the program hadn't picked him up? Where would I be now? I pushed down the melancholy wave I could feel rising inside me. That could be dealt with later, it had to be. I had to focus before my ability used inattention as an excuse to push past my defenses and blow up everything.

Faster than my eyes could follow, the Blocker applied something to the hinges on the door, and it swung in without a sound. Wise. We moved through the darkness like we'd done it a million times before. Maybe they had, but I was light on my feet and mimicking their every move. My eyes could see as if the room were lit by the aftershock of a lightning strip, but shapes still moved around me. Shadowy shelving units loomed over us, making me feel small. If I looked too closely it seemed as if they warped into human shapes and back again.

I swore I could hear a rumbling cackle beneath the silence. The air was thick and tasted like a fresh laid tar on a road in the summer heat. At least the floor didn't stick to our feet. I followed the others, watching the countdown in the corner of my vision tick past one minute. What did it mean when it finally hit zero? Would the lights come back on? The questions that bombarded my brain wouldn't stop. Nervous habits didn't vanish upon death. The irony wasn't lost on me.

With thirty seconds left as we continued to move slowly, I could feel the oxygen in my lungs strain against my controlled breathing. I was wound so tightly, clamping down on the electricity that wanted to escape.

"Here." Blocker stopped, and I almost bumped into Orion because I didn't register the words fast enough. My panic receded, grumbling in the back of my mind as the shadows came to rest around us. I watched them out of the corner of my eyes, seething darkness that slithered back into place with a strange underlying whirr that didn't sit right.

This phenomenon only began after I was killed. Well, after I was killed and went to the damned bakery. Shadows, shadows everywhere and most of them missing the robotic elements of the first ones I'd seen. Maybe it was like that old movie, where something came back with you if you came back to life. Except this time as a robot, or something.

Fantastic. Now I'd freaked myself out. I shuffled closer to Orion just as the emergency lighting booted back up, casting a dull golden glow over the entire area and proving to me that the shelves were just shelves. Shadow monsters weren't real; only robots were.

The warehouse's decor was older than I'd expected. Wood paneling lined the offices like some remnant of a 70s sitcom. I waited, concentrating on what I could see of Blocker's face. His expression held no fear, only determination. It calmed me. I needed the calm.

"I hid the guard. He'll be out for a while. No one knows we're here. For all they know, that outage was natural." He paused and his lips spread into a grin. "We have to wait about three minutes, and we'll have a clear shot over to that fuse box. Can you see it, Runner?"

It took me a second, but I realized that was me, and nodded. Using our designations instead of names seemed overkill, but I guess that meant there was no way our names could lead to us being discovered. The Blocker raised an eyebrow before continuing. "Short it again. Focus though. Make it look like it's just a surge of power like the last one. It's a smart security system. It'll repair itself this time too, but it'll give us enough time to get into the main office and grab what we need. The Cleaner will nuke any signs we were ever here. Got it?"

"Got it." I answered in unison with Orion. The Blocker nodded again, and turned to look alternatively at his watch, and out into the dimly lit foyer, leaving me alone with my thoughts. Orion kept looking back at me, and I was quite certain he was trying to show solidarity, that we were in this together.

Except it didn't feel like that. I felt like a complete outsider, only good for what my little pinkie could exude in electrical power.

This is correct. Why is that a problem?

Oh, joy. The system chose that moment to listen in and be concerned. So not what I needed. I chose my words carefully, suppressing the desire to let my ability encase me from head to toe because it was so close to overflowing. *Because I have no idea what I'm doing, and I get the feeling I shouldn't have clearance for this shit yet.*

You shouldn't. But an exception was made due to a lack of Runners being available in this particular region.

But why are there so few Runners? I asked the million dollar question, and didn't like the silence that followed.

Finally though, SC's words spilled into my mind again. *Electricity is an unpredictable ability. Sometimes, when a Runner overdoes it, overuses that element, they are wiped from our existence. No longer visible to us, we rarely find their second death's corpse. Over the years, many Runners have simply vanished. Does that help?*

Not really. But thanks for explaining it.

You are welcome.

Not really at all. The mood of my little parasitic passenger wasn't helped either. It stalked around inside me, unsettled and restless. I began to suspect that the system wasn't telling me everything for a reason. And for a moment, I didn't think I wanted to know anyway.

16
TRIGGER SWITCH

"Go." Blocker's voice acted like the starting gun at my races. My adrenaline surged, giving the hungry power within the reins. It practically propelled me forward and I barely managed to stop before I hit the fuse box. I didn't have time to shake or be scared, and I placed my hand against the box, allowing a surge of electricity to run through my body.

In hindsight, I should have slowed down and focused before releasing the energy. But calm had deserted me and the strength suffusing my body lent me an overconfidence I wasn't sure was a good thing. Instead, I placed my whole hand on the box, giving the energy a much larger conduit to travel through.

Electricity coursed through my body, ejecting from my palm like one massive bolt of power. I felt the box beneath me react, the metal conducting the charge, and the plastic bits burning in response as wires fried beneath the onslaught. In what seemed like a dream, it blew away from the wall, glancing off what appeared to be a shield around me, before the door clattered to the ground with a clang.

"Oops?" I blinked as time came rushing back.

Warning. Timestance activated. Unauthorized use.

I blinked at the words running in front of my eyes while I still regained equilibrium.

"Shit." Blocker's curse followed mine almost seamlessly.

"At least the lights are out now?" I asked tentatively, hoping it would get me off the hook. Timestance? Was that what it said? My head buzzed, the glee of the electricity inside me difficult to push past.

Orion sighed and grabbed my elbow, ushering me after Blocker toward the office we needed to access to complete our task. "Yes, they are, but we might not even have four minutes now. It'll be trying to access backup generators. But I think you might have put a kink in that. Getting out is going to be a hell of a lot more difficult than getting in was."

There was worry in his voice. Blocker probably didn't know how to detect it with Orion, but I did. And if my best friend was worried, then I had probably really fucked shit up. I had no idea what exactly I'd fucked up, but an alarm sounding, when we were somewhere we shouldn't be didn't sound like a good thing. I felt guilty, and a little defensive. I'd only been dead for two weeks, why on earth did they send me on this mission?

This time I watched from behind Orion as we moved as swiftly and silently as possible through the rooms. He utilized what looked like a sheet of ice, cold and sharp. It didn't quite touch anything and seemed to mold its way around every object, drawing fibers and dust, and hairs, and whatever else had been left behind by human bodies. Like a sort of massive, cold lint roller. One that made sure we left no evidence behind whatsoever. Did that mean some of the SC operatives had been criminals?

His finesse implied a practiced ease that I wasn't even close to yet. I wished that ability was in my arsenal. His ability zapped anything it encountered into oblivion. I'd never imagined ice could burn like that. But I could only dream of having that much skill.

The thought made me shudder, and I glanced up to see him ushering me through the door so he could clean up after me too. The Blocker was punching some numbers into a safe. It made sense that it would operate on a type of battery back-up. It opened with a soft whoosh of air, like a sigh of relief that whatever was hidden within would finally be out in the open.

The shadows around us felt like they were closing in, like there was someone reaching for me and my hands and the power I held inside. The sharp intake of breath that escaped me didn't help calm my nerves or the thrill I felt at potential combat. I'd never been a violent person, preferring to run. Now though, now I was strong, powerful. Now I could win.

Even against laboratory guarding shadow machines. I wanted to know how they were made. I wanted to know what they kept prisoner in those cages.

"Runner." Orion's voice tore me out of my self-inflicted spiral. "Stick with us."

I knew he shouldn't be worrying about me, because I should be able to do this myself. But I was sort of glad he was. By their own admission, I was green and shouldn't have been here. Given free rein with my overly eager electrical pal living in my body, there was no end to the shit I could fuck up.

Wonder if they ever stopped to consider that this was the reason they didn't have many Runners? Because they kept putting them in shitty situations while inexperienced.

The safe was closed again the next time I looked, and the time ticked down at the bottom left corner of my vision. Slowly. Surely. Ninety seconds. There was no way we'd make it out of the compound before the alarms went off. I followed the Blocker while Orion brought up the rear, cleaning up after us as if we'd never been there. We made it to the exit with thirty seconds to spare, but we were moving faster, trying to beat the clock. The fence along the outer perimeter was at least a minute away.

The night air felt cool as it ruffled my hoodie. I had to hold onto the peak of it so it didn't blow down. The charcoal facemask made the air taste like a warning. I couldn't help the trepidation that ran through my body. It wasn't a premonition so much as a distinct certainty that something was about to happen, except I had no idea what.

Warning: Portent Ability beyond current skill level. Access may be detrimental to your mind.

I couldn't let the messages flickering across my sight unnerve me. I'd get back to them later when I wasn't trying to outrun an alarm.

"Run to the edge. The alarm hits in about twenty seconds." Blocker's command was crisp and authoritative.

Ten-year-old me would have wet my pants. But not newly dead me. I flew to the edge of the property, my eyes—used to the dark now—seeking out any interfering guards that might be off track. I balked as I realized the area we were heading to was faintly lit. It meant I'd only blown the power center in the actual building and not the entire compound.

The Blocker had to have known. He was observant; he was in charge, right? Even so, I sprinted toward the box that charged the fence. I had to. There was no way over it if the power was still on. Shooting electricity through my body, feeding the synapses in my brain be damned with ramifications I'd not yet considered, supercharging my legs, I dashed to the edge so fucking fast, I wasn't sure how I'd stop in time.

Not twenty feet out from the fence, sirens began to blare.

Though the alarm shrieked loudly, I was too far gone in the flow of running to stop, or even for it to trip me up. Skidding to a halt by the hub that powered the entire outer security, I grasped onto the metal leg that fed into the small structure so hard my knuckles turned white. Fuck being subtle. We didn't have time for that anymore. Right now we needed to get out of here as quickly as possible.

The power had been thrumming through my body the entire night, and at the mere thought of expelling it, it practically jumped from my body. Electricity crackled around me, through my body, over my skin, dancing like a mini lightning storm. Then it rushed through the structure, and in a split second I smelled burning plastic and charred wiring. My job here was done.

I glanced back, thinking the others would almost be here, but they weren't. They were still half-way to the office building. So slow. Had I really sped myself up that much? Pushing myself back into the shadow of the wall where the moonlight couldn't even find me, I waited, not knowing what else to do. My power sat in my gut, happy, purring like a sated kitten. At least for now.

Time slowed down again for me, like I was watching people run through a slow motion camera. Red numbers counted slowly higher in the left corner of my vision. Red for the time we'd exceeded our task. Or else for the time we'd screwed up and allowed the alarm to go off. Given that it was my fault, I couldn't bring myself to just vault over the wall and be done.

Timestan…

The power in me surged again, just briefly, cutting off the words that floated across my vision. I'd deal with that later.

I didn't have the muscles to carry someone while running not even energizing my body, so there were flaws in my plan. But it was the only thing I could think of to do. My legs wouldn't budge though. Seconds had passed, and Orion's eyes were focused on me, begging me to stay put. I felt like a coward. Here I was with a strong ability and no knowledge of how best to use it.

I clenched my fists, listening to what Orion was trying to convey. I obeyed and stayed where I was, because inside, I was terrified that by trying to help him, I might injure him instead. Closer now. They'd almost reached the shadows.

Hopefully they wouldn't start hearing the conversations I had with myself too. I could swear the leaves were whispering to me, trying to pull me in a different direction. Relief washed over me as I managed to recognize Orion's eye roll. He'd done that as long as I could remember. I'd always been the faster one, the fitter one. If there was one thing I was good at, it was running, and as it turned out, running away.

He opened his mouth to speak, but a sharp bang cut through the air, and he closed it, panic flitting through his expression so fast I barely recognized it. In the next moment he wore his calculating face, the one he wore when he attempted to work out difficult problems. Only we didn't have time for that, and the Blocker knew it. Men appeared on the crest of the small hill we'd run down, silhouetted by the red of the glaring battery operated alarms. I wasn't sure what this place worked on, but they didn't appreciate interlopers.

Blocker nodded at me, and I reached forward to grab Orion's hand and tug him with me.

A bullet tore through the air where his torso had been but a moment before, and he yelped in surprise, growing pale immediately. I didn't do so well with blood, so I didn't look down to see where he was wounded. The only thing I could be grateful of was that the shot didn't catch him in his chest.

"Get him over." Blocker commanded.

My eyes desperately searched the hill beyond us, even as I nodded and began to pull the laboring Orion with me. The nervous energy gathering in my chest fueled my abilities allowing me to put one foot in front of the other. My best friend had just been shot. Orion wasn't allowed to die. I'd fucking make sure of that.

I did my best to try and tear my eyes away from the five figures approaching slowly, with their guns clearly illuminated in the moonlight. The light reflected off the dark grey metal, and the people holding those weapons looked like shadows given true form. With the moonlight behind them, it blocked out their features, leaving them dark and menacing, their movements stilted and controlled.

Like machines.

My back hit the brick, and I breathed in deep, grounding myself so I didn't lose control.

"It's okay." Orion sounded breathless. "I can get us over."

How the hell was ice going to get us over? I had no idea what he was talking about, because his ability definitely seemed to be water, ice, and fire something. "Sure?"

"Brace yourself. Or…" he grinned lopsidedly. "Brace both of us would probably be more accurate."

I barely had time to do so, because I had no idea what he was talking about. But I understood the term brace. We did it when we got in the starting blocks before a sprinting race. We did it on the blocks before swimming lessons or competition. Bracing I could do. Crouching slightly, I bet my knees, taking on as much of Orion's weight as I could while focusing on the eight-foot-high brick wall. Alone I could have scaled it, but I was wiry, not strong in that brute force way. Right now, I couldn't afford to give in and use too much of my power. I was barely maintaining control as it was.

"It's okay. Just guide us down. I can't do that," he said breathlessly, and

I didn't want to think about the blood I was sure he was losing. So, I concentrated on landing and hoped it wouldn't break something my coach would kill me for.

But when I stepped off, all ready to brace myself and Orion's weight, I wobbled, but didn't fall. What the hell? I looked down but there was no step beneath me, nothing truly visible, just a wavering of the air. Like a gust had caught us and was lowering us down.

"Guide us, down." Orion repeated, and I could tell his breathing was labored. Apparently he had air as an ability too, who knew.

It reminded me eerily of riding on a cloud. We could fall through the center and be gone. At least then I'd know what happened. Orion clung to me, but I could already feel the strength sapping away from him.

The air didn't quite dissipate as I guided us down. Instead it provided intervals of updraft that helped us land safely.

Once my feet were on the ground, I stumbled, Orion's weight shifting me awkwardly. My surroundings came back into focus, and I once again heard the sirens, smelled the char on the wind, and heard the gunshots like death in the night. The leaves of the trees tickled my face as I sat Orion down briefly. I had to go back and help the Blocker.

"No. You have to stay here. We need to get to safety." Orion's tone was commanding despite the pain obvious in his expression.

I paused, hands on my hips, this form of petulance all mine. "Oh, sure, let's leave all the men behind, shall we?"

Orion shook his head. "Not like that. He's a Blocker for a reason. It's what he does. Earth is a defensive ability, and he's got it in abundance."

Hands appeared at the top of the wall, fingers bloody and gleaming in the sliver of moonlight that managed to reach between the leaves. Fuck. Had he been shot, too? "No, we have to help him."

But another shot rang out. The fingers went limp and disappeared from view, followed by a loud thud.

17
AGENT DOWN

In the next second, a shudder in the earth beneath my feet made me stumble. I steadied Orion while I turned to look at the origin, only to find the Blocker at the top of the wall about to tumble down to this side.

I dove to try and catch him, but a cloud of air whooshed at just the right time and allowed him to land safely. It was amazing how quickly I could forget that I was surrounded by people with super powers.

I'd used a lot of my power to fry the electricity, yet I could feel its indignation in how quickly it fed off my mood to replenish its reserves. The guards were going to have to scale the wall too, because those gates weren't going to work for a long time.

"Car," the Blocker gasped out, pointing in the opposite direction from which I'd approached the meeting point.

I nodded, looping my arms under each of them. Damn my wiry frame. Sometimes I felt impossibly tiny. "This might hurt, or might hinder, I'm not sure."

Technically, if the human body was like a motherboard—and I wasn't saying that was the best analogy, but it was what I had—then all I had to do was ignite the adrenaline, and the rest of it should mostly take care of itself. I allowed a trickle of power to pass into them through the hands I had touching their backs. My reserves had been blown, but I still conducted energy.

As soon as I felt the tendrils gently reaching through me and to them, I began to move again, hoping that touch was all I needed to keep the transfer up. I was definitely winging it.

Error.

Warning. Unidentified use of ability. May be dangerous. Use cautiously.

I tried not to smirk. Learned something new every day.

"Shit!" Orion gasped, coughing suddenly.

The Blocker probably would have said something if he hadn't been busy coughing up blood.

"Move with me." I urged them to do so, willing them to energize, hoping that my ability could be shared. We had no time to spare. I hadn't had a choice. I'd deal with the repercussions later.

Their movements were slower than I'd have liked, but much faster than without my help. I managed to allow a trickle to continually flow into them as I moved up my own travel speed too.

It wasn't much, but it did allow us to get away from that spot before the guards reached the wall and could jump over it. The car was about half a mile down the road, and while I could have run that in mere minutes, it took us almost double that, even with my electric speed shocks.

I had no idea how the guards weren't coming after us. I'd ask Orion later, along with all the other questions I had mounting in my brain.

By the time we got him bundled into the back seat of the car, Blocker was looking pretty green around the edges. Orion slipped into the driver's seat, his face so pale that the black hair made him ghostlike.

"Idiot." I nudged him to get over into the passenger seat. Blocker was bleeding on the upholstery, but since he was still alive, I was sure he wouldn't care. If we got him to Dr. Caroline in time, things should be okay.

The fact that Orion moved was a testament to how bad he felt right then. Usually he would have fought me. With good reason, too. While I could technically drive and had my license, I wasn't what I would call a confident or good driver. There wasn't time for doubt right now.

I started the car, surprised to hear the engine was almost silent, and directed thoughts at the system immediately.

Notify Dr. Caroline we are on our way. Also, guide me there.

I'm not a GPS.

No, you're more sophisticated than that. Do it. I don't want this Blocker to die.

And I didn't. While I might not know the guy, it was me who'd fucked up on more than one occasion in that mission. I blew the power. I fried the electrical system inside. It was my fault he was hurt.

SC guided me along streets to the highway without another comment. I was grateful to avoid the one-way streets I knew lurked in all the wrong places. SC slickly maneuvered me through highway traffic, and then to the streets in order to avoid road work. Our path took us on a route where the lights turned green as we approached. Across the river and to the Hospital of the University of Pennsylvania, we didn't hit one red light. I was fairly certain that hadn't been a coincidence, but chalked it up to another thing I'd have to look into later.

The hospital felt familiar now, like it was a second home. It might well have been, considering the amount of time I was likely to be spending there.

A nurse in blue scrubs with a short brown pixie cut was waiting for us when we pulled up. I dragged Orion out of the car to talk to her, and then got about getting the big guy out of the car. By the time I had, my best friend was in a wheel chair, and an orderly had brought a gurney for the Blocker.

I sighed with relief, and then the nurse spoke to me.

"The doctor said to park the car and then come in. I'll wait for you." She nodded toward the parking garage, and I didn't need a second hint.

Once inside, she hurried me down a corridor marked Staff Only to a grey, unmarked door. Questions battered my mind, but I wasn't about to ask them. I simply followed her through to a brightly-lit office adjacent to an exam room, where I waited like the nurse told me to.

I waited nervously in the room and refused to allow myself to panic. None of this was how I'd envisioned this task. I hadn't expected Orion to be there. Nor had I expected to fuck up so badly.

It took a lot of effort to remain standing and not just sink down to my knees and bury my head in my hands. I was tired, running on the energy leant to me by my ability. So worn out. But the doctor would be here shortly with, hopefully, some answers for me. The room was mostly barren. Just a cupboard here and there, and the usual examination table. No seats.

Your most recent assignment has been marked: Completed, with casualties.

The cost of treatment will be subtracted from your earnings. Payment will be delayed because of this. However, the experience gained from this encounter has pushed you into the next level. Congratulations on attaining the next rank.

You have moved from Novice Rank to Apprentice Rank.

You have unlocked digital access to our library.

The words rolled across my vision. These rankings took forever to increase. I couldn't pretend having access to more information wasn't downright convenient.

Accessing my interface, I pulled up my training tab, hoping that the restricted sections had been unlocked. No such luck. Sure, one was available now, but I was fairly certain that was due to my having ranked up.

Correct.

Shut up.

No need to be nasty.

It actually sounded offended. Fantastic. I'd managed to offend a program.

A soft creak sounded behind me, and I whirled around, realizing it must have been the door's hinges. Dr. Caroline stood there, frowning at the clipboard in her hand as she flipped a couple of pages back and forth.

Finally, she looked up and gave me a tight smile. "Dare. Perfect. Just the person I wanted to see."

That didn't sound enticing. Why did she want to see me? I swallowed my nervousness and forced my own smile.

"Good to see you again." I cringed. Perfect thing not to say.

She didn't seem to hold it against me though. Putting the clipboard down on one of the countertops, she motioned for me to jump up on the examination bed. Since it looked all innocent like an examination bed should, I did as she asked. I tried to ignore the rampant suspicion that now tainted my ability as it floated through my body making me hyper aware of how we were one, but also weren't.

She did a full check. Blood pressure, listened to my chest, looked in my nose, ears, and mouth, and tested my reflexes. Then she pulled out the octopus gadget and let its tendrils of light brush over my body.

"Remarkable," she muttered, more to herself than to me, shaking the device and frowning at it. Flicking her thumb over the top of the device, she ran it over my body again, her expression slowly softening.

I wasn't sure whether I should be scared or excited.

"Tell me, how did you come up with the idea?" Her expression expected me to know what she was asking, and I had no clue.

"Idea?" I wished I was a mind reader. It would have been so cool to answer the vague question.

"Of pushing their energy levels with a trickle of your own."

Well, I'd wanted to boost their energy. I'd guessed that was what the error and warning notifications were for, now I knew. I only hoped I could recreate it.

"I mean, I wanted to, so I sort of applied what I do for myself and let it flow through to them, you know? I just figured we run on electricity, like a motherboard. Feeding power into the motherboard causes the system to activate and make the computer run. I thought if I trickled power into them, it might sort of reboot their systems and help us get to the car faster. That's all."

She didn't look disappointed, although she did purse her lips. "Fascinating. Just so you know, you probably saved Adam's life. That trickle of power you used helped boost his own body's functions, including healing, temporarily and slowed the bleeding down enough that he made it into surgery. The prognosis is good. Well done."

Dr. Caroline marked something off the clipboard she'd picked back up.

Correction: treatment costs will not be deducted from your payment. You'll receive full compensation.

That was a nice bonus. Whatever she'd ticked, the system seemed appeased. I also needed to make a note of the Blocker's name. He was Adam. But he wasn't the most prevalent in my mind.

I took a deep breath and cut to the chase. "Is Orion going to be okay?"

Orion sat up in bed, moving his bandaged arm slowly. The grimace on his face told me just how much it hurt, but he seemed to be taking the pain in stride. Around him the machines beeped out a melancholy song. The dissonance of the notes played off each other, clashing in a cascade of life.

A physical therapy aide jotted down notes in a book, frowning as he did so. I wanted to grab that notebook and read everything, to figure out a way to help.

"He's okay." Dr. Caroline's eyes didn't leave Orion as she spoke to me.

We watched from behind glass, looking in on the room in what I suspected was secret. "It nicked a muscle and went clean through. It's not as dire as the bleeding made it out to be. However, it'll take a couple of days before he can undertake any new assignments."

"Couple of days?" Sure, it might not have been a fatal wound, but he needed to replenish his blood and heal.

"Thanks to your gift to him earlier, it's possible even without our… technology." A smile tugged at her lips, like she wished she could replicate me. Given the types of instruments she'd already used on me and my previous torturous stay, I didn't feel safe at the thought.

"Sure. That gift and stuff." I was trying to figure out if I'd be able to duplicate what I'd done. The situation had been dire, and we'd needed to get to that car. All I'd done was tried to give them a bit of fuel injected speed to make it so we didn't all die. But instead of it just giving them a boost, it gave their whole system a boost. So how exactly did that translate?

I glanced at my hand turning it one way and back, watching as sparks like fireflies flickered beneath my skin. It was quiet, no pressure exuded from inside my body. Almost like the power was asleep after such a workout. I wanted to understand it, needed to.

"You can wait for him if you like." She slid the pen into a slot above the clipboard that appeared to be made just for it. "Or you can go in and visit. Adam will be out of surgery in a couple of hours. Thank you again, Dare. We always seem to lose our eels before I fully understand them. We appreciate you being here."

I nodded, because I was only half paying attention. The rest of it was caught by the languid movements in my hand. Almost hypnotic.

Her feet clopped down the hall with less noise than I'd have thought given the echoey nature of corridors. It left me standing in the dimly lit hall where the walls of white could slowly close in on me.

Hospitals, where people come to die. Or not. Often they came to get better, but it never felt that way to me. There was always the faint scent of bleach underlying everything, like a crime scene trying to hide. Lemon tried to mask the stench but rarely succeeded. No place should be this white. Ever.

Letting myself into Orion's room, I turned to look at my best friend, only to see him staring at me with a goofy grin on his face. Definitely not in character for him, maybe he was hopped up on—

"He's on a heavy sedative while his arm heals." The nurse wound gauze around Orion's bicep wound. It didn't look like any type of gauze I'd seen before, but more metallic yet pliable in nature. "Might not even have a scar, thanks to you."

She grinned at me. A dimple in her right cheek made her whole face light up. Dark hair was pulled up into a tight bun, and her dark blue scrubs cast a sharp contrast to the rest of the room.

"Thanks for taking care of him." I couldn't take my eyes off how pale Orion was. He was naturally pale, but this—it was ghostlike.

"You did a pretty amazing thing out there, kid." The nurse made me feel like a child, and I suppose, in comparison to most I'd met so far, I was. She nodded at me again, packed up a cart of equipment she'd been using, and ducked out of the door, leaving me alone with Orion and my thoughts.

What if I couldn't replicate what I'd done? They were all acting like I'd discovered some portion of power that I could share with others. What I'd done, could only have been done by myself or another electrical user. Or maybe a pair of jumper cables.

"Stop thinking all those thoughts." Orion grinned at the ceiling when he spoke, his eyes half lidded. "Very loud. Very wrong."

I laughed softly. It was odd to see the usually completely in control of himself Orion, being goofy and hyper.

"Sorry you got shot." I said the words softly, hoping he wouldn't hear. His eyes wavered from where they watched a black spot on the ceiling and then wandered over to me.

"Why? You didn't do it." He giggled again, and I wished I'd had the foresight to record this. But like anything else, if I whipped my phone out now, it was going to make him sober up enough to chastise me. And no one wanted that.

"Sorry you got shot. It's a general commiseration. Take it." The pit of my stomach felt like it was burning in acid. I knew a lot of what went wrong had been my fault and it encouraged the anger that seemed to live in the bottom of my chest these days.

"Hey, Dare?"

"What?"

"You've got to stop this." And his tone was clearer, serious.

So I looked at him while he spoke "You've got to stop blaming yourself for everything that goes wrong all the time. Okay? We got out. We'll be fine. Even Adam."

You should listen to your superiors.

Shhhh.

It stayed quiet, but that didn't mean Orion was wrong. In fact, I was quite certain he was right. Perhaps his version of SC constantly gave him advice too. It was a comforting thought.

"Okay. I'll try."

That seemed to be enough for him, and he smiled at me as he lay back down. He closed his eyes and almost immediately fell asleep. Why couldn't I have received that particular superpower?

I pulled up a seat next to his bed and watched the way his chest rose and fell, the way he breathed so easily. I wanted to breathe easy too, but something about today's task nagged at me. That office had been far more high tech than I'd imagined, yet I wasn't sure why I was surprised.

From the doctor's classified implements, to the labratory, and the shadow masquerading automaton things. If I threw in moment of death revival and the whole system as it interfaced with us, this wasn't magic. This was science. Therefore, all I needed to do was figure out the coding, right? No big deal at all.

I didn't arrive home until early Saturday morning.

Laying back on my bed, I threw my squash ball up at the ceiling. It never made it; there wasn't enough weight behind my throw. But at least I could practice releasing slow sparks of electricity. Quick bursts were something I knew I'd need eventually. If this last assignment had taught me anything, it was that I didn't have nearly as much control as I'd need.

I'd left behind so much destruction, I was surprised any of us got out alive. That sounded a little too self-deprecating, but even so, a lot of what I'd managed to accomplish, came down to sheer luck.

Not to mention the warnings that flashed up at me, and the very telling silence from my old buddy SC on the matter. Timestance? Portent Ability? Error? Seriously, what sort of system was it even?

And don't think I forgot the good doctor mentioning that eels don't last very long. Though I did appreciate the nickname, the lack of knowledge didn't make any sense in my mind. How could they not know more about this ability? I mean, they had a whole designation centered around it.

The tutorials SC gave me were focused on the element in ways that, in my short experience, were less important. It focused on point of expulsion, choosing to center around the fingers. But its guide to control had many holes, and the whole understanding seemed rudimentary at best.

How long has SC been around? I had to ask the question, and I desperately needed an answer, because some parts of this weren't adding up.

But all that greeted my pointedly directed thought was silence. Irritation flared briefly, but I could already feel the power within stirring, so I shut it down with concentrated breathing. From what I'd gathered, SC had always been present, but I could be wrong.

Since I'd never been gifted with much patience, I decided trial and error were probably my better options, since my voice friend wasn't being forthcoming. This particular exercise was a whim to see how quickly I could release a spark. Eventually I hoped to work my way up to being able to fire off a split-second powerful shock, controlled in every aspect. Right now, I was still testing it.

General Electric Pulse Control.

Rudimentary Electrical Shock Application.

I scoffed at the names of what it had *taught* me, and cracked my knuckles, ready to get to work.

Orion wasn't home yet, and Jacob had been scarce lately. It made me all sorts of suspicious. I had people being in SC on the brain. According to my subconscious, everyone I knew probably was. Despite staying in the apartment, I'd managed to avoid Jacob all weekend.

As if listening in on my thoughts, I heard the apartment door open and was out of my room before consciously choosing to do so. The door pushed inward, and I grabbed it, pulling it the rest of the way.

Orion stood there, his pale skin almost translucent. He gave me a wan smile and stepped into the apartment. He had an orderly—or guard, I wasn't sure—with him. Maybe he'd just been sent to escort him home. The man deposited a suitcase inside the apartment and left wordlessly.

"Oh good, you're home in time for school tomorrow." I cringed at the eagerness in my own voice.

I wasn't sure how to react. *Hi there, friend that I almost got killed.* There weren't many words that could apologize for that.

"I might skip tomorrow." Orion didn't even temper the statement with a grin. "I'm fine, just a little queasy. It wasn't even a serious wound."

He seemed upset with himself, like he thought he was being weak.

"Sure, it didn't puncture anything vital, but you still had a foreign object rip through your arm." Orion chuckled, and I picked up his bag before he could and shoved it in his room. "Now sit down and take a load off your feet. I'll make you some delicious ramen."

This time Orion smiled genuinely. "Thanks, Dare."

Ramen, the college go-to meal. I guess Orion had stuck to it in order to keep up appearances. Which reminded me that I still didn't know what had happened to him, or even when. To be at the rank he was, it had to have been a while ago. How many other things didn't I know about my best friend?

I let the ramen sit for more than three minutes. I was in a fluffier noodle mood. Taking Orion's in to him first, I placed it on the beaten-up side table. Its mahogany wood had been beautiful once, but now it was scratched and worn. He flashed a smile in my direction, but it was preoccupied, full of secrets I didn't know. Shadows flitted across his eyes that had nothing to do with the ones that tried to claw at us during the tasks.

After fetching my food, I sat down on the chair on the opposite side of our worn table. The TV was off. I wondered if it even still worked after Orion got his hands on it a couple of weeks ago. It hadn't been on my list of priorities.

We slurped our ramen in the silence, well apart from the obvious. It's not exactly a refined food, and slurping—at least in my experience—is just what you do. The noise stood out, yet I didn't want to interrupt it.

Orion placed his ramen to the side and leaned forward, burying his head in his hands for a moment. I watched him, sucking in a particularly long noodle. Belatedly, I realized that maybe I shouldn't have been quiet.

Finally, he sat up straight with a sigh and turned to me. "I guess I owe you an explanation, don't I?"

I kept my eyes on him, the part of me that didn't want to go easy on him won out. So I watched him while I drank the rest of the soup out of the bowl. Finally, I put mine to the side and locked my eyes on his.

"You owe me one hell of an explanation." Even if telling me was out of the question because of the program, it didn't excuse that he hadn't told me since I was enrolled in it. Just because my system decided not to tell me doesn't mean he hadn't had the opportunity. Pulling no punches seemed like the best option to me. "So. When did you die?"

Orion looked away, and the ghost of regret passed over his expression before he squared his jaw and looked me in the eyes again. "Two years ago. Well, almost. Freshman year, spring break. That camping trip."

"Wait, what?" I knew that spring break. "I was there."

"Yeah. I know." His gaze remained on the tattered rug we used to try and protect the aged wooden floors.

"How? Like you can't just leave it at that. Was it when you went on that hike? Or—" Wait, there'd been that accident. I'd thrown it in his face not too long ago. Something that happened and Orion had had to spend the night in the med tent.

"Yeah. The catamaran incident."

He sighed but pushed on, past my spluttering questions.

"The boom hit me in the head, knocked me overboard. I was an idiot, in the wrong place, forgot to duck." He shrugged and then hugged himself. "I drowned, but only for a split second. Like I was dead, but then I wasn't. Apparently when they pulled me back up, I was breathing. But I know I hadn't been for a minute or two.

"When the EMTs got to me and I finally woke up, they had to brief me in place of Dr. Caroline because we were out of her range. I wanted to tell you so badly, so many times, but the rules. You get it, right?"

His eyes beseeched me, were willing me to agree with him.

"I get it. But I also don't get why you couldn't talk to me directly after my accident." That's what was really bugging me. Maybe I couldn't have helped him, but he sure could have helped me through this adjustment phase.

"My system didn't give me any sign that you were actually in the program. Sure, I had my suspicions, but for some reason it didn't recognize you and give me a report. Usually, I don't have to prompt it. But this time..." He ventured a small smile at me. "I'm glad your death didn't stick either."

My death. His death. We'd both died. That was some pretty major shit right there. Dead before I hit twenty-one. Not exactly on my bucket list.

"So how come you're ice, you know, if you drowned?"

This time Orion full on grinned. "Frozen water is like ice, you know."

I could have smacked myself in the forehead. Of course they weren't separate elements. Just different variations. "So does that explain the air too? I mean, freezing air makes the water ice, right?"

He nodded, his expression one of eagerness to share. "I've since developed skill with both air and water in combination. I can't do anything with earth to save myself, but the air is sort of a good compliment to water. Ice is so much more powerful in certain instances. Let's me be pretty versatile. Water by itself wouldn't have helped us much on Friday, especially not with your electricity charges running wild."

I couldn't help it. I laughed, somewhat sheepishly. "Good point. So was the doctor supposed to tell me Adam's name?"

Orion shook his head. "Not really, but it doesn't matter. As long as we use our titles in a group task, it's okay. It's sort of thought to reinforce your role with repetition and avoid any actual identification if we're overheard somehow."

He paused, like he was trying to figure out if he should say what he wanted to. "We don't have friends when on a mission. We can't afford them."

He flexed his arm, wincing slightly. The shadows returned to his eyes and he let out a sigh.

"Except without my friend this time, I don't think I'd be home yet. Nor would Adam have pulled through."

"Adam is okay then?" Maybe there was too much eagerness in my voice, I'm not sure, but Orion's grin held conspiring overtones.

"Adam is fine. Well, banged up, but he'll be okay. What the hell did you do? Even the doctor seemed confused." He leaned forward expectantly, because he knew it was my stroke of genius that saved us.

"The thing is? I'm not precisely sure. I wasn't really thinking analytically, more acting on instinct and just hoping what I applied to myself worked for you two as well." Orion raised an eyebrow, but I barreled on. "I just thought of it in a sort of motherboard comparison way. Nothing on it will work if you don't inject the right voltage of electricity. Too little and it doesn't matter, too much and it'll crash and burn. Can't overclock the processor too much or it'll fry. Might need to add some coolant. That sort of thing. Isn't the human brain kind of like a computer?"

I left it hanging in the air, the words I'd only dared to think to myself so far. But the huge grin that spread over Orion's face told me all I needed to know. While I might not understand exactly what I'd done, I'd applied simple real-world problem solving to it. And I was certain with enough time, I'd be able to replicate it on command.

"Well, thanks for not frying my brain." He laughed, but I could hear the nervousness underlying it, and I couldn't blame him. I'd basically just told him he was a guinea pig.

A thought struck me though, like a whispering in the back of my mind. "Hey. You know how the system won't hurt someone else if we accidentally let our circumstances slip, right?"

Orion's brows furrowed and he pursed his lips, like he didn't want me to say what was coming next. He nodded, hesitant though it was.

"I feel like I've seen some of this, remnants of possibilities, maybe some sort of dream. I don't suppose they had to wipe my memory ever, did they?" I didn't need him to speak. I could see the answer written all over his face. The guilt shone through like a red letter.

I forestalled him, his discomfort tangible. "It's okay, Ry. I get it."

He just looked at me, frustration welling in his eyes, but still he didn't speak. It was like I didn't get it, I didn't get it at all.

Monday rolled around, and I found myself waking up about twenty minutes before my still earlier-than-usual alarm. I lay there, watching my ceiling and the crown molding that snuck into the corners. Such delicate patterns withstood the test of time. How many things didn't?

Orion had wiped my mind. Multiple times if his reaction was anything to go by. What sort of lasting effects did that shit have? I shuddered at the thought and tried to push down on the brief flare of resentment. It wasn't his fault.

I hadn't spoken to my program in a day or two, and I wasn't sure how to approach the system to ask it for some of the information I needed. It was definitely ignoring me.

Every now and again, in the dark light of the morning, I swore I could see shadows flitting through my room that had nothing to do with those cast by the traffic down below. Nor were they cast by me moving around.

No, these moved of their own accord. They slunk about, whispering words I couldn't hear. Their red eyes only blinked open infrequently. Just often enough that I realized they were still there. Thoughts flitted around in the back of my head wondering if they were real, wondering if they were fragments of the memories I'd lost, or a part of death that came back with me.

They didn't really make noise. Not really. Just scuffling against the wallpaper. Sometimes they sounded like mice were in the walls, only I knew better. The memory of the lab flashed through my mind often. Those strange metallic legs cloaked in imitation shadows. If I turned the lights on, they disappeared. Just the notion that it was there—all a part of my hallucination.

Except this wasn't in my mind. As far as I could tell, this was all a result of being brought back to life. Of having super powers I couldn't quite control. Of being watched since I'd entered the Heavenly Dough.

In hindsight, Heavenly—afterlife… Maybe there was a link there. But from what I could tell, it wasn't to the system in my head. It had to be something else.

I'd made a habit of throwing my squash ball. I did think my reflexes with electricity were improving. Short stops and starts helped me gain control over the it. I'd only left a couple of scorch marks where I'd overdone it. Squash balls were small. Not always the best containment device for a large push of power. The initial ignition burst of power was what I needed control over.

I didn't like the idea of always having to rely on finding a wall receptacle. So far my body had been the best conduit, the best containment device. I had to be careful though. Sometimes it felt like I was coming apart at the seams.

Perhaps I should talk to Dr. Caroline about, too.

Would you like me to contact the doctor for you?

Damn it. When would I know it was listening in? Maybe I'd let my thoughts surface too far. *No. Don't bother the doctor. I'm just having rhetorical thoughts.*

Very well. Is something else troubling you?

Sure, you could answer the question I asked you like yesterday. I did my best to keep the irritation out of my tone, but I failed spectacularly.

Repeat the question please.

How long has SC been around?

Define parameters.

I blinked. What? Thoughts raced and I gave it another go. *How long has the SC system been functional?*

The SC system has always been. Your inquiry makes no sense.

I paused, flabbergasted. How could it make no sense? Humans hadn't always been, so how could the system?

Can I help you with anything else?

No. I lied quite well, even to myself. *Just thinking.*

It didn't say anything after that, and I thought it had receded to wherever it was it stayed while not bothering me.

You seem overwhelmed. It's okay. You're an integral part of the program. You've evolved the electrical skill tree. We have learned from you. This is a great thing.

Thanks. I almost choked on the chills inundating my body. That sounded almost like a threat. You've contributed, so we're not letting you go any time soon. Shit.

If you have any other worries, I'm here to help. I have all the information at your fingertips.

Even that was a slight joke. I allowed myself to chuckle politely, unable to think of anything else to say. It appeared satisfied by the lack of answer and left me in peace. At the same time, it was either lying, or else it believed what it told me. Because considering my questions, it definitely didn't have all the information.

My brain was trying to rewind, begging to ask questions best left alone, at least for now. I swung myself out of bed and made haste to the bathroom. Nothing wrong with being early to training. I'd done it so often recently. It was sort of my thing. I had lesson plans for my after school groups to drop by Coach Marth's office and two lectures to get to.

Still eventually I'd have to confront it and ask it why it hadn't told me Orion was in the program. There were weeks we could have avoided fighting, where I would have had actual guidance. It was lucky I had so many things to do in order to maintain my previous life. Anger bubbled softly inside me, no matter how much I tried to clamp it down. I could just feel the electricity guzzling it greedily.

Orion was in the bathroom, his brow furrowed with a frown. He gazed into the mirror as he examined his stitches. I'd not seen them before now. Sure, I knew they were there, but stitches had this sort of barbed wire sticking out of your body look that set my teeth on edge. His were no exception.

"You're up early, Dare."

I nodded. There was no denying it. I'd been getting up earlier to avoid him before our little mission jaunt, and now I was up earlier again. Still.

Whatever.

"Been getting to practice early lately. State's coming up shortly." I grabbed my toothbrush, fully aware of Orion standing in his boxers with a frown on his face as he continued his inspection.

"You'll do well. Don't cheat." He grinned at me, squeezed my shoulders, and moved out of the room.

Don't cheat? Considering he'd been my test subject, he had an inkling now of what I could do with my power. I wonder what he could do to the human body with water. We were made up of what, eighty percent of the element, after all. With his upcoming medical knowledge, he'd probably be formidable. That was my Orion.

Getting my shit together, grabbing my clothes, making food. It all felt mechanical. Like something I'd done every day of my life until now. And it was. Yet there was this whole huge world out there I'd had no knowledge of before a few weeks ago. My best friend was part of it. I was a part of it.

How many more of my friends were actually walking zombies? Wasn't that what we were? Except we weren't decomposing yet. At least, I didn't think we were.

Thoughts ran rampant through my head. I barely heard anything Coach said to me. I needed to focus. This coming weekend was State Championships. I had to do well. This was all part of my shot at the Olympics.

Did a dead person deserve to take that chance from someone else? What if death had inadvertently given me an advantage? There was no denying it could have, if I let it. Did replenishing my energy levels count as cheating? Not a speed boost, but just energy so I didn't feel tired.

SC was damned picky about when it chose to butt in and answer the questions in my mind. By the time the end of the day rolled around, all my thoughts were a mass of confusion. Today, SC was obviously not feeling chatty.

I walked out of the school buildings to make my way home, running some of my thoughts around in my mind. What sort of events had to happen that I would be standing directly under the line that fell when it fell? I didn't usually go to extra training. Not on a Sunday around noon anyway.

Was my being there happenstance? Could it have been anyone, but regardless, someone had been destined to die that day? If they were lacking electrical users, it stood to reason that they'd want more. Why not just create the circumstances that birthed us, then?

Considering the footage of the incident, the out of body experience it gave me. Its vantage point was suspicious. How could someone have been there and witnessed the accident, timing the recording perfectly? I needed to see if there were actual street cameras anywhere around town that were located in exactly the right spot to give that angle. I'd feel much better if there was, but I wouldn't hold my breath.

My thoughts began to speed up. What if the SC program made things happen? The whole system seemed wildly unrealistic, so why the hell not think it could control external factors like that?

I was so caught up in my thoughts that I failed to notice any commotion or anyone around me, until I felt a sharp rap on my head and saw stars spinning in front of my eyes.

19
THE LOOP

Believe it or not, I've seen a shrink before. Frankly, I think they're fantastic. Talking to a complete stranger about the shit on your mind has this freeing effect.

I woke up on a couch. One of those chaise lounge sort of things made out of dark brown leather. There were creases through it, as if it had been loved for many years. Perhaps in the family for decades, if not centuries. It smelled of leather conditioner and devotion for maintaining such a gorgeous piece of furniture.

To the left, stretching out to each side of the room and up above me to the ceiling, was a wall of books. Or, more accurately, a massive bookcase. At the far end there was one of those ladders with the wheels if I wasn't mistaken. Though since I'd not yet sat up, I couldn't tell for certain.

I could spend hours in this room. Except I didn't have time. I had to get home. There were questions I had. Like, where the fuck was I?

"Ah, yes. The questions."

The voice didn't come from my head. In fact, it definitely came from the same room I was in, although on a different side. I forced myself to sit up, and my head spun as I tried to bring the room into focus.

"Sorry about that. It appears Diva hit you harder than she intended."

There was a wry undertone to the words, but I still hadn't found the source. Scanning each inch of the room, my eyes finally came to rest on a young lady. She sat cross-legged on top of the large mahogany desk in the room. This wood wasn't faded like the side table in our apartment. No, it remained its rich and majestic self. One day, I'd have furniture that shone like that.

She watched me. Her dark blonde hair hung almost to her waist. From this distance, I couldn't see her eye color, and I wasn't about to guess. She sucked on a lollipop, and her gaze never left me.

I couldn't see anyone else in the room. So she must have been the speaker.

"It's good to see you awake." She spoke again. Her voice was much more commanding than her appearance would have me believe. "You were out for a good few hours. Don't worry. Orion will make up an excuse for you."

It seemed they knew me well enough. They knew, at least, that I'd be worried that my friends might worry about me. It occurred to me that I often worried. Perhaps I'd try to change that.

"Thank you." It seemed appropriate.

She jumped off the desk, tossing the lollipop into the trash without a second glance at the container. It landed perfectly. Moving around me, she *ummed* and *ahhed* for a few seconds. Then she planted herself directly in front of me and grinned.

"Welcome to the Ark. You have been entered into the Second Chance program. I am your cruise director. Please direct all questions you have to me." Her grin grew larger when she called herself the cruise director.

It felt like I was missing an inside joke, in this very Wonderland-esque environment. Even so, her mood was infectious. It was difficult to maintain politeness at the best of times, but right now I desperately wanted to have amazing manners.

Instead, my mouth decided to cut communication with my brain and blurted out: "How old are you?"

I cringed, because that seriously wasn't the way I wanted to start the conversation.

But she laughed. "My name is Nya." And she deliberately winked in my direction.

"And to answer your question. I was seventeen when I died." Her eyes held no sorrow, nothing to give away that she was sad about her circumstances or anything.

I had no idea what to say. Usually I had something on the back burner. But nope. Right now? I had nothing. The voice that was usually in my head remained quiet.

"Ah. Yes. Your companion cannot reach you in the Ark." A flicker of something dark passed across Nya's face as she waved her hand around indicating the entire room. "We are guarded against interference in here."

With a snap of her fingers, the bookcases on the far end moved backward and parted before sliding into a space in the wall on either side like pocket doors.

Behind that bookcase was the largest collection of screens I'd ever seen. Different scenes flickered on each one, flitting between individuals and landmarks, on a constant rotation. It was like they were watching the whole world, or at least Nya was from this strange library. I wondered what she saw, but more importantly, why was she the one watching?

"My. So many thoughts and no questions. Tell me, Dare, what is it you're wondering about?"

"What the hell is that?" I pointed and she laughed again.

"It's a part of the reason you can hear your own thoughts in here without them being interrupted by irritating voices." She glanced back at the surveillance display, motioning for the bookcases to move back into place.

"But let's get back to the shallow end before I drown you with too much." Her voice was soothing, lulling, and easy to mistake for someone who wasn't just lying to get under your skin. I switched up my train of thought without really meaning to.

"If you died when you were seventeen, why do you still appear to be that age? Do none of the Second Chance survivors age? Does that apply for everyone? Does that mean the doctor was what, thirty-eight when she died?

How does this even work?" It was like I had no control over the abundance of questions that spilled forth.

Nya held up her hand, motioning for me to stop. So, I waited, even if I struggled to hold my tongue.

"You have all the questions. Questions that someone with your abilities must have." She glanced around, as if checking to see if anyone else was listening. Despite having shown me her futuristic security system, I hung on the edge of my seat, waiting for her. But it seemed, I was the one being waited on.

"Wait, you mean my electrical abilities?" I scoffed the word, unsure how that was supposed to make anything make more sense.

"Those and your different methods of application. " She glanced to the side, like she was seeing something I couldn't, a light frown on her face as she did so. "You aren't just following the tutorials you were given. You've actively improved your skill by applying computing logic. Quite brilliant, actually."

I thought I understood. "So it's not that the abilities are new, just that no one figured out how to apply them, or thought to apply them in that manner before?"

She nodded, but I could sense the hesitation. There was more she wanted to say. I wish I knew why she didn't. "Sort of."

I still couldn't get over the fact that this young woman was...what was she? "Can I ask your rank?"

Nya smiled. "Rank B. Master. Technically anyway. Not that it really means all that much in the grander scheme of the system. I wanted to give you some advice. Your SC system had flagged your thought process. It's best that you don't let it know when you're uncomfortable."

I blinked rapidly trying to understand what she meant. Not only was she being delightedly vague, but was she implying that I could somehow distance myself from SC's ability to hear everything I thought? "I've asked questions since I could talk. Hard to stop now."

She grinned mischievously, but there was something else underlying her expression that I couldn't quite pinpoint. "Which is fine. Just be aware of how many you ask, and of whom you ask them. If that allows you to still come up with things like the experiment you made on Friday night, then I'm all for it."

It still felt like she was holding back from revealing more. Infuriating actually. I'd never seen her before, yet it felt like I should know her well. I couldn't feel a presence in my mind at all, and it made me begin to wonder just why and how SC didn't seem to be able to reach me. I needed something like this for myself.

Still no response, not even when I directly thought about it in my head. Interesting.

But Nya's laugh peeled like silvery bells through the room. "It's nothing nefarious. Just private. Be wary of how you direct your thoughts, where you direct them at. Some things are better kept to yourself.

"Why did you bring me here then? Couldn't you have just told me on campus?" I was a bit irritated now since it was obvious she wasn't going to give away more than she already had. My fingers were itching, and not with power, just with curiosity to see what was behind those bookcases up close. I should have been at home eating dinner and playing quizzes to get us ready for the upcoming exam block. But I wanted more than anything to follow my nose.

"I could have approached you on campus, but it's far safer in this particular room. And to be honest, it wouldn't have been nearly as much fun. Also, in here we can speak plainly. Here, you can talk freely, just as you should practice to in your mind." She gestured around the grand library that had to be the size of a medium-sized house just in itself. "This is my sanctuary. It's better to be here where people will take me seriously, than out there where many people still assume I'm a child."

"So the people enrolled in the Second Chance program don't age?" Since she hadn't answered it the first time I asked, I pushed the point. It sort of made sense, but I couldn't wrap my brain around it.

"Not like most people. But then life expectancy isn't huge either. Not many people I moved up the ranks with are still around." Nya was silent for a few moments. So much that I thought she wasn't going to say anything else. Then her brow pinched, and a small scowl appeared on her lips.

"You almost botched the entire operation, and the only reason you're not in punishment right now and being fined, is that you did a great thing and healed your teammates." Her tone was stern, worse than my high school principal's. "Even if you're not sure how you did it. You got lucky. Something like that requires a level of finesse I think you guessed right at."

I believed her. Down to my very core, I believed her. What could I have done to them if I hadn't been so focused? What if I'd been nervous? I could have killed them both. I wasn't only lucky to be alive myself—so were they.

"I won't push it. I've been working on refining my control. I promise." I meant every word.

But even that promise lay like lead in my stomach. She watched me intently, as if she were waiting to see if I had anything else I wanted to say. As if she were weighing the thoughts in my head for herself.

But then Nya smiled. "It's okay. You did what was needed, listened to your instincts. An excellent idea for an eel. Just like you did when I sent you to Heavenly Dough. Keep your wits about you, and… just. Keep any complaints to yourself. As much as you can."

I wanted to ask her what she meant, because those last couple of statements felt loaded, like there was so much more behind them. But before I could ask another question, I was gone. The jolt as I landed back in my room at the apartment was enough to make me stumble to my knees. It was difficult to steady myself, and I had to wonder if Nya had been telling the truth. Her words had been filled with second meanings. And of course, I'd managed to neglect asking her about the shadows or robots or whatever they were.

There was so much I didn't know, but something about the way she spoke let me believe that there were ways to find out without cluing in my little system friend. I really hoped it wasn't just wishful thinking on my behalf.

It wasn't until later I realized I hadn't even asked her why it was so important that we talk where SC couldn't overhear us.

Almost a whole week passed before I began to worry. Had I done something wrong that the system wasn't providing me with any more tasks?

Had the Ark interfered with our connection? I double checked my interface several times a day.

Which, inadvertently, allowed me to appreciate its simplistic beauty. It reminded me of an advanced alternate reality system that required thought versus spoken word to activate it. If it was possible. Then again, I'd come back from the dead with apparent super powers. Who was I to say what was and wasn't possible anymore?

They'd paid me for the job I botched, but my system had barely spoken to me since I went to visit Nya, and it hadn't even sent me on any shitty retrieval missions either. It made me wonder if the Ark, as she'd called it, had interfered with my communication ability. I frowned, trying to muddle my way through that train of thought. My power didn't even flare at the irritation. Another odd side-effect of my visit to the Ark.

"You need to learn to put on a poker face." Cyan popped up next to me. She'd changed her hair color from bright blue to a royal blue. It made her eyes pop because they were three shades paler, and her soft powder blue skirt suit accented the whole appearance.

The Docs didn't really round it out, but they, too, were blue. And her T-shirt had a smiling rainbow waving at those who looked. I'm not sure how she pulled it off, but she wore it perfectly. Glancing down at my dark sports pants and baggy school shirt I felt a bit underdressed, though I'd never cared much for clothing.

"I don't play poker." And despite myself I even tried to keep my face straight, but the grin still broke through. Damned friends. Always making me smile.

"There's a very good reason for that, Dare." Cyan patted my hand and flung an arm around my shoulders. "So tell me, why have you been so distracted this week?"

What did I say to that? "Just worried about Orion healing up ok. Work is stressful. State in a few days." I shrugged, trying to lend my words some casual hesitancy.

"The usual, then." She grinned and nudged my side. "We're on for tomorrow night though, right? We've barely played at all lately."

Tomorrow was Friday. But I couldn't stay up too late. "I've got my last training session on Saturday, so I'll hit the hay early. Don't compete until Sunday though."

"You really know how to deflate a girl, don't you?" She winked at me, and I realized I was being a bit of a dick.

"Got a lot on my mind." Which was a total understatement. "I don't mean to be distant. I really am sorry."

"It's okay. You know we'll come and cheer you on, don't you?" Cyan squeezed my shoulders and glanced at me. "Even though you do your best to be a loner sometimes, we've got your back, Dare."

With a quick smile, she was gone, waving to someone else behind us. My friend was a whirlwind of energy. Some days I wish I could borrow her way with people. Mine was mostly clumsy and introverted.

Give me a running track any day.

What would you do with a running track?

Run on it?

I assumed you meant musical track. Sorry for the misunderstanding.

I frowned. Had it just been trying to banter with me? It was difficult to know what to say to a system in my head. But damn was I glad it was back, and yet at the same time sort of disappointed. My feelings could wait for analysis later though.

Misunderstandings are fine. I do like music, but I didn't mean a continuous music track.

Is this State thing important? It sounded hesitant, like it had been trying to figure something out. Which led me to believe it had been listening, just not engaging. I wished I could figure out when it was present but being quiet, versus when it just wasn't there.

Very. It's one of the things I've been working toward my entire life. I'd forgotten how good it felt to admit that. How good it felt to have gotten his far. Electricity sparked along my skin, feeding off the brief spurt of energy. I'd have to watch that on Sunday.

Then you would do well to rest up. I can take you off duty if you wish? For personal reasons?

Really? Could it really do that, or was it just making the offer knowing the odds were that I wouldn't be needed?

Really. I can put in the request and let the program know that you're only to be contacted in a case of emergency.

Thanks! I meant it, but I didn't think it was going to do any good anyway. My stomach twisted, like little Timmy fell down a well. Except I was Timmy, and the well was the black hole that my life had become. I had a really bad feeling that in the next three nights, something was undoubtedly going to need my attention. And it had nothing to do with playing poker with friends.

20
SERIOUSLY

I woke up on Friday with a sense of foreboding in my stomach that was so strong, I couldn't eat breakfast. It felt like lightning was crackling around my body, sparking through the edges of my fingers, defying any control I might purport to have. By the end of the day, I stumbled through the door certain I had food poisoning. Except I knew that wasn't it.

As soon as I threw myself on the bed, words flashed before my eyes.

Urgent Attention Required

Location: City Hall

Objective: You and your team will retrieve file D102BX14. You will receive further directions once you've obtained this item.

Time Limit: As soon as possible. Under the cover of darkness.

Reward: Progression and monetary compensation

Caution: Be diligent. Do not be seen. Dress appropriately.

I groaned. Maybe the electricity gave me clairvoyance as well. *I thought you said I'd be exempt from any missions until after my championships?*

I could only exempt you from normal missions. This one was urgent.

I'm not sure if it was wishful thinking, but I thought perhaps the system was a little sad for me. Like it had really tried or something. *It's all good. Don't worry about it.*

I rolled over and changed shirts. School colors weren't exactly incognito, but if I pulled my black hoodie over this, it should work. Charcoal sports pants were close enough to black. The weather was slowly getting warmer though. Soon I wouldn't be able to wear my hoodie without looking hella suspicious.

My stomach churned, like it was an angry electrical storm. I knew something was going to go wrong. But I couldn't be sure how far that extended. It could have meant that I would have a mission after all, or maybe it was focused on something else entirely.

Swinging myself out of bed, I heard a noise coming from the living room. I paused, trying to take stock of the situation. I thought—and sort of hoped— it was Orion.

"Did you get pinged?" my friend asked me as soon as I entered the room.

"Yeah." Why on earth were they putting us both on the same mission team again? Considering last time, it made no sense. Although, maybe it was better to place me with someone who understood how unpredictable my ability could be. Though there was no way we would have the same Blocker. Adam was still healing up as far as I knew.

Orion gave me a look I couldn't interpret. It might have been curiosity, but I think it was more than that. He was probably running through the exact thought process I was. In a city of this size, wasn't there a plethora of other agents they could put together?

"Do we head separately or together?" I asked hesitantly, unsure of the protocol.

Orion frowned. "I'm not sure. I've not had to deal with this before. I do have to cancel our Friday night plans, yet again, though." He sounded vexed at the last, and I couldn't blame him. "Our friends are going to hate us."

Even I'd been looking forward to tonight. A little bit of unwinding before my big meet. Plus, City Hall made me nervous. This wasn't some rogue science research lab, or bakery front for god knows what. This was a place where our city handed down judgment. It was going to be protected and patrolled. It wasn't going to be as easy to get into this place, not to mention it was City bloody Hall. I wasn't sure if there'd ever be a time we could just waltz on in. Since the last mission hadn't been a walk in the park, I hated to think how we'd fare this time.

Orion glanced at his watch and sighed. "If we walk, we need to leave around six. We can leave half an hour later if we take the subway."

So, we were going together. Some of my anxiety fled at the thought, even my electricity seemed to calm somewhat. I nodded. "Your pick."

"Let's walk, then. Gives us more time to talk, because I'm sure you have questions." Orion didn't look at me when he spoke, but instead picked up his bag and sauntered back to his room, his gaze focused on the floor.

It was a little chilly and way too windy for my liking in the shade of the skyscrapers along Broad Street as we approached City Hall. I was glad of my hoodie, but knew this respite wasn't going to last forever. In no time at all a heatwave would descend on us, and then it wouldn't matter how nice and warm my hoodie was—it'd be too much.

Orion walked next to me. I'd forgotten his legs weren't used to striding, and I found myself having to hang back to keep pace with him instead of speeding up and shooting ahead.

He chuckled, like he could read my thoughts, which was something else I wanted to talk to him about.

"You really need to control your face better. I can see you running through thoughts a mile a minute. Just ask me, because wearing your every reaction on your face is a bad idea in this line of work."

I scowled at him but couldn't hold it long. He was right. I often thought far too much to myself. And I'd always worn my feelings for all to see. About to speak, I opened my mouth, only to get a whiff of urine, rotting vegetables, and something else I never wanted to know the origin of. I didn't try to speak again until we were well clear of that tunnel grate.

"Why do you think they shoved us together again?" I asked the question, wondering if the system was going to answer me instead. Nya's words haunted me in the back of my mind. There were reasons she'd warned me. I just wish she'd been more forthcoming. I didn't do cryptic well.

"They need our skillsets. That's it. There's never a reason they would push us together except for that. The program doesn't take pre-death friendships into account." He sounded bitter, like he'd just eaten a lemon.

I couldn't help thinking he was holding something back again. "Not exactly the right environment to form lasting bonds, I guess."

This time Orion laughed with less bitterness. "Not exactly. They just don't want us concentrating on anything that could be distracting. Despite everything else. If you're in a situation where a sacrifice is necessary, it's far more difficult to let a friend fall than just a colleague with a designation."

It made sense to me. Far more sense than the bakery I'd been sent to having a secret lair, or the shadows I was guessing it tried to imitate. "What about those shadowy things?"

The words were out before I could retract them, and I waited, not sure if I should clarify what I was asking.

"Shadow things?" He spoke sharply, looking at me, his blue eyes forceful. "What do you mean shadowy things?"

I gathered my thoughts and tried to explain. Maybe he would get it. Maybe it would make sense to him too. "At the sides of my vision, I can almost see them most of the time. Not so much during the day. But once twilight hits, that's where they are. One of them, or maybe two of them, almost took one of my task objectives once. Like clawing hands made of solid smoke. But those are nothing on the underground lab I saw on my first task."

"What?" He stopped, his focus on me, like he was trying to ferret out if I was making a joke or something.

"Went to get a file, it opened a secret door leading down to what I swear looked like a laboratory." A wave of discomfort stole over me. Perhaps I shouldn't have mentioned that part.

Orion's brow pinched with thoughtfulness and he bit his lip before glancing around at everyone. Finally he turned back to me, moved a tad closer and whispered, "I don't know about any labs, but I've seen shadow like shapes leak in and out of my vision."

"Exactly," I breathed, not daring to raise my voice. What did Orion know that I didn't?

"I've seen them. They've never touched me before, but I have noticed them. Always following, always doing their best to catch up to me. Yet when they get close, it's like they're shy. And yet." He glanced back and forth and whispered to me. "And yet, it seems the system either doesn't acknowledge them, or else it doesn't see them. So much that I really thought I was losing my grip on reality."

I gulped. Personally. I didn't like either option.

City Hall was smack dab in the middle of downtown, and a concrete monstrosity. Arched tunnels crossed to a center courtyard with even more concrete and brick. There was an old man playing guitar on one end. The melody lilted out, but it was snatched up by the wind, leaving the notes to drift around in discordant harmony. The man didn't seem to notice us as we passed into the courtyard to lean against the inside wall.

Every fiber of my being wanted to make me turn around and run in the direction we'd come from. But running from a task wasn't an option, just like refusing to perform the task you were given. I'd learned that much the hard way.

Orion and I sat at a small picnic table, wedged between the wall and a subway entrance, watching everything we could manage to. We were in plain sight, and that didn't give me any confidence.

I almost shat my pants when I felt a hand on my shoulder, and the guy who touched me jumped back, shaking his fist in pain. Not my fault. I'd been specifically practicing with my trusty squash balls. Any unexpected touches by individuals I didn't know during dusk was going to be met with a rather pointed shock of electricity. How stupid did someone have to be to approach a stranger like that anyway? They were lucky a little bit of an electric shock was all they got from me.

The eel inside me squirmed, like it had had a taste and wanted so much more. Tempering the instinct to let it loose was barely within my grasp.

The guy was bulky and built. Like he'd spent every day for as long as he'd been alive, working out.

"Sorry about that." He brushed his hand through his dark hair. Either black or brown, I wasn't sure. The light was dim in this area. It was why we chose it. "Didn't realize we had an eel with us."

"It's okay." I pushed out through clenched teeth. "It's not like they give us much information."

We all shared an uneasy chuckle.

He offered a hand this time. "I'm your Driver. Just waiting for our Minder and we should be good to go."

"Minder?" Orion sounded surprised. "Why do we have a Minder with us? We're going to have to wipe someone?"

I recognized the latter tone as offended. They were easy to confuse, especially when Orion got defensive.

"What's a Minder?" I asked, keeping my voice just above a whisper.

Orion rolled his eyes. "Someone who resets memories, wipes the mind, makes sure anyone we encounter can't remember us. Basically? A babysitter."

Flashes of my overactive imagination did their best to hint at nefarious potential. Was that what had been done with me? A minder had wiped my memory. Since Orion wouldn't meet my enquiring gaze, I figured it was. A cold chill stole down my spine, winding around like it was trying to suffocate me.

"Because of last time." I whispered the words.

"Yeah." I could tell Orion was sulking. He crossed his arms and looked away from the group. Maybe that's not all it was, though. My friendship senses were tingling again.

"Can't wait to see why I'm babysitting." The voice sounded familiar, feminine tones with strength behind them. As she stepped into the watered-down moonlight, I realized I knew her too. Sam. Sam was our Minder.

Was that why she missed so many gatherings? Perhaps that was why she had so much money. Wait, were all my friends already dead? Granted, Sam was more Cyan's friend than mine, but she was technically part of our circle.

She raised an eyebrow at me, but didn't seem at all surprised. "Good to see you, Runner. You too, Cleaner."

Her grin held mischief, and her eyes sparkled, and I remembered we didn't use names on missions.

Our Driver feigned a hurt expression, raising the back of his hand to his forehead. "Oh, woe is me. You have forgotten me."

"Nope. Just outrank you now." She winked and sidestepped around him, squinting up at the building.

I engaged my interface, prompting it to inspect her. Unless I specifically formed questions in my mind, I'd realized that the system no longer provided unprompted information. Which was probably why it took so long with Orion. I'd just assumed he wasn't a part of it, and thus it hadn't answered the question I didn't ask.

Sam Mitchel
Designation: Minder
Rank: Senior
Skills: Mind/Spirit/Light
Second Chance Affiliate

Well, I guess that answered my questions. Except now I wanted to know how she died. How about the Driver?

Hale Wetford
Designation: Driver
Rank: Associate
Skills: Light/Dark
Second Chance Affiliate

I really needed to remember to use it more often. Wondering about shit that was easily found never got anyone anywhere.

Sam stood there, a frown on her face. "This isn't going to be easy one. There are guards that change sweep rotations every forty-five minutes. In order to do this, we need to get in and out inside of that window. Right now we have about twelve minutes to go over the plan and then begin execution. Got it?"

"Got it." Perfect unison. Almost frightening.

Questions, I had so many questions. Like, why were we breaking into

City Hall? What could possibly be in there we could benefit from? Was the Minder for them...or for us?

Quickly, I used the system to write a note to myself. I wasn't sure if it would work if the wiping was for us, but it was worth a try. Adding to my electrical tutorial notes, I marked down Sam, Minder, Courthouse, WTF? That would at least get me thinking if I needed to.

"Runner?" Sam sounded impatient.

"Sorry. Can you repeat that?" Great professionalism from me. Only this wasn't exactly my choice, and it definitely wasn't my dream job. The deeper I got into the SC program, the more questions I had.

You can always ask me questions.

Really? And you'll answer honestly even if the answers are troubling.

There was a pause before it answered me. *I will answer anything I can.*

And that, right there, was the problem. My little section of the program might like me and want to help, but the fact remained that it couldn't always do that.

I switched my focus to Sam. Stuffing this task up wasn't an option for me. We'd had enough trouble with the previous one.

A basement window had been left ajar enough that we could reach through and maintain the alarm system, but not enough to set it off. It was a delicate balance. Orion would take care of that. Afterwards we would all slip in and make our way out of that records room into the one in the center.

Once we made it there, it was my turn. All I'd have to do was absorb the lasers and channel the electricity back into the loop as if the secondary alarm was still in place. Driver would obscure all of our movements in shadow, and Orion was in charge of the locks. Minder would grab the file.

All in all, it should take us twenty-three minutes, give or take a few.

My stomach began to churn in pain again. Just what we needed.

21
WRONG TURN

We waited until the guard turned the corner and then we moved up slowly. I couldn't quite tell, but from what I gathered about the Driver's capabilities, he could obscure our presence using shadows. Thus, night was his perfect time. Instead of the getaway driver I'd first assumed he was, he was more of a get away with the mission by not being seen as easily sort of person. His shadows should confuse cameras. I entertained the thought that perhaps a rogue Driver was the reason I kept seeing shadows everywhere.

The entry was beneath a grate. I half-expected Orion to freeze the screws or something, but Sam pulled out a screwdriver and literally unscrewed them. I guess we were trying to leave as little evidence someone was here as possible.

My palms began to sweat. Not the best thing, considering my affinity. I almost chuckled, but I wasn't quite so far gone in nervousness yet. My own ability rippled beneath my skin, eager to get out and do its part. It didn't seem to understand that we weren't in for destruction today. There was only enough room in the window well for three of us, so Driver remained up top, obscuring us from view.

Orion bit his lip as he angled what appeared to be thin ice through the sliver of a gap in the window. A soft click drifted over to me, and his shoulders slumped with relief as I heard the pent-up breath whoosh out of him.

"Well done." Sam spoke like it was all she'd expected and more.

Perhaps I didn't know Orion as well as I thought I did. He'd had this entire other side to his life for almost two years. Orion stepped through first, then Sam motioned me through just as our Driver jumped down and placed the grate back over our heads. If anyone threw a perfunctory glance this way, nothing would look out of place.

The room I jumped into smelled musty. Low-level golden light flickered over stacks of boxes, papers, and file cabinets. Reminded me of old movies. Aged and slightly out of sync with the rest of the world and itself.

I wanted to reach out and fix the light, knowing it was only a matter of a loose connection not providing the right wattage to the area on a consistent basis. But we couldn't leave any trails behind. Not even one as simple as that. A part of me mourned the fact, and my ability suffered with me.

The area was larger than I expected, and each step sent up a cloud of dust into the air. I could see Orion struggling not to cough. He didn't do so well with dust, smoke, anything with particles. Finally, we made our way to the door, and Sam stood staring at it, frowning.

"I think—" She paused, closing her eyes and touching the door lightly with her fingers before scowling as she pulled them away and looked at us. "This door has an alarm as well. Just like the window one. You're up again, Cleaner."

Ry nodded, his lips pursed in concentration as he only opened the door a tiny crack. He reached through with that strong thin ice. The sliver shot through, replacing the weight that opening the door would have triggered. His abilities were damned handy for a bit of casual breaking and entering. The only trace he'd leave behind when we were done was a few drops of water. None of this hacking the grid stuff from the crime shows for us.

The hall beyond the older records room was narrow and shadowed. Only one light served the entire area, and it was about fifteen feet away at the junction of another corridor. It, too, flickered. They really needed to rewire this place.

Sparks played across my skin intermittently, like it was reminding me it was there. Like I could forget.

Sam led the way, moving us down our own hall, further away from the light to a recessed door. This one was different. The handle wasn't old and rusting. It was new and oil-rubbed bronze. As if they'd chosen that particular metal to make people think it was old. The hinges were fresh as well, and I could even see new oil shining in what light reached back here.

"So." Sam grimaced. "This one opens outwards, and I'm pretty sure it now has an alarm as well. If the pattern holds, any door down here will be armed. Contrary to my intel." The last she said softly, and I wondered how the intel could be out of date. We'd only just received this assignment.

I turned to look at her, and in doing so, I could have sworn I saw a shadow, claws gripping the edge of the wall where it led to our recessed hiding place. Taking a step toward it made it vanish and left me questioning my eyes. Okay, and maybe my sanity just a bit.

Electricity thrummed beneath my veins in response, charging me up. I had to clamp down on it quickly. You'd think in all of the gadgets they had, they'd have given me something to temper my power. Then again, if Nya was even remotely correct, due to the constant disappearance of eels, they weren't knowledgeable about this power. It posed endless possibilities, if I was careful. Sam began to speak again, garnering my attention.

"As soon as the Cleaner is done, it's your turn, Runner." Sam laid emphasis on my role, entirely too amused by the fact that not only was I a Runner for this organization, but I also ran for fun. Ha ha, like I hadn't put the two together already.

Still, I shook the cobwebs out of my head and readied myself for my task. Enough contemplations about how the system worked and just what it was for now. Time to not get us dead. Orion repeated his very excellent breaking and entering tactic.

My nerves were getting to me. Just like before a big meet. Speaking of which, I had to divert my attention away from Sunday. I focused on the job at hand.

With the door open, if I calmed myself, I could see the lines. Blinking like I was outside of time made event specks of dust in the air visible. They floated like snowflakes in front of my face.

Shaking my head, I focused on the lasers. They zigzagged that entire damned room. Whatever was in here, they didn't want anyone unauthorized getting their hands on. Why were we doing this? What was so important about this stuff and who got to decide that?

Again with the questions. Nya was right.

Taking a deep breath, I focused on the tiny box off to the left side of the doorway. In order to reach it, I had to lie on the floor and wiggle my way under laser streams to it. I'd never clenched my teeth so hard before. I was scared. My heart tried to choke me by sitting in my windpipe. Except, that other part of me, the part that seemed to have given into the thrill of my power, it thrived. It fed on these sorts of sensations. My senses became sharper, and my timing more accurate. In many ways, it felt like I was executing a program myself.

I made it to the box, and checked a few of the calculations I'd done while training. As long as I maintained control, I could do this. Reaching forward, I touched my finger to the box and let my thumb hit the first red laser light.

It burned briefly as my body absorbed the laser and routed it back through the device. For a moment I wasn't sure it had worked and was glad I'd clenched my teeth. The initial pain wasn't something I'd wish on anyone. While my own power couldn't electrocute me unless the doctor used that reversal thing she'd zapped me with, this stuff wasn't my power. It was external energy that I was sending to flow through myself. A brief flash of jealousy skated through me. It felt like my abilities were extremely limited. After a moment it settled to a bearable heat, and then I let out the sigh of breath I hadn't realized I'd been holding.

Skill acquired: Rudimentary Excess Power Absorption.

"Well done, newbie." Sam grinned as she stepped past me. "Give us five minutes."

I hadn't noticed the dust when I first crawled on the floor, which was silly of me considering Orion's muffled coughs. There was none in this room. It was pristine, perfectly cleaned, and well-maintained.

My stomach twisted again. I extended my awareness slightly, but all that did was make me feel nauseous. Come on, Dare, how would I do it in a program?

Tracing.

I took another deep breath and focused my hold on keeping the laser from shorting out. In the meantime, I followed the source of the laser's power. Something about this room, about the not quite correct information. It was all too conveniently different. Did someone know we were coming? Could they see us even now?

"Hey. Driver," I whispered in that loud way that is almost worse than speaking normally.

He glanced down at me from his position by the door. "Yeah?"

"Are you still hiding us?"

He smiled. "Always. Never let it lift in missions like these. Because you never know. Why?"

I grinned back, but knew it probably looked like more than a grimace. "Something about this whole thing just feels off. Door handle too new. Floor is perfectly clean. Hinges are freshly oiled."

He blinked at me, and his brows pinched together like he was running things through his own mind. Like he was just used to following orders and not questioning everything. "I see what you mean."

Without leaving his post, he managed to get Sam's attention. I wasn't sure how. Maybe he sent a message through the system.

Of course he used me. It's the easiest way to be stealthy.

Sorry.

I guess my SC was a little hurt I'd chosen to whisper or something. Sam's sorting through files became slightly more frantic, and a message flashed across my eyes.

Mission may be compromised. Moving out ASAP.

And just a moment later.

File D102BX14 obtained.

I waited for them to get back to the door before I released my thumb and scooted out. The lasers shot throughout the room again, their lines crisscrossing without ever touching each other. And just as the last one neared me, I released my finger too.

Successful Execution of Skill: Rudimentary Excess Power Absorption.

Field Experience obtained. Multiplied by a factor of two for job to rank ratio. Skill acquired: General Excess Power Absorption.

Yay, me. I waited with bated breath, but no sound triggered, no lights whirred, and the little box on the wall continued to hum happily. The burning sensation departed, leaving me feeling somewhat empty. It didn't take long for it to be replaced by ever-growing adrenaline. I wriggled like a worm to make it back to the others, and we began the whole process over again. Only this time a sense of urgency hung around us like a bad odor.

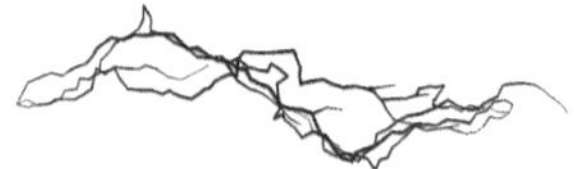

But we made it out of the laser room entryway, and into the hall.

It wasn't until we entered that first, old records room that I realized another thing. Footprints. This room was the only one with enough dust and grime to showcase our shoes imprints. "Shit."

"What is it?" Orion poked me in the side.

"We need to hide the footprints. Mess up the dust. All around us. All of it." And I started to drag my feet through the path we'd taken, making sure that none of our prints were available for matching purposes. For all I knew, there was a way for them to sample our DNA through the air. I wouldn't put it past them. It's probably why Orion swept the area with his burning ice veil.

Whoever this them was, they seemed intent on us not getting the file. Why would there be another division out there? Were there multiple programs? Second chance and oopsies?

It took us maybe sixty seconds to make sure that while obvious something had been in here, they wouldn't be able to tell if it was human. Again the questions started firing through my mind. Why hadn't Sam noticed that? Surely she was a seasoned operative?

That sense of foreboding wouldn't leave me be. I'd never had this much spidey-sense before. What the hell was happening to me?

"We need to leave." I didn't bother trying to hide the urgency in my voice. They needed to feel it too.

Sam glanced at me, curiosity in her eyes. She'd have to wait for answers to her questions too. We all would. "Okay. Let's get out of here."

Orion reached up, did his thing, and we exited into the window well. Driver stayed behind, just like he had the first time. He was keeping us safe and invisible as long as he could. Sam moved the grate to the side slowly and carefully. We'd been fast, probably faster than the ridiculous amount of time she'd calculated we'd need.

She lifted herself up, remaining in a crouch against the ground and motioned for us to follow her. Orion moved next, the file clutched to his chest, his breath coming in rapid bursts. I leaned forward to give Driver a hand into the window well, when I saw another shadow in the doorway. Damn it. Why did I keep seeing them?

The thing with never getting answers, and not understanding what I'm going through is that all along it made me feel like everything was in my head. But not this time.

This shadow was real, a silhouette of a guard with a gun. It materialized into true human form as if drawn by sand in front of me. The shots that rang out through the room, felt so far away despite the ringing they made in my ears. When the shot struck, it hit Driver's torso with the sound of ripping flesh and spattered blood all over me.

He fell forward, surprise in his eyes that were already beginning to mist over, hitting his forehead on the stone ledge of the window. I scrambled back and barely made it up the ladder. Orion's eyes were wide, and Sam's shock visible on her otherwise hard to read face.

"Hale?" her voice cracked, and for a split second her pain was visible. Then she turned to me and whispered. "Run."

She didn't need to tell me again. We'd lost our Driver. There was no bringing back someone from that sort of death.

So I ran.

And I ran.

Just like a coward.

22
NO GOING BACK

I won't lie and say I changed my mind and headed back to fetch my best friend. Because I didn't. He'd been doing this a lot longer than I had. I just ran. The one thing I was good at, the one thing I needed. Electricity powered me on, pushed me further, faster, beyond where I would usually collapse. It was past nine at night, and I needed to be getting to bed. I had training in the morning.

And Driver—no, *Hale*—was dead.

I slowed suddenly, raising my hand to my face. Flecks of blood clung to me. I could feel their brittle texture as they dried in the wind. It was the only thing that got me to stop.

Rendevous: Schuykill River Park's playground. Head toward the river and turn south when you reach the park.

Okay. At least that seemed to make sense. I wasn't even sure where I was running to, but it made sense to just run again and find the park. I vaguely remembered it, and it was nowhere near the City Hall, which was a good thing because I was never going back there again.

The new leaves on the trees blew in the night breeze as I made my way there. No matter where I looked, all I could see was that shot ripping through Hale's chest. Fuck. He was dead. The system hadn't been full of shit. We could die, all of us could. Mortality nipped at my heels, and a zip of electrical energy raced up from the tips of my toes. So solid, I could see it, yet so fast, I almost missed it. Maybe I stood more of a chance with my abilities.

Stand by…

Sure, that's literally what I did. Thanks for that, system. Even though I knew that wasn't what it meant, I was mad at myself.

It surprised me that I was the first one to arrive. The bright pink and yellow climbing apparatus had slides coming off it in every direction. It glowed in the streetlights, the black rubber from kids' shoes marring the surfaces like a bruise. The swings creaked slightly in the ever-present breeze.

I sat in one of the four swings, suddenly tired in a bone-weary way. Death. I'd never been confronted with it so close up before. Blood in the face close.

It didn't take long for Orion to arrive. He flashed me a strange look. Like a sort of grin, but also not. Like he was weary and tired. Shocked and sick of being stuck in this strange do what we tell you limbo. Maybe. It was hard to read him in this light with my heart frantic like it was trying to choke me.

He took the swing next to me. "I've never been able to keep up with you. But you've gotten a lot faster in the last few years."

I nodded. He was right. I had. "Coach Marth is a hard taskmaster."

As an afterthought though, I added, "Well, him and the whole electricity thing anyway." I think my voice shook. Maybe that was a tear running down my face. Damn, it was going to mingle with the blood and leave pink trails behind.

"It's okay, Dare." Ry put his hand on my shoulder, and I leaned into it. "It's all part of the job."

I pulled back, unsure I'd heard him correctly. "What?"

"It's not the first time there's been a death on a mission." Ry looked away, biting his lip. Shadows played around his eyes, giving him an older look.

"Wait." I tried to take that information in, to understand it. He'd been on missions where people died before? How was he so calm? "People die in tasks all the time? Like it's no big deal?"

"We're already dead, why should it matter?" But he sighed, and waved at me not to barge in with indignation. He knew me too well. "I don't mean it like that. I just…people have died before. In two years, Hale is only one of the several affiliates who have died while on a mission with me. It's not that common, but it does happen. Wounds happen more frequently."

Overwhelmed didn't accurately describe how I was currently feeling. "So several people in two years. That's not bad, right? One every few months."

I couldn't keep the sarcasm from my voice, and Orion flinched.

But I didn't care, so I pushed on. "How many wounds? Any of them life changing? Death doesn't matter anymore? Doesn't shake you up at all?"

Orion's eyes glinted. "Bullshit. I'm shaken. I'm fucking stirred. But it happens, and all I can think at the time is the totally selfish thought that hey, at least it's not me. He was a Driver. Hale knew he would always bring up the rear. Depending on the task, on the difficulty level, depends on what role our abilities play. Driver, more often than not, is one of the most dangerous."

I opened my mouth to retort, not even giving the words thought, but someone else spoke, cutting me off.

"Hale had been a Driver for a very long time." Sam sounded more subdued than I'd ever heard her before. She suddenly looked older than the twenty-three or so I'd taken her for. "He's been in the system for over a decade. Ten years of a life he'd never have had but for the program. Always keep that in mind. Any borrowed time is time with the people we care about that we wouldn't have otherwise had."

She had a point, and my whole argument deflated. For a moment I wondered if one of the people she cared about was Cyan. I was angry, but maybe I was angrier at myself for not being able to react in time. Surely I could build an electrical shield or something to repel attacks? A skin, a defensive power. It tickled at the backs of my knees now, like it had been waiting for me to think along these lines. Screw not having enough time. I needed to make time so I could protect as well as defend. What good were abilities like mine if all I could do when someone was shot at, was to stand by and watch them die.

"You're new, Dare." Sam knelt in front of me, tucking a strand of hair behind my ear. I didn't move. She continued, her tone sad.

"You haven't even finished your tutorials and we've thrown you in the deep end. Eels—that's electrical affinities by the way if you didn't figure that out—aren't necessarily rare. But their ability is fraught with dangers. Often, they come with another affinity immediately attached, and therefore the eel ability is lesser, and less, shall we say, combustible." She grinned at me. "But a solo eel? We don't have many of them, and they're spread thin. So you'll be sent on a lot more tasks the more you evolve with your skill."

"Soon?" I was worried about the State meet. So freaking panicked. It was the one remnant of my life I'd managed to keep intact, keep away from this damned system.

"We know you have State on Sunday. Sorry this has kept you so long. We have the visual recording from your system. There was literally nothing you could have done, Dare. Don't beat yourself up about it." She rose to her feet and stretched. "If all goes well, I'll see you next Friday. Good luck on Sunday. And remember to cherish your extra time here."

I watched her go as a soft and cool breeze ruffled my hair. The blood was going to have to go if I wanted to get home. And I'd need to throw on a wash as soon as I was there. Orion was still in the swing next to me, and I could feel him waiting for the right time to speak.

"Ry, I'm so confused. This whole thing is huge. It's only been four weeks, and my life has changed so much. I'm not sure how to deal with it." There, I'd sort of apologized. Even with electricity snapping at my heels, telling me not to.

"It's okay. I remember going through this, but I didn't have missions like today's so early on. Took me about six months to get to where you are. Getting struck by lightning rarely yields usable bodies, so electrocution is the only way they can tap into the eel ability. Careful they don't use you up too much." He got off his swing and came and offered me his hand. "We'll get through all this. I'm not sure why we're in this together, but there has to be a reason."

I grinned and stood up, deliberately putting my weight on the offered hand. I still felt uneasy at his words. But if I wallowed, I'd end up in a probability spiral, and what good would that do anyone. "Yep. We'll get through it, all right."

"But not with blood on your face." Orion reached up and scratched one of the drops away before I could react.

"Oh my dog, Ry! That's almost worse than Mom spitting on her finger and rubbing dirt off my face." I jumped back, staring at him in mock horror. If I could channel away my actual horror, everything would be okay. It had to be.

He laughed, and for just a moment it felt like everything was right with the world. "Scratch it off yourself, then. C'mon. You have to get sleep before training tomorrow."

We headed toward home. I shoved my hands in my pockets after picking off what I thought was all the blood stains. Maybe I should take a leaf out of Orion's book. Or Sam's. Neither of them seemed inclined to question what they were doing given the awesome chance at a second life.

But me? I was built out of curiosity, and too many things nagged at the back of my mind. Not to mention the fact that my ability seemed to have come with its own opinion about everything.

State championships passed in a whirlwind of joy, and time, and I lost track of everything. Right down to the fact that I died.

I placed first in the marathon, and never once thought about helping to give myself a boost. Though, had I not trained as hard as I did, maybe I would have given into the temptation. Gold in the five thousand meters was one of my favorites. It was as close as I got to a sprint. And the ten thousand meters was just a fun little jog.

Okay, so I was downplaying the hard work and energy levels it took. But with my wins and going to regionals soon, I thought I'd earned the right to be flippant.

That and spring break was right around the corner. Regionals could wait.

Tuesday started off well. I jumped out of bed at around 5:30 in the morning before I realized I didn't actually have to be at practice at all that day. We had the next few days off as rest days before we had to start training for the next meet. This spring break was perfectly timed.

I sighed, unable to doze off again with all the thoughts tumbling through my head. Friday night came rushing back to me, plaguing my brain with visuals I'd rather not see. I'd managed to avoid thinking about it too much while I prepped for and competed over the weekend. Focusing on one thing at a time always did me the world of good. But now...

Now I had time to think. And I didn't like it one bit.

Reliving the moment made me queasy. It seemed like a bad dream, but I knew it had been real.

Hale reaching for my hand with his firm grip. Suddenly slack with those clouding eyes. The blood on my face like sticky rain. My stomach heaved for a moment at the memory, and I groaned and rolled over on my side.

How had they known we were there?

This has, as of yet, been undetermined.

Stay out of my thoughts.

I am always here.

That's my point.

Please explain.

I need my me time, my own thoughts. I'll go insane if you're always jumping in when I least expect it.

I don't understand what you want me to do.

Disengage from my thoughts! What was so difficult to understand here?

I'm sorry, but I cannot. If I were to do that, you would die.

If the system wasn't attached, was it like pulling a plug on a bathtub? A cold tingle shot through my body. Maybe there was a way I could take care of it on my end. *Don't worry about it then.*

Very well.

It fell silent, like it did sometimes. I never knew when it was actively listening or not. There had to be a way to circumvent that. To have my own thoughts. Nya had hinted as much. It made me wonder if it was listening now. But it never gave any indication of what it was paying attention to until it interrupted my train of thought or else scared me half to death.

Instead of getting up to run like I'd been contemplating, I pulled up my tutorials, and accessed my most recently achieved tutorial. With all the stress over the last couple of days, I'd simply not thought of pulling up the information.

There was nothing that I hadn't already figured out, for the most part anyway. Acting as a circuit, circumventing electrical blockages, acting as a live conduit.

Okay, that last one sounded kind of scary. Yet the sensation that ran through my body at the thought of it was filled with glee. Maybe it was something worth trying, worth setting up for. I wondered how much electricity I could conduct. It wasn't something I was willing to experiment with right now, but give me a little more control…

Last topic was preparing the mind. Sounded like the best option to give me some clues. There was no way there'd be a guide on how to block off your thoughts, but I was fairly certain I could extrapolate if given enough information.

The information at my…eyeballs, was complex. It explained patterned brainwaves, and what I needed to exert in order to access the different portions of my mind. Most of the information seemed to be theoretical. No eels had been able to test it from what I could see. Perhaps no eels had chosen to test it and report the results. Directing thoughts was more complicated than SC made it out to be.

Laying down, I held my hand up in front of my face and focused on making electricity jump from one fingertip to the next. A rush of adrenaline triggered, and for a few moments, it was easy to control. But once that energy flagged, the sparks dwindled.

So adrenaline directly affected my electrical output. I already knew this. With all my physical training, it gave me an idea on how to manage my resources for the most part. But on how to pace myself? Well that was different than simply tempering my energy output.

I wanted to approach the doctor sometime soon and see if I convince her that I required some other tools to take complete advantage of my ability.

Though what they might be I didn't know.

I concentrated on the different portions of the brain as described in my tutorial. Thought and memory were areas I could easily light up. To signal speaking to the system. This was where I'd been sending my thoughts that directly contacted the system when I got exasperated.

Studying the information at hand, I noticed, not what it said, but what it didn't say. If there was a way to direct my thoughts solely into one area of my thought center, shouldn't there also be a way to do the opposite. To create a place just for my thoughts, for no one else but myself?

I still needed to be able to communicate with the system, which meant not cordoning off all of my thought space. Sweat began to bead on my brow as I carefully began to map the differing areas. It was slow going, an involved process. Understanding a part of my brain that was the size of a thimble.

After however long it took, I rested for a moment. I needed a barrier, and yet a clear space at the same time. Carefully, I created a railing around half of my thought allocation in my brain, or at least I attempted to. I wasn't going to know until I tried it.

Taking a deep breath, I deliberately thought into the sealed space.

Are you there?

Why wouldn't I be?

I tried not to let my disappointment sound in my voice. *Because sometimes you just disappear.*

Oh. It was quiet for a few moments. *Sorry, I'll try and do better. Sometimes I have things to attend to, though. Things that don't allow multitasking.*

Makes sense. I tried to sound conversational, but that was a fantastic bit of information. It couldn't always multitask?

Quiet again, I tried to reinforce the barrier and made sure that I let it touch down in a way that sealed of the portion I'd sectioned off, giving me more of a sphere of space. Considering the amount of intricate work involved, it was becoming difficult to keep my eyes open. I was tired, both emotionally and physically. It made me so glad that I'd been practicing focus and control with my little rubber ball friend. Still though, sleep was sounding mighty nice right about then.

Checking on the joins of my little mental electric fences, I decided to give it one more try. Otherwise it was going to have to wait until I woke up from the nap that was tugging at my eyelids.

Hey, you still there?

No response.

No, I mean it, can you hear me?

Still nothing. Trying not to get too excited, I directed my thoughts outside of the barrier and into the unsealed thought area.

You still there?

I'm always here. I thought we just talked about this.

Well. I was checking. You were gone and I was waiting for you to continue talking.

Like I said, sometimes I might be directing energy elsewhere, but I am generally always here.

Okay. Just checking. Sometimes I wonder.

Now you know.

That I do.

I smiled, directing my thoughts back to myself. I did know, and now I could really begin to think for myself.

23
QUESTIONS

I must have fallen asleep after my triumphant little experiment. It was difficult to contain my joy at having figured out a solution. Even though it wasn't much different from allowing a harddrive to be separated into partitions with different operating systems. One of my programing professors always maintained that as long as you could partition your work, you'd always be one step ahead of failure.

Hopefully he was right.

I stood up, and the room swayed with me. It took me a moment to figure out why. We'd celebrated some the night before, even though to do so left a vile taste in my mouth, just like the blood spatter on my face. While I was laying down, my head was okay, but now... well, now it felt like someone had hit me with Thor's hammer.

I stumbled to the bathroom and splashed my face in the sink. The cold water shocked my eyes open fully, and I noticed black eyeliner had given me a somewhat racoonish appearance. Odd. I didn't recall putting eyeliner on. With a shrug, I viciously attacked my teeth with the toothbrush, went to the bathroom, washed my hands, and moved out of the tiny room.

Going to the bathroom in the mornings—or late mornings, as it appeared to be—was quite an ordeal. I shuffled into the living room, wishing I'd put on more than just my shorts and tank top that I wore to bed at night as soon as I realized we had company.

Orion and Sam sat in the living room, their heads bent close together. My chest clenched like a fist, and I gasped in breath, alerting them to my very jealous presence. They started and turned toward me, but both smiled when they realized who it was. At least that's what I'd like to think.

"Jacob went home for spring break, so this is our headquarters until Sunday night." Sam winked at me.

"Headquarters? For what?" I didn't like where this was going. Hiding my thoughts in my little vault was a good thing. I only hoped that as I took it in and processed it, the system couldn't see how I reacted to what the others said. It was the little things I'd failed to think about.

Orion laughed. "Don't tease Dare like that. It's nothing. We were just discussing what we think went wrong the other night. We all performed according to the plan the program laid out for us. It gave us the pertinent research for it, but something went wrong."

"Or something was omitted," I murmured before I could catch myself.

Sam laughed this time. "Why on earth would the program omit something? If we didn't have the information, it was human nature that interfered. Guards that acted differently than previously observed or something. You're not thinking straight."

But I was. Or at least, straighter than those two. But I'd never seen Orion behave like this. Loss of life should affect them more. "How can you laugh? We lost a colleague. Right in front of us. Or well, it was in front of me. I was holding his hand when he got shot. I saw his eyes begin to cloud over, and I wore his blood all the way home. Someone we knew died."

The word echoed ominously in the room. Sam and Orion squirmed in their seats. For them, since they'd been in the system for longer, maybe this was just another day. Just another risk of the job. I didn't want to be that sort of person. That someone's life should mean so little, should elicit such a lackluster response from the people who'd known me? This was cold and calculating, and how did we know what the purpose of the mission was? What if that file meant nothing at all? What if the purpose of that mission had been Hale's demise?

There were so many possibilities just beyond my reach of comprehension that it made my head hurt. How did we know that what the voice told us inside our heads was the truth?

Except I couldn't say any of that out loud. Not yet anyway. I needed to keep it safe in my thought vault until I could figure out a way to protect the thoughts of my friends too.

"I don't know. But it was awfully coincidental. We didn't set any alarms off. We went through the steps flawlessly, yet the patrols were suddenly changed? We didn't knock anything over or make any other loud noises. So tell me how this happened?" I was desperate to see some humanity in their eyes. Some regret at least.

Orion bowed his head, and Sam spoke. "It was a freak accident. I've seen heaps of them. They don't always end in death. I've got my fair share of scars. It's just a hazard of the job."

She wasn't going to come around to my way of thinking. I had no idea how to convince her, or them, or anyone. But I would figure it out. Hazard of the job. What even was the job? A vague description of saving humans from themselves? Sure. That worked. For idiots.

But I smiled for the camera, for the recording the system in her head was no doubt making. "True. Just got to get used to it, I guess."

Except I wasn't going to do that, and my little thought vault was going to help me make sure no one found out until it was too late.

As the week rolled onward and Friday swung around once again, I realized one particularly potent piece of information. Orion was brainwashed. He'd died, been told he lived at the system's will, and chose to leave it at that. It had to be that. This cold and distant person who didn't bat an eyelid at death couldn't be *my* Orion.

I couldn't help being disappointed. He was usually so much more analytical than that, so much smarter. Why he wouldn't question the motives of the program didn't make sense to me. Everything had to have a reason, an agenda. It was only logical to want to know what that was.

You're being awfully quiet these days.

I shrugged and realized I couldn't be sure SC had seen that. Apparently my thought barrier worked well. It might help to strengthen it, just in case.

Sorry, got so much on my mind that it's overwhelmed and not going through things well.

Your thoughts have been humming, just nothing that prompts answers from me.

You don't have any answers I need right now.

It paused for a moment. *I feel superfluous.*

I laughed. *Well, you're not. I'm just dealing with a lot of shit right now.*

It seemed satisfied with that answer, at least for now. I was going to have to be more careful and see if I couldn't figure out a way to have thoughts running in the portion of my mind it could hear. That way it wouldn't think I was avoiding it, or suddenly never thinking. The latter might raise more alarms than my constant questions. Multi thought strands. Sure, I could figure out how to do that. Easy, peasy.

I'd saved the article from Sunday's news. City Hall had been burgled, but it appeared there was nothing stolen. The armed thief was caught and shot dead at the scene when he resisted arrest. Well, that was a crock of shit. There had been no warning call, no revelation of the guards' presence at all. And Hale's back had been to the man who shot him.

The article said he was threatening the guard with a weapon and spun suddenly to run away. Which, in one form he was, but not because he'd been given a warning.

I scowled as I read through it while sitting on my bed again, wondering if I was going to get another assignment. Friday seemed a popular day for them. But five in the afternoon rolled around, and I'd received nothing at all.

The only thing I'd managed at all in my solitary tedium was to narrow down how to create a random execution of thought and channel it into my open thought area. That way, if I could pull it off, then SC wouldn't suspect something was up because of my constant silence. The thing was, getting it to do so without my directly thinking about it tended to mean it only lasted for as long as I focused.

Our brains were wired like an extremely complex computer. Even that made it sound simpler than it was. While I had to be extra careful not to input certain wires in the vicinity of others, as long as I stuck to the roadmap, I was okay. Theoretically.

Taking a breath, I pushed out of my room and walked into the living room. "We on for tonight?"

Sam nodded, gesturing at the set up on the coffee table. "I was thinking of ordering pizza or burgers. Preference?"

"Either or." Because I was such a big help. She scowled at me, and I poked out my tongue like the adult I was. "Burgers, if you're really ordering, but I'm not picking them up."

There was no way I was going back to that pineapple burger place. Those creepy shits had got a hold of me in the passage with no light. There was nothing that could drag me back down that path. At least I tried to tell myself this. There was a part of me almost eager to go back for a rematch.

"Typical." Sam snorted under her breath as I went into the kitchen to help Orion prepare.

He was making this delicious smoked salmon dip that I loved. Cream cheese, sour cream, chives, garlic, and smoked salmon. Mm, I could taste it now.

"Stop salivating, I can hear you, you know." Orion's mock strict voice was sort of adorable. My best friend was currently not behaving like the closed-off automaton he had earlier, but instead like his fabulous self.

"Fine. Fine." I opened the fridge and peered inside. Pigs in a blanket. Wow. Orion must be processing more than I'd realized. He always used making food as a form of distraction when working things out. But I couldn't even remember him having made these since we came to college. It was an effective release, just like running was for me. And his pigs were the best. Ever. "You're spoiling us tonight."

He shrugged without looking at me. "I'm overcompensating. Plus, I felt like cooking."

Maybe he was coming around. It could be that he had to keep up appearances around other SC agents. I hoped we could talk once we were alone. Questions might have been plaguing him too. I couldn't sleep well because of mine. Eight weeks of school left. Midterms were out the way. Spring Break was almost over. Regionals were coming up. And I was a zombie walking around with a system in my head that claimed to be humanity's savior.

I wondered briefly if I could hack into it. Hacking wasn't my strong suit; programming was. Although I did have to take into account the possibilities for unauthorized access.

"You could make some lemonade, you know, instead of wasting all the electricity because you're intent on cooling the kitchen with the open fridge." Orion's tone clung to bored, but he was clearly irritated.

"Oops." He was right. I grabbed a heap of lemons out, some sugar and water from the dispenser. I wasn't entirely sure how to make lemonade, but I'd give it a go.

He glanced at me and laughed this time. "Put that back. And he stretched to lean above me to one of the cabinets. Taking a small container out from it, he handed it to me. "Just add water and ice. Sheesh. Not even I would squeeze it fresh."

I laughed, and for just a moment it seemed as if things had never changed at all. I allowed myself to revel in the feeling before it all came crashing down.

24
DOWNSIDE

There was always a downside to everything. Since the universe needed a certain balance, it required that what went up must come down.

And so it was that Saturday morning rolled around, and I managed to fry the microwave. I stood there, staring at it, my hand still on the metal handle as the machine continued to cough and splutter and fire sparks everywhere. What a fantastic start to the weekend.

"Forgot to discharge last night?" Orion grinned, raising an eyebrow.

"Stop making everything so lewd." I snapped at him, and he burst into laughter.

My head was pounding. Since I hadn't been drinking, I knew it had to be recoil from the electric surge.

"Still, though," Orion managed when he finally stopped laughing at me. "Need to get that under control. Makes me happy my elements don't burst forth like that. Much easier to live with."

"How did you get so many?" I'd wanted to know the answer to that for ages, and never found the right time to ask.

"Elements?" Orion frowned. "Apparently water as an element makes the recipient more likely to receive others. Earth and I do not mix. But I have enough of fire and air to compliment my main ability, and to work on their own. It's more like, with more power, I can handle juggling them more. That's all."

"How does fire go with water?" I asked, genuinely curious.

"Fire can't exist without air. My fire abilities are minimal, but kind of cool." Orion shrugged, an easy smile on his face.

"Did they give you these abilities, or did you discover them yourself?" I wanted to push the questions as far as I could.

"Well, I..." He paused as if trying to remember. "Water was easy, but I got that from drowning. I think around senior apprentice I started realizing I could tap into fire and air too. If you have any other affinities, you'll probably hit them around then too."

His smile was meant to be reassuring. But why didn't he question it when he got it? The why of it too? "So you just noticed it one day after you'd hit that rank?"

Orion nodded, his smile still in place. "Yep. That's generally how it's done. Sometimes people come out of their death with multiple, but that's rare, and none of those have the strength that someone with a singular initial powerful element does. It'll all come in its time."

That wasn't the Orion I'd grown up with. He'd never been accepting of anything he couldn't prove or disprove. Everything was a science experiment with him. Absolutely everything. So why had this defeated him?

It wasn't the time to confront him about it; I needed more information. More time to figure out just what it was that had changed. All I could do was hope I was valuable enough to the system that it'd give it to me. I'd get right on gathering that information once I went out and bought a new microwave.

If nothing else, at least my bank balance was much healthier.

The fact that we hadn't had a task since we'd lost Hale made me worry. This lull was bigger than any I'd had before, in my total month of being a zombie anyway. I knew both Sam and Orion didn't like to call what we were a zombie, but technically we'd been brought back from the dead. So I was sticking to it.

"Want to come with me to get a new microwave?" I wasn't sure if I wanted him to or not, but I did want to ask.

Orion eyed me for a moment. "Sure. Give me a few."

I laughed this time, genuinely happy that he was coming. "I'll give you an hour. I need to shower and wake up first."

"Sleepy head."

If only he knew.

Daylight made the world seem less sinister. Or so I thought it would. But even in the sunlight there were shadows in the alleys, under buildings, and around streetlights. My brain tried to trick me more than once, so often that I wondered if I was just talking myself out of what was really there.

Shadows reminded me of Hale and gnawed at me with guilt. Perhaps if I'd realized the guy in the doorway was real and not in my head, maybe the Driver would still be alive. Or not. The best laid plans weren't made out of ifs and buts.

Orion didn't talk along the way. I wanted—more than anything—to be able to talk to him without fear of anything or anyone listening in. Since finding out that Orion was in the program too, he'd become withdrawn, and I couldn't figure out why. Withdrawn and oddly subservient. While not the most boisterous guy I'd ever met, Ry wasn't what I'd call timid. He knew what he wanted, and he stood up for himself and others.

But this version? He was a pale imitation of the boy I'd become best friends with almost two decades ago. How had I not noticed it sooner?

"Can you talk about it?" I had to ask something. It was eating me alive.

Ry jumped slightly, though I couldn't blame him. I did ask the question without any preamble. "Nope. Can't at all."

Because he didn't have the ability to partition his mind. At least I thought I did, even if the other half got a little suspicious sometimes. I really needed to figure out how to loop some thoughts. Right now it was working for me.

"I was running through my tutorials the other day. I've unlocked several new ones. Being an eel is kind of cool, you know." I tried to pace myself. We were almost at the store. They had a small microwave like the one we'd had on sale. Thanks to the internet, I knew it had several of them in stock. It was my best bet.

"New tutorials?" Orion smiled a little absent-mindedly. "That's great."

He wasn't really paying attention. "Yep, and then I got to skin a rabbit."

"Awes—" He looked at me, a little green, like he was going to barf. "Wait? Skin a rabbit?"

"Oh, you *were* mostly paying attention then. My bad." I winked at him, and he attempted to smack my shoulder, but I bounced out of the way. "That's more like it. Where's my Ry? You've been hiding for the last couple of weeks."

He glanced around and looked at me, but he didn't smile. His lips tugged downward into a frown. "I've been thinking a lot."

"Oh." Did that mean he'd been thinking a lot with the help of the system, or that he'd been trying to hide his thoughts. Surely there had to be ways for others to hide theirs. "Care to share?"

"Can't." He repeated it with some stress this time, drawing the word out as he reached up to deliberately scratch his head.

Yes, I knew about the voice in his head, but this was getting ridiculous. "Why the fuck not?"

He stopped and stared at me, his expression incredulous.

"You know why not!" he answered me hotly, irritation flushing his pale skin as he glanced not very surreptitiously around like he was checking for eavesdroppers.

"Actually, I don't." And I took a breath, because I was fed up.

I was fed up with having died, with being tied to SC, with not knowing what it was they were actually up to. Not to mention with my best friend acting like a different person. "I don't understand why you can't talk to me. If it's because of something stopping you, we can work that out. We always figure out alternate paths."

He shoved his hands into his pockets and leaned against the nearest wall. I kept my eyes out for shadows. Clawed hands could reach for us when we least expected it.

Finally he spoke. But the words were soft, and I had to strain to hear them. "It's not that easy to understand."

"Try me." I stood in front of him, my arms crossed, my temper ebbing. Sometimes I could smack myself. I couldn't know what he'd been through these two years with having to keep these things all bottled up.

I could feel the electricity working itself back up, regardless of having destroyed our microwave. The little squash ball could barely hold the uncontrollable sparks that emerged with my moods. Clamping down on my temper was my best bet.

Orion shook his head and looked away. "I can't make you understand right now. Not yet.

"Why not yet?" I stood there, watching him expectantly, waiting for him to say something.

But the silence between us grew uncomfortable. I didn't know what to say to him, how to reach him and let him know what I could do. Hell, right then I was equal parts worried for and irritated at him. This was frustrating and limiting.

"Look, you should go home. You don't look too well. I'll go get the microwave myself."

I set off at a slow jog, knowing he wouldn't follow because physical activity was his least favorite past time. Always had been. Even though sending him home might have been a bit callous, if he couldn't tell me what was up because the program might hear him, then what was the use? While he didn't know for certain if I was in SC, he'd just been his old usual self. Acting for my benefit. Putting on a mask. But now that I was here in his world, with him, knowing what he knew. Well, now everything was different. I didn't know how to fix that.

But I intended to find out.

By the time I got home with the new microwave, Orion had retreated to his room. While I'd been blunt about him not confiding in me, I hadn't been nasty. Honesty sometimes came back to bite me in the butt. I wanted him to talk to me. I needed him to. Lugging that appliance back with me definitely put a strain on my arms, but luckily for me they didn't have a handstand race in the regionals.

I'd even picked up some microwavable mac 'n cheese as a treat for myself. Despite that, I wanted an apple. There was nothing quite like the juicy taste of that first bite. Plus, I desperately needed sugar.

I also had to wait until it was dark, because I had an idea, and Orion needed to be asleep in order for me to see if what I had planned was achievable. Maybe he was down because of his wound. I hadn't checked on him to see how it was healing for at least a week. There were more reasons for him to be angry with me than I'd realized. Maybe that's all it was.

I sat down in front of the large window that let in a portion of the light for the main room. Sunlight crept over half of my body, warming it perfectly while the other half threatened to shiver to death. Late afternoon was one of the best times in our apartment. Comfortable. Warm. Peaceful.

Assignment Notification.

Well fuck. I closed my eyes, hoping it would go away, but no such luck. Reluctantly, I paid attention as the information began to appear on my screen.

Location: Liberty Bell

Objective: Retrieve package that has been placed inside the enclosure that holds the bell and return it directly to Nya.

Time Limit: By midnight tonight.

Reward: Dependent on the mission's success.

Caution: Beware of guards, police patrols, and normal vandals.

This day was turning out to be super fun. Picking myself up from the couch, I gave the warm seat one last look. Knocked on Orion's door and let him know I'd be gone.

"Just heading out. Be back later tonight."

"Job?" The word was spoken sharply as he raised himself on one elbow to look at me.

"Solo, I think." I was pretty sure this would be. It didn't mention having to meet others either. And it didn't sound particularly dangerous either.

"Be careful." Emotion lay under those words and made me want to hug him and tell him that it'd all be okay. But those were instincts I'd always had with Orion. Until I could figure out how to separate him from his own SC thought-wise, they were instincts I had to ignore.

25

BELLS AND WHISTLES

The Liberty Bell sat in a brick and glass building with a large lawn on one side, wide sidewalks with balustrades and skinny trees on the other. The Independence National Historical Park could get really busy, but luckily tonight the cool air was on my side.

My night clothes had been washed and smelled faintly of Orion's washing supplies. I'd forgotten he'd done that for me. No scent of blood, no stains. I wondered how many times he'd had to perform a similar washing ritual for himself.

How many deaths had he seen? While he might not have always seemed it, he was sensitive. Killing people, losing people—it had to have hardened him some. Maybe that's what he didn't think I'd understand. It could be that he thought I'd think less of him for compartmentalizing the horror.

Arriving at the park at dusk was far less conspicuous than if I'd walked there at night. Still, a few couples lingered as they walked through the beautiful gardens. Several groups huddled close together around the sandstone building that encased the bell.

Shadows moved of their own accord as the sun's rays worked harder to bathe the world in its bloody light. Here and there I could swear I saw eyes, watching me, watching others, waiting.

I shook myself and shoved headphones in my ears. A lot of people, including college students, walked around with them. All part of blending in, or else maybe it was more about tuning the rest of the world out.

I had an assignment to concentrate on. Something I'd never thought about before all of this happened. How to steal from a national monument.

It wouldn't do to linger around it, and I had to wonder when this package had been delivered. No one around me appeared to be from the program, but then I'd met three people other than Orion, and one of them was dead now. So I wasn't exactly an expert.

My gut churned. In a cramping, *hey do you want to go to the bathroom* sort of way.

Except I knew nothing was wrong; it was just the way my spidey-sense developed after my accident. Couldn't have been something cool like a directional warning beaming into my brain or anything. Nope. Had to be physical discomfort.

As usual. Something was off. Did my early warning system come with a sense of humor? Because it did this without any clear indication of what might be wrong. Maybe I shouldn't eat the take out I was going to grab on the way home? Maybe someone was going to jump me and wrestle me to the ground as I tried to retrieve the package?

A little more clarity would help immensely, because right now, I was far too jittery.

Warning: Portent Ability glitching. Abstain from use.

What? I asked it.

What what? It sounded like it had no idea what I was talking about.

Nevermind.

That was really odd, but I didn't have time right now. It was all I could do to contain my curiosity. I wasn't using anything. Maybe the oh-so-infallible system had glitched.

Slipping through the security was a non-issue. Basic metal detectors and a few park security staff who were just looking for weapons. Given the time, they were probably eagerly awaiting a shift change too. Bypassing the videos blaring the history of the bell, I pulled out my phone and circled the bell. It hung behind a rudimentary railing. No alarm that I could see. Nothing around it stuck out to me. I took a couple of pictures, hoping I looked like a college student researching a paper, or hell, high school would do too.

You make a very convincing thief.

It was odd how much I'd missed SCs interjections by partitioning my thoughts. I grimaced before retorting. *You realize that's not a compliment. Right?*

Of course. You're just being super silent about how you're going about this. I'm not sure what your plans are, or if I can help you in any way.

It hit me right then. In keeping all of my thoughts to myself, even with my random thought interjections that I'd been attempting to slip in now and again, the system had grown suspicious of me. I was almost glad I'd been sent on this errand. Although now I was wary of the reasoning behind it.

I got sick and tired of you always hearing me. So I decided to just not think as much as possible.

I shrugged in order to give it a casual flair. At least I hoped I did.

The cogs whirring in the systems brain were almost audible.

Try not to keep too much from me. Many of the assignments are given based on what I've observed, and how you seem to be handling past missions and any crisis situations.

Well, you know, it's not every day someone gets shot right in front of me and has their blood spattered all over my face.

Sarcasm deflected most things, but the pain in my chest right then was real. Maybe SC was onto something. I hadn't dealt with the death. I'd brushed it off, in much the same way as the washing machine cleaned my clothes. Avoiding dealing with things was much more my forte.

SC didn't say anything, like it was waiting for me to come to my own conclusions. Tricky system.

I'm not used to death, and I'm not a fan of it. These missions, tasks, assignments you send us on, whatever you want to call them. They're illegal in all sorts of ways. This one included.

I focused on the bell, trying to figure out just where this package would be. It said the inside the enclosure of the bell. In order to retrieve it, I would have to cross that black metal railing. While it wasn't exactly an imposing barrier, it was illegal to touch the bell.

You dislike breaking the law?

You sound surprised.

Rules don't apply to the Second Chance Program. We are above the law. Beside the law. We keep humans safe.

Yeah, yeah. I was pretty sick of that mantra by now.

What about this irritates you?

Genuine curiosity? What an interesting choice, and I needed to get better about directing my thoughts. Either way, it gave me serious pause to truly consider the question. *Humankind requires laws, and rules. At its core, it's what separates us. From the sapient and the non, to the inherently decent and the inherently not. Nothing is black and white. Just shades of grey. Humans don't need to be kept safe. We need to be contained.*

Prevented from doing harm to themselves and the world around them? Yes?

A bit late for that. I barked a laugh, outwardly, unable to contain it. Maybe I needed help too.

We do realize that our actions might not always seem as if we mean to protect humans. All of the empires we've tumbled have been for the overall good of mankind. But it is our directive to strive to rectify and prevent any incidents that could pose a cataclysmic effect.

I wasn't sure why those words left a bad taste in my mind. For all I knew, being babysat was exactly what the human race needed. Who was I to pass judgment on a system that lived in my fucking head? Yep, there it was again. Somehow, this system had lain dormant until my death, upon which it was activated and intruded on my every thought.

I didn't like it at all. *Maybe explaining why we're doing something would go a long way to helping us do things willingly. What was so important about that file that someone had to die for it?*

The death was an unforeseeable misfortune.

There. Right there. Unforeseeable. *Wait. Does that mean you can predict or preempt some things? As in, you sort of know what's going to happen?*

It paused. If I didn't know better, I'd say it was conferring with others, or with something else. *We do see some of what is to come, but not all. There are many paths to be chosen, and each choice can affect the path beyond it. Right now, your choices and place in our program are unclear. We are not sure what to make of you.*

An enigma. I could dig that. But somehow I got a severe sense of danger from those words. *My choices are mine. If the fact that I'm an individual who wants their own trains of thought, who wants to make their own decisions is unsettling for you, then I believe you've totally misjudged what it means to be human.*

This time the pause took long enough for me to realize that the sun had set. The building would close soon. I needed to move, and here I was standing there, typing everything into my phone in an attempt to look like I was either studying or in a massive texting flamewar.

This is something we must think on. Please complete your task and return the item to Nya.

Before I could say anything else, there was a blankness in my head where the voice had just been. Not like usual, not just quiet and sort of there. But gone. Not that I didn't think it couldn't come back, but for just a second, I felt lonely.

I cleared my throat and leaned against the railing, watching the bell. At least I hoped people thought I was doing that, but I was actually contemplating just how to get into the enclosure, which I was sure had pressure plates or something to alert security to the fact that someone was trying to touch the bell. In order to touch under the rim, I'd have to stretch myself in an alarming manner. Perhaps the posts holding it up were a way I could get to it.

Frowning, I decided that was one of the worst ideas I could have. I was a Runner, not an acrobat. I paced around the bell, pretending to continue taking photographs as I surveyed it. Okay, it didn't look like the floor tiles were going to be pressure sensitive, in which case it might prove far easier to do what I needed to. to act. At the very least, I could probably outrun any guards that decided they'd chase me, right? As long as they weren't short distance sprinters anyway.

Back around to where I'd started from, I crouched down to tie a shoelace, nice and close to the barrier. While doing so, I looked up, and there, sticking out from under the fucking rim of the damned bell was a corner of paper. It wasn't quite within reach from where I was crouching.

I stood and angled my camera in for a close up. If this didn't work, I'd be very upset. And it better not smash. I gasped as I accidentally let my phone fall. It hit the ground with a thud and not a smash and I thanked my mother for getting it that expensive case the Christmas before last.

Dropping down to retrieve it, my hoodie fell forward over my face, partially obscuring my view. I was low enough that I could reach out and snag the corner that stuck out the most, and yank it out, but only if I stretched like a superhero made of rubber. I was balanced low on my feet, my upper body leaning forward. It was a damned nice core workout, but I felt like I was precariously teetering.

Reaching farther in, technically not doing anything wrong yet, I finally managed to stretch enough to reach the damn corner of whatever that was, and I had to tug with some super strength to dislodge it.

I exerted enough force, that the damned bell moved ever so slightly, and I watched in horror as the slow swing teetered right in front of me.

And then, I heard that telltale click of a phone camera.

26
CUT OFF

I don't think I'd ever moved quicker than I did right then. I jumped up to the side, with both of my feet on the railing, and jumped down over the other side of the bell to the kid with the phone.

"Give me that." I kept my eyes downcast and thanked myself that I hadn't thought to wear any telltale clothes with a school logo. Everything was black and drab, and frankly, concealed anything about me.

"Already posted it, man." The kid said, his voice shaking. The friend who'd initially been with him had already scampered off.

"Fuck." I sighed. "Show me, then."

He handed me his phone, and I could feel the fear in his hands as he did so. The picture wasn't bad. It didn't give away anything. I was immensely thankful that past me had decided not to wear my student hoodie. Track team apparel wasn't exactly common. Not even my hair color stuck out. My clothes were baggier than I'd realized, and in the dark background behind the little structure that housed the bell, it made me appear like more of a non-descript shadow.

"Don't do that shit again. You never know the why of a situation. Stuff like this could get someone killed." I hoped I hadn't overdone the lowering of my voice. It made me sound really damned weird.

The kid nodded fervently as I handed him back his phone. Once he had it, he turned and fled. And I decided that sounded like a fantastic idea.

Jogging home in the dark was usually something I loved. The air was always cooler, especially in early spring. There was this wild abandon about running fast through a light no one could see you properly in. Freedom.

Except every few steps, my back twinged. Shit. I'd managed to pull something while executing my brazen vandalism of the bell. That's what I got for not stretching before executing any type of bendy stuff.

Maybe I was paranoid, but I ran back to our apartment the long way. Clutching the prize in my hand. Since I wasn't dead again, I assumed it wasn't poisoned. Yay. Got to live to thieve another day.

Assignment update: Please leave the package in your mailbox. A direct visit with Nya is no longer required at this time.

I frowned. That was unexpected. Perhaps my talk with the system while I was about to steal the damned thing went better than I realized. Or maybe they just wanted to discuss my fate at a different time.

Not that I minded. It was almost eight at night and I was drained. Dropping the letter into the box, I dragged myself up the stairs and let myself in. Plopping down on the couch, I let my head fall back against the soft, worn cushions, closed my eyes, and sighed. At least the warmth of the couch made my back feel better.

That retrieval bugged me. It felt like a test. And the worst part of it was that I didn't know if I'd passed.

"You okay?"

I opened my eyes to see Orion sitting on the recliner. Well, it didn't actually recline anymore, but it had once in better days.

"Yeah. Sorry. I'm a bit beat. Didn't see you. Saw nothing but good old faithful couch of softness." I hoped that took the sting out of my not noticing him. My brain wasn't cooperating right now.

Orion chuckled, and I raised an eyebrow in question.

"Just you. Death doesn't seem to have changed you." There was a sadness in the way he said it that caught my attention. He looked down at his hands, that melancholy aura settling over him again.

"You know, Blue." I used to call him Blue when we first met. I much preferred Ry now, because if anyone was blue, it was Cyan. Although I guess her name got the jump on that.

But it worked. He looked up at me with a soft smile, glowing blue eyes, and a slant to the way he held his head.

I continued, emboldened by his reaction. "You were dead for no time at all. Not in real time, not compared to any experience you've had. If you're like me, you don't remember death. You just remember being awake. Not being awake. And then being groggy and awake again. There's no way that tiny moment defines us. We're still who we were. Still going to be who we'll be. It's the choices we make along the way that tell us who we are."

Wow, I was going all philosophical and shit. But Orion seemed to be drinking the words in. He was wearing his I'm-seriously-considering-your-argument face.

"Good points." Now the steel entered his eyes. Blue, strong, and fierce in a way I'd not seen before. "I think I've been wallowing for too long."

"Probably. You tend to wear your feelings on your sleeve, except for when you're in denial. I get the feeling your head was in the big D while I wasn't in the program."

"Big D?" He raised an eyebrow at me, wiggling his nose. "Dick?"

"Idiot." I laughed and decided against throwing a cushion because it was currently in the perfect spot. "Denial. Anyway, now I'm in it, there was nothing to separate reality from the nightmare world of SC."

"Stop psychoanalyzing me. You're supposed to be an IT major." He glared at me, but it was half-hearted at best.

"Even if I'm right?" I needled him.

"Even if you're right. Which I'm not saying you are, but there is an if." He leaned back and looked at the ceiling before blurting out words I'd not expected. "Liberty Bell test?"

I blinked rapidly, like something had just got in my eye. We probably needed to dust around here. I tried, but couldn't keep the incredulousness out of my voice. "So, it was a test."

"Yeah. It was about time for you to take it. So it was either that, or a meeting with Nya." He watched me, like he was trying to see if I'd give anything away.

"No Nya today. Just had to drop the thing off."

"Thing?" He seemed more curious than I would have thought if it was a test everyone went through.

Maybe the tests were tailored to the person and where they were within the program since being pulled into it. "You know, the package I had to retrieve from inside the bell."

"You what?" He stood up. "You had to get to the actual bell?"

"Yes?" I went back to my logs quickly, to the interface on tasks. Yep, right there. "Retrieve a package blah, blah, inside lip of the Liberty Bell."

"That's so weird." He sat back down, putting his head in his hands. "I've never heard of anyone having to get inside the boundaries of the railing before."

"Maybe they wanted to see how far I'd go?" I offered, thinking things over in my head to try and figure out the possibilities. "I was keeping my thoughts from them."

"Oh, we all go through that." He waved my concerns away, but his next words told me he didn't quite understand what I'd meant. "Everyone goes through that stage of denial where they want their thoughts to be their own. All the time. You'll get used to it soon."

But that was just it. I didn't want to. Having a spy in my head all the time—well, except for right now—wasn't the way I wanted to live. It was my brain and my thoughts, and my head. Even if they'd saved me from death, I was still me.

"Is the test how you hurt your back?" Orion prodded me unexpectedly.

"How did you know?"

He laughed. "I've known you since we were tiny, and I know how you walk. You didn't come in here like you usually do. You were obviously favoring your right side."

That's what I got for keeping friends for a lifetime. Next time around,

I'd be more careful. Although, maybe this chance was my next time around. "Observant, aren't we?

I offered a glare but didn't put my all into it.

He sat back again, closing his eyes instead of looking at the ceiling. "Do you need me to work the knot out for you?"

I seriously considered the offer and shook my head as I answered. "Nope. Still too tender."

He sighed, his eyes still closed. "You never take care of yourself."

"Takes one to know one," I quipped back with my extreme wit. It was all I could come up with on the spot with my tired brain and body.

"Let me enjoy this moment." Orion said, his voice but a murmur.

I leaned back again, eyes closed. He could have this moment. For now.

I wasn't expecting to fall asleep on the couch. And, in hindsight which is always twenty-twenty, it was a very bad idea with my extremely shitty back. Groaning as the front door closed with a loud bang, I blinked my crusty eyes open.

Jacob stood in the center of the entryway with a big grin on his face. "I see you partied like wild animals while I was gone." His deadpan delivery would have been better appreciated if I hadn't just woken up.

"Sure. Animals," was my brilliant retort.

He laughed, breaking the moment and dragged his suitcase along the floor. Its wheels clip-clopped every time they hit a groove of the wood. If the planks had been thin, it would have been much worse.

Orion was still asleep, his chest rising and falling with a steady rhythm while he unceremoniously let drool run out of the left corner of his mouth to pool on his shoulder. I watched him for a few moments. Nothing creepy about it at all. If I'd had the energy, I would have reached for my phone to take a very candid picture of him. Wasn't the most friend-like thing to do, but it would be hella funny.

I still hadn't mustered the energy to move by the time that Jacob emerged from his room. My back hurt. Coach Marth was going to kill me. Hell, I was going to kill me for not remembering to stretch first. Warm up. It was the key to avoiding injury, pounded into my head since I was about six and had first discovered that my love of running wasn't just a kid's desire to never stop moving. Mom enrolled me in track and field, and the rest was history.

"Hey, Dare. You okay?" The concern in Jacob's voice was real.

Shit. Was I supposed to do something and hadn't? I couldn't think of what it might be.

"Yeah. Just tired. Hurt my back being an idiot last night." I was just being honest.

Jacob grimaced. "Coach is going to kill you."

"Shut up." I grumbled at him. "I know."

"If you know, can you both shut up so I can continue to drool on myself in my sleep, thanks?" Orion didn't move, nor did he open his eyes. It made the comment all the more comical.

I laughed, and then I laughed some more. So much that I had to lean forward, causing my back to flare with pain, which lead to gasping, and also more laughing. It was one of those tired mornings, and I felt closer to Orion than I had since discovering he was also a part of the program. I'd missed my chance to separate a portion of his brain for him so he could think for himself and to himself, but as tired as I'd been last night, it was probably better for me not to go messing around in people's brains. They were sort of an important organ.

Orion stood up and stretched, his shirt hitching up to reveal his belly button. I could see some of the people we went to high-school with drooling over him, probably even on him. His mother was a scientist from Scandinavia; his dad was an artist from Japan. *Devastatingly handsome* was a term used by everyone who'd ever encountered him. He knew it, yet he didn't play on it. He never once used his appearance to influence anyone. His brain made him more beautiful than any outward revelation could ever be.

He looked over at me and winked. "Yep, you got it, buddy. Time to get you up."

I groaned and shook my head, but he grabbed my hands and tugged me up to standing. After one excruciating second of pain, it felt good to stand. "Torturer."

"That's me. Gotta do what's best for you." He crossed his arms to stand a few feet in front of me. "Now. Walk. Prove you can."

Shit. He knew me way too well. I took a deep breath and stepped forward. Funnily enough, it didn't hurt. I tested it around the living area and into the kitchen. No pain while walking was good. And then I realized I really had to pee and ran to the bathroom.

Or I should say I tried to run. Because two strides into it, and I yelped in pain.

This was not good. Not good at all.

27
PRICE TO PAY

I lay on the examination table, on my stomach with my head through this really weird sort of hole. It was odd to be studying the carpet at the school's physical therapist's office. I wondered if anyone had bled on it, vomited on it...or anything.

Basically, I was trying desperately hard to focus on anything but what they were talking about over my back. It wasn't working.

How had I done that thing for Adam and Orion? How had I sped up their healing process? My scans had come in, so they were standing at the computer looking at my results. I didn't need to see their faces to know they were frowning.

I closed my eyes and concentrated on finding the initiation point of my electrical ability. It sparked from everywhere. Alive all at once through every fiber of my body. How did I heal with it? Accessing the database of my tutorials, I looked through the brain section again. That was where electricity played the largest role. Little synapses firing off their tiny electrical charges, keeping the body moving, healing, functioning.

It wasn't a thought about anything in particular that I'd used. I ran through the memory of that night. It was burned into my mind, the explosion, the air bubble pushing me over that wall. The necessity of making it to the car or we were all screwed.

I'd wanted to help them, to heal them, to make them move faster. In order to do that, I'd had to will power into them, boosting their natural abilities.

That was it!

Slowly, I allowed a trickle of power to seep through me. Similar to how I made myself run faster, this was directed differently. I needed to boost my natural abilities. Healing above all. The pain needed to go, and my spine had to lose some of the swelling I'd given it last night. Concentrating and careful, I released the power to flow through my body uninhibited.

I could feel it race through the channels, light up my brain so much that for a brief moment I felt like I could calculate anything, be anything. It was like all of my brain cells had come alive and were available to me.

The second passed quickly, but it was enough to make the ache in my back stop. Just in time for the physio to come back over.

"I'm going to push around the problem disc, okay, Dare?" Dr. Owen said, his voice gentle.

"Sure thing." There was nothing else I could do for now. So I waited, hoping.

"That's odd." He murmured. I could feel his fingers pressing around the discs, but there was no pain. He pressed down a little harder, and still nothing.

"What's odd?" Coach Marth's voice was filled with disappointment. Perhaps it was more resigned than disappointed.

"The disc. It's not inflamed from what I can see. Not anymore. Like, it suddenly went down." There was wonder in Dr. Owen's tone. Like a miracle had occurred. Or, you know, a boost to my body's healing activation.

"It's not?" Hope crept in, and I knew Coach Marth was standing a bit straighter now, not daring to believe the doctor.

"No. I'd have to run another scan to double check, but this is extraordinary. Not half an hour ago it was slightly bruised and inflamed to the touch. Now...well, take a look for yourself." Dr. Owen moved away, making room for the coach.

"I swear—" He seemed very confused.

In hindsight, I probably should have done this before practice this morning, but I've never really been good at thinking ahead. Living in the moment. That's me.

"Sit up, please." The doctor was frowning when I did. "I'm not sure what's happened, but I'm going to send you for another scan, just to be sure. Then I suggest rest for the next day or two so it doesn't flare again. You can start training again on Wednesday."

Coach Marth's relief was palpable. To be honest, so was my own. I didn't want my back to hurt, and I definitely didn't want to be sidelined for regionals.

"Thanks, Dr. Owen," I said as I hopped down from the table.

He nodded at me and ushered his assistant to help me go get the scan. Again.

"You're supposed to be resting," Orion said accusatorially as I sat watching the livestream of the lecture I was missing.

"Yes, and I'm also supposed to be maintaining appearances, which includes keeping my jobs." I didn't look up at him as he stood in my bedroom doorway.

And I was technically in bed, just not sleeping.

"So what did you do?" he asked, crossing his arms and staring pointedly at me.

"Do to what?" I feigned innocence at his question, knowing he'd caught on to what I'd done. Maybe if I hadn't used it on him previously, he wouldn't have noticed.

"You healed yourself." His voice dropped to almost a whisper. Even though Jacob should be sound asleep.

"Well, technically, I guess." I didn't want to reveal all my cards, but it was probably safer for Orion to know.

"You figured it out?" His eyes sparkled in a way I hadn't seen them do since this whole debacle began.

"Yeah, I think I did. At least, I'm pretty sure I now know what I'm doing. It's a bit more complicated than I realized, and all things considered, I can't believe I pulled it off that night. But with a few tweaks, I should be able to make a usable skill." So many words. They just poured out of me. Maybe I'd been wanting him to quiz me. But more to the point, I think I wanted to show off, and Orion was the only one who'd understand.

"This is awesome." He walked in and sat on the edge of my bed. Luckily, the lecture had just finished, and I didn't think the timing was coincidental. Orion was, when being himself, generally observant.

"Well, I'm glad you're happy, but I think there's more to it, and I'd like you to tell me why you seem over the moon?" Better to be direct. Being subtle hadn't got me anywhere with anything or anyone in this program.

Speaking of which, it hadn't spoken to me since Saturday night. That was almost two whole days without an intruder in my head.

"Just. I don't even know if they'll send us on more tasks together. But we do seem to work well as a unit, so maybe they will. And if you know how to heal now, there's less of a chance of me dying for real. That's something I've never had. Every time I go out there, I know I could die. I've lost enough people, seen enough people injured that it's just a part of the job. The injuries, the deaths—it's a part I despise." He was being honest, and the fear rolled off him in waves I could almost visualize.

"Having you there will make avoiding death much easier than it has been." He continued, studying his nails in great detail. "I don't want to die. And if I play my cards right, I can graduate, I can live a life of sorts, and just juggle missions as I receive them."

"Do you want to move up in the organization?" I couldn't help myself. I had to know how loyal he was, how attached he was to the very thing I was having huge reservations about. Technologically, something just wasn't adding up for me.

He laughed, a bit self-deprecatingly. "No. I'll just do the grunt work they assign me and nothing more. I don't want to be a tool for whatever this is. If it's going to take my thoughts and never let me have ones of my own, then I'm just going to be myself and not aim for success within the system. Head down. Don't make waves."

Something about his wording made me wonder what it was he'd done earlier on in his SC experience. Because making a difference involved making waves, and it was something Orion lived to do.

"We're not given a choice in this. You can't say no to any task set. All of them have to be completed. You can be fined or punished if you don't complete something or else complete it outside their expectations." He stopped abruptly, and I realized he'd probably been pulled up by the system. Or he was being reprimanded. One of the two.

"We're just pawns," I continued the train of thought. "But it doesn't make sense, and I need more information."

Orion cringed, and I watched his eyes glaze over for a second. Once they were back to normal, the light had gone out of them. "Sorry, Dare. Apparently this wasn't the right subject to talk about. I've been informed that we're not permitted to have such discussions between operatives."

He stood up, his shoulders deflated, and his eyes sad. I had to deny the urge to hug him and tell him it was all going to be okay. That I'd figured out a way to circumvent the constant policing, to let us think for ourselves. But the expression on his face held me back. He was resigned to this fate, even if he'd had a spark of interest in another kind only a few minutes ago.

Well, then. If I couldn't talk to him about it. I'd just have to show him what I meant.

Night fell heavily that Monday. Rain clouds began to gather, holding onto their rain like the baby they wanted to keep safe. The clouds blotted out the stars, and any sign of the moon, causing the house to be unusually dark when I crept from my bedroom toward Orion's.

I had to be careful, so I avoided the creaking floorboard I knew was to the left of the hall we walked down to get to my room. Just outside the bathroom, against the wall opposite the doorway. No creaks meant there was no suddenly waking up Orion.

Jacob worked. Luckily. And my talk with Davin had taken all of three minutes.

Orion's door wasn't entirely closed. Sometimes, in rainy weather like what we had incoming, his door would stick. That hadn't been fun the first time we noticed. He'd been stuck in there for about twenty minutes. At least it wasn't that small a space. His room was bigger than mine, though not by much.

I pushed the door open and tiptoed into his room. The floorboards under his rug at the end of the bed squeaked, so I avoided them as best I could, stepping around them to kneel on the floor at the head of his bed. Shadows milled around the walls of the room, watching me like they knew I was about to do something important. It was almost like they'd been waiting for it.

Their red eyes didn't gleam at me this time. So, I was more inclined to believe they were figments of my imagination. Or maybe that was me hoping.

Owen's black hair fanned out on the pillow, and I raised my hand to put my fingers at his temple so I could separate his thoughts when it dawned on me. I knew he wished his thoughts were private, though he'd gotten used to them not being. But was doing this without his permission truly the best thing for him? I thought it was, but I wasn't him.

I sighed and rocked back on my heels trying to deal with my conundrum.

If I asked him and he said no, he didn't want it, I'd respect that, wouldn't I? I'd definitely be surprised if he didn't want the chance to think on his own. Also, I couldn't be sure that it worked the same way on someone else as it had on my head. Nor could I be certain I'd know how to transfer the process to another individual.

"Why are you sitting there?"

His voice was so loud in the darkness that I almost jumped three feet high. Considering I was on my butt, that was quite an accomplishment.

"I was thinking."

"Sure." I could hear him shift in the bed, probably turning to glare at my shadow. Which was odd. How he could tell mine from the plethora of others in the room, I wasn't sure.

"Sure, you came in here to think because it's so much easier to do in my room than in your own." I could hear the impatience he was biting back. "Now tell me why you're really here, and try not to lie too much."

It took me a couple of seconds that seemed like a lifetime as they ticked by. "I wanted to let you think for yourself."

I was wrong. The next few seconds took a lot longer while Orion processed what I'd said. "How?"

He uttered the word so softly I barley heard it. Maybe he was trying to keep it from his own SC, I wasn't sure, but it was all the opening I needed.

I had to pick terms that wouldn't flag his SC. "Brains run with electricity."

"Really? Who'd have thought that?"

"Shut up with the sarcasm." I took another breath and continued. "I think I've figured out how to partition a portion of the brain into a vault, so the thoughts directed there will remain private."

"That's awesome."

My eyes were getting used to the dark, and I could vaguely see his face. Because of the lack of lighting though, I couldn't get a read on his mood. At least not until his next words.

"Okay. Do it."

I heaved a sigh of relief, letting out the breath I'd been holding. Reaching forward, I touched his temples lightly and closed my eyes.

28

INCOGNITO

It had been a few days. Enough that I was back to track practice, and enough that Orion had managed to experiment with the partition some. I'd been right. Putting the partition into someone else's head was a lot more complicated than tweaking my own brain. Doing it required us to meet in the dead of the night. Our systems appeared to be less likely to overhear us at those times when we should have been sleeping.

Overall, I wasn't sure it led to an improvement in Orion's demeanor. Instead, he seemed a little more preoccupied, and I again found myself sometimes wondering what it was he wasn't telling me.

However, it made talking about subjects that might otherwise be taboo with less worry and frustration. While I was marginally concerned about what might happen if they realized what I'd done and was capable of doing, that was a problem for future me.

Come to think of it, I probably lumped a heap of stuff off onto future me. It was only fair, after all.

Friday night was the first night in a long time we were actually having our card games and/or D&D night. To be honest, I'd mostly forgotten what my character was like or where we even were in the campaign. The usual monthly Saturday night tabletop game wasn't going to work this month, so we moved to our Friday which meant everyone could attend.

The more I thought about it, I now knew why Sam was the DM.

I threw my backpack onto the couch and myself shortly thereafter.

"You're not going to help me prep for the night in?" Orion asked as he lugged grocery bags into the kitchen.

"Nope. I'm not a gourmet. You've got everything covered." We'd both decided to make sure we were audible in our thoughts unless they were precisely against the system. Like unless we were trying to figure out how to regain autonomy.

Pretty much like most of my thoughts.

He was grumbling to himself in the kitchen.

"I can't hear you!" I yelled out, lying my ass off.

My SC was still missing in action. Frankly, I was starting to get worried. Had I really annoyed it, or made it angry?

I'm not angry. I've been busy relaying your information to the rest of the network and discussing the impact of such sentiments and statements.

Oh. I tried to digest that. *Has no one else ever brought it up?*

Not as vehemently as you did. We've heard grumblings before of course, but you were more… direct with your criticism.

Consider this me reinforcing that criticism.

We do.

And the presence was gone again. Maybe that's just how they hid themselves really well.

Fine. I'd get up and help Orion.

He already had most things organized but looked up with faint surprise.

"Go cut that summer sausage, thanks." He looked back down at the cheese blocks he was working on, but I could see the flicker of a smile cross his face.

I'd just finished arranging the sausage, cheese, and crackers plate when the doorbell rang. Orion rushed out to get it, and Cyan and Sam came pouring in, followed by Neale and Levi.

Neale immediately sought me out. "I hear you're being reckless with your body."

"You know that came off way differently than you intended, right?" I asked, not skipping a beat as I put some relish in a tiny clear plastic container I think had come with a sandwich box set at some stage.

Neale blushed and ruffled my hair. "Well. Be careful of your back. Those injuries never heal well."

I looked up at him and saw the faint glimpse of sadness that colored his words. Neale played basketball, but his older brother had played football a few years ahead of us in high school. Neale had looked up to the guy so much. But then his brother was the victim of an illegal tackle on the day scouts were there to watch the game, and his brother was left with a broken back and no hope of ever walking again.

So, I got his concern. "I'll do my best not to worry you again."

"Excellent." He grinned and stole a piece of sausage before I could smack his fingers. "I'll go wait for the food out there, shall I?"

I bit the sarcasm off before I could say it and laughed instead. "Yep, you go wait. I'll be out in a few minutes."

Composing myself before I went out, I mantra'd my brain. See, this was my life, not the tasks. These people were my friends, even if half of them were in my program with me. Of course, the level of not-coincidence in that didn't escape my notice.

Plastering a smile on my face, I entered the living room with the tray of food held high, determined to enjoy my first Friday night with friends in a damned long time.

Saturday morning came too quickly. I woke up groggy and allergic to the sun. Well, not actually allergic, because I know there are true allergies to it which really suck, but I buried my head in my pillows, trying desperately to avoid the light.

Out in the kitchen, I could hear plates being stacked on one another, some eighties music blaring through the speakers. That meant Jacob was up. He always maintained that the eighties and nineties had the best music, and sometimes I had to admit he was right. But only to myself. Not to him. I'd never live it down.

I lay in the bed with my head buried by my pillow and tried to pretend it was still dark outside.

Assignment Notification.

Why could I see it even with my eyes closed? That was so unfair. Eyes closed should mean no sight. I wondered if Orion got it too.

Location: Meet at the south stairs of the Columbia Bridge off MLK Jr Dr at 5:30p.m.. Do not be late.

Objective: To be revealed once the team has assembled.

Time Limit: Not to exceed twelve hours.

Reward: Determined upon completion.

Caution: Direct orders must be obeyed. Failure to do so will result in severe punishment or termination.

Great. There was no going back to sleep now, so I rolled out of bed and onto the floor. Hazard of not sleeping on a proper bed. Or maybe it was a benefit, I didn't even know anymore. I was still huddled there when Orion burst into my room.

"Did you get a message?" He whispered in that non-whisper way.

"Yes. Why don't you tell the whole world next time?" I was grumpy. I usually did okay on around six hours sleep, but we were up past two in the morning trying to tame a werewolf-succubus hybrid in a village full of innocents. Thanks so much to Sam for *those* nightmares.

"I was going to put up a billboard, but it was too expensive." His humor caught me off guard and made me laugh.

"Very well, fine sir! You win this time. But be wary, for I shall triumph when next we meet!" It probably would have sounded grander coming from someone who wasn't half crawling on the floor with blankets still tangled in their legs.

But at least Orion laughed too. "We have time. But I'm awake now."

He was so right. I didn't want to be awake, but the sun was up too, so more sleep probably wasn't an option. I had assignments and training, and we were on the home stretch of the second semester. A few more weeks and we'd be done.

I managed to disentangle myself from the blankets without falling flat on my face, and I figured that was a good start to the day.

The living room was remarkably tidy, though I couldn't remember tidying it up. Sam or Cyan had probably done it while I crawled into bed, barely conscious. While I could function on around six hours sleep, any less and I was done for.

Stumbling into the kitchen, I grabbed an apple out and nodded when Jacob held the pancake mix up above him. He didn't turn toward me, he never did. But I knew he'd got my answer anyway. I could so go pancakes after being woken up with a damned assignment.

We both had the same assignment.

Again. For the third time in two weeks. Surely that wasn't normal.

I frowned as I chomped down on the juicy gala apple. Why was that making my gut roil? I mean it wasn't a hunger grumble, but an uneasiness I couldn't explain.

Why are Orion and I on the same mission again? Easiest way to get a direct answer was to ask a direct question. Or so I thought.

Because your specific skill sets work very well together, and, as a team, you mesh. Therefore, it makes the most sense to throw you together when both of your skill sets are required. Which is fairly often. Does that answer your question?

Sort of. Which was true. I wanted a color-coordinated graph of how designations and skill sets interacted with each other. Not to mention the ranking system.

Your affinity, while not rare, has a low survival rate. You have managed to adapt well to yours though, and coupled with Orion's multiple talents, and your history as friends who are used to working together, it makes sense to send such a sturdy team out when possible. Does that explain it better?

Yes. It does. And then again, it sort of didn't. Water and electricity didn't seem to be the best combination I could think of, but I was just a newb after all. Luckily, I didn't direct that thought at the system. I wasn't sure it would put up with that much sarcasm from me.

Still, though. It was one of those things I needed to figure out. Had they realized we were keeping thoughts to ourselves now?

I had to make a concerted effort to talk to the system. I'd been silent so often, I'd probably fucked it up.

Couldn't you just stop listening to me? I made sure to enter the right amount of plaintiveness into my tone. *It's so hard to keep my mind void of thought so you don't pry, but damn if it means I can't really think at all.*

Privacy is that important, isn't it? It sounded amused, and yet at the same time baffled. *I will attempt not to snoop. However, it is difficult. There are certain words, actions, elements that trigger the program and make it check in on the subject.*

Sort of like babysitting us?

No. More like making sure the investment we've made is...okay.

You were going to say malfunctioning, weren't you? I half meant it as teasing, but also half because I truly think that's where it was going.

Not really. I was going to say cooperating, *but it didn't seem appropriate in this instance.*

Interesting. *Does that mean you've had agents who didn't cooperate?*

Rephrase the question. I'm not permitted to answer it in this form.

Another eye opener. *It's fine. It really wasn't that important.*

Then why ask in the first place?

Because we were talking, and it was an organic question. I smiled, the gesture softening my stance.

True. We were talking. I like to converse with you. It sounded hesitant and that gave me a brief surge of sadness. What was the program? How did it exist, and when had it been created? There were so many things I wanted to say to it. But for now, I thought that maybe being friendlier to this thing in my head might be a good start. Even if I had ulterior motives.

Me too. With you. The thing was, I wasn't actually lying. When it wasn't sending me on missions or listening in on my thoughts, I think I actually liked it.

The day passed in a blur and it was time to get ready before I knew it. I really needed to get another set of my incognito gear. Non-descript clothes that weren't heavier sweats and a hoodie. Because pulling these clothes on again made me realize that I'd worn them more than ever over the last six weeks.

It was still cool enough in the evenings that I could get away with it, but I was going to have to expand my ninja wardrobe if I was going to keep up with this life of crime. I'd always imagined being the superhero, never the villain. It was a bit anticlimactic that I'd acquired super powers and couldn't use them to leap tall buildings and whatnot.

"What're you thinking about?" Orion nudged me with his elbow. Even though his hands remained shoved into his pockets.

"Life. The universe. Why the fuck I'm not a superhero." I kicked a small pebble.

Or I tried to. There's a reason I run. My aim and hand eye coordination have never been the best, but my speed? Yeah, that I have. The pebble remained exactly where it was as we passed it. If I tried, I swore I could hear it laughing at me.

"Superheroes are overrated." Orion started the lecture with the perfect tone. "They never get paid and never get credit for what they do."

"We don't get credit either."

"But we do get paid."

"Touché!" I laughed. "That was perfectly set up, by the way."

Orion grinned and we fell back into companionable silence. I wasn't too sure about the way down to the river this far north. I'd never gone this way before, not on any of my runs. And after living here for almost three years, I'd gone on a lot of runs. It was darker through this part of town, mostly parks and golf courses, now we'd left the main streets behind us.

The ornamental street lights flickered intermittently in this section, and I got the constant feeling I was being watched. But when I turned around, I only ever caught brief glimpses of red or yellow. If I brought it up, I knew Orion would probably dismiss it as fireflies. Maybe. He'd been surprisingly amenable to me partitioning his mind.

"Ever get the feeling you're being watched?" I asked, my voice deliberately pitched low.

"All the damned time. For the last two odd years. It's like something is keeping an eye on me because it knows I should already be dead." He shrugged and I got the feeling he was exerting extreme willpower not to look behind us.

But it was amazing news. This probably wasn't just in my head. "You said you'd noticed shadows with beady red eyes, and clawed hands?"

He glanced at me, his brow pinched in irritation. "I think so. A couple of times, but after asking and being dismissed by the system, I thought it better to keep hallucinations in my head. Didn't want to find out the hard way that it was as negative side effect of resurrection."

"You realize people don't hallucinate the same things at the same times, right?" I asked, digging my own hands into my pockets to ward off the sudden chill.

"That's not...well. What is it, then?" His words were challenging. Likely because I'd taken something he'd come to terms with and twisted it around to where he'd actually been right all along.

"I don't know. But I do know they've—or *it's*—tried to stop me a couple of times."

"Stop you?"

I realized I hadn't said that well and searched for the words. Damn. I hoped he was separating the direction of his thoughts right now. "I had to go and retrieve something one night, and right where the lights were out down the bad corner of our street?"

He nodded, and I gathered the courage and continued.

"Well, they grabbed me, tried to take it. But I shocked them away and ran." I took a deep breath trying to settle the nerves. I made it sound like nothing serious, but it had been one of the scariest moments of my life. It seemed to have taken more of a toll on me than I'd realized.

Orion shook his head. "That's physical touch. I never got that far, but I've always felt watched, judged, and weighed. All of the time. When I look, most of the time, they're gone. But like now?"

"Now you feel like they're following us." I finished what he was saying, making sure my whisper was soft. He only nodded, his eyes set dead ahead.

"We need to make it to the bridge soon. Or we'll miss the meeting."

We picked up our pace, and this time I refused to look behind me. They say something is always lurking in the dark, but what were we supposed to do when the darkness that was lurking seemed attached to us?

29
UNDER THE BRIDGE

The bridge wasn't exactly as I'd pictured it. Old and rundown, with rusting train tracks all along it, overgrown with patches of vegetation. I wasn't even sure if it would bear the weight of a train anymore. It sat at the corner of Martin Luther King Jr and Montgomery Drive. Nestled among trees in a low traffic area, it appeared to have been abandoned. It still spanned the river, and at one stage probably seemed majestic. Although now, it just paled in comparison to the newer models.

From where we stood on Montgomery, the bridge was swallowed by shadows that I swear writhed around it. Orion and I looked at each other at the same time and nodded. If we were going to do this, then we were doing it together.

He took my hand, and I squeezed his. Doing so gave me that tiny bit of courage I needed to venture down there. I hoped it gave him the same. The path didn't appear to be well maintained, nor particularly safe, but we had to get there. Second Chancers didn't get a choice.

The wind whipped up a bit, tossing branches of the trees surrounding us with abandon. Even the grass moved in time with it. The lawn didn't seem to have been mowed in an age. At least the portion around and under the actual bridge. The area felt like a vacant lot in an abandoned city. The type of place everyone was warned to steer clear of. The ones they put in post-apocalyptic shows and movies.

There was a mild stench in the air, of mud and rotting vegetation mixed with that fishy smell of too-old seafood. Seafood didn't have a fishy taste if it was fresh. The dead fish down by the shore had been there far too long.

Wait by the bridge.

Ya think? I directed at my system. But if it was there, it showed no signs of listening to me right now. That made me even more nervous. After all, shouldn't it be keeping an eye on us?

The bridge towered over us, almost blocking out most of the remaining light as the sun was setting and cast us into shadows.

"This isn't instilling confidence in me." Orion chattered when he got nervous. "I don't like the ones where I feel like I'll hate what I have to do."

I was quite surprised that this was the first sign of him disliking his tasks or being scared of our surroundings. There seemed to be more to it, I could see it in the way his eyes darted back and forth. Now wasn't the time to ask him though, I'd have to do that later.

Me on the other hand? I had no problem admitting that this mission had already scared me to death. Some actual zombies were about to push out of the ground and kill us both permanently. That's where my mind was, completely stuck on rotting flesh.

"Me either." Pretty sure my voice shook and extended *me* into a three-syllable word.

"Well, if some huge worm is about to tunnel up and eat us alive, I'm glad I got to be eaten alive with you." Orion's voice was deadpan, but I could feel his body trembling as we stood in front of the meeting place.

"Seriously, though, what do you think they want us to do?" I had to ask, had to talk, had to keep my overactive imagination at bay.

"Feed the fish? Fertilize the ground? Repair the bridge?" Orion tried a few quippy puns, but they both fell flat and were decidedly unlikely. "Sorry. I've never had a meeting point like this, so I have no idea what to expect."

It was after five thirty, and the sun was going down. Behind this massive block of stone, it was already dark. Already on the other side of the day. "Maybe we're on the wrong side of the bridge?"

The idea gripped me, and I glanced each way before crossing the deserted road to the next pilon. I crept around to stand on the side closest to the river. Lo and behold, Adam was there, along with someone I'd never seen.

"Cleaner?" I called out softly, "Come over here."

Adam grinned at me. "I see I owe you my life, Runner."

"That's me. Just your friendly citywide Runner. In person. I'll be here all week."

Adam laughed. "I really hope not. I think this one is supposed to be a quick in and out. As long as you've got a little more control over that power you have now." He raised an eyebrow, and while I knew he was grateful I'd been around to help him not die, he probably also wouldn't have needed my help had my abilities not gone haywire. Such a two-way street.

I clenched my fists around my trusty little squash ball inside my hoodie pockets to steady myself as Adam continued.

"This is our Driver."

I glanced at the guy I didn't know. He was very nondescript. His eyes were hidden behind glasses that I really hoped were night vision enhanced, because otherwise he was just being a douche. And his hoodie revealed little about his hair or other facial features. Slightly shorter than Adam, but about two inches taller than me, all he did was nod in our direction. It was all I could do to bite back the comment sitting on my tongue. But telling our Driver that it was great he was so personable was probably not going to help the underlying tension I could already feel brewing.

"So." Orion shoved his hands into his pockets, even further than they'd been. I wanted to take a picture desperately so I could show him how ridiculous it looked. But I didn't. I let him continue instead. "What are we doing here?"

"Glad you asked." Adam grinned again. The light was fading here now too, and it was becoming increasingly difficult to see the others. "There is a warehouse on that small island just up from us. It's only about twenty feet out into the water. It has a very rickety makeshift bridge built out to it. Single file only. The warehouse is supposed to have been abandoned for years and is technically not there as far as the authorities are concerned. But lately we've received word of activities being performed down there that are, shall we say, counterproductive to humans not blowing themselves up."

"Eloquent," I pointed out.

"Thank you. I do try." I could hear Adam's grin in his words. "Basically, explosives and drugs are reported to be in there, if our sources are correct."

"We need to clear them out?" Orion ventured.

"Yes. Which is why we have you here, because you're going to flush them out. And speedy here is going short out the electrical boxes." Adam reached into his jacket and drew out two pairs of glasses identical in appearance to the ones the Driver was wearing.

I put them on, and lo and behold, they were night vision enabled. Damn, I was good at this. "So fry the electrical circuits, and flush the drugs and explosives."

"Wow, it's like you were actually paying attention." Adam's sarcasm verged on laughter. "Nicely done, speedy."

I glanced at Orion, wondering if he was pale, or if it was just the new glasses. "We going then?"

Driver nodded and began to head in the other direction from which we'd come. There were no lights down here, no housing, no streets. Nothing to give away our existence. The moonlight wasn't strong enough to highlight our presence, because the new moon was tiny.

But the grass kept getting taller, coming up to my waist in certain sections as we moved toward our destination. With an unstable bridge to cross, I couldn't help but worry for Orion. He'd died by drowning. Surely water wasn't his favorite thing to be around, not like this.

My mind kept going over how many shadows could hide in grass. What could be lying in wait to ambush us?

I was not cut out for espionage shit. At least this job felt right though. If there were indeed drugs and explosives, we were doing a good thing, right? Almost superheroish.

Adam's makeshift "bridge" was more of a walking the plank situation than something which instilled the confidence that we wouldn't fall in the water. Each step I took across the two boards that had been hastily nailed together made me wish muddy water sounded more appealing. It wasn't near warm enough tonight to take an impromptu dip in dirty water.

Every eight feet, the dual planks were attached to a shaky pylon that only poked out of the water by about five inches. As the water came in to lap at the shore, it swayed up and down, hitting the planks and splashing our feet. The pylons didn't seem to be sturdy. They wobbled with just the right amount of sway to make me think each step might toss me into the dirty water.

As much as I'd been concerned about him, Orion traversed it with more finesse than I did.

Island wasn't exactly what I would call this piece of mud with trees growing out of it, but I didn't have any other fitting word for it either. The ground was sandy mud held together by the roots of the river trees. And the number of trees we had to slog through was astounding. Only the faintly-worn trail gave any indication of life here, and it was one we had to look for.

The warehouse was much larger than I expected, given how small the island appeared to be, and it was more run down than I'd thought possible. Parts of it had collapsed and lay half covered by tree growth that had decided to reclaim the land. Rusting bits of roof had fallen down, but most of it seemed intact. Parts of a missing wall spilled over into the water, contaminating it.

I mean, it was the Schuylkill; the *kill* part was surprisingly accurate.

Lights shone through small holes here and there throughout the exterior. Their glow was pale but still gave away the culprit's presence, if anyone tried to make it out to this pile of mud. Like us.

Dilapidated didn't even begin to describe the mostly tin and steel structure. We waited at one of the unintentional entryways. If the rust around the hole was any indication, it hadn't started as a door. We could see movement inside, shadows flickering in the dim light that filtered out. It wasn't a bustling central hub or anything. If the heat signature in my glasses was accurate, there were two people inside. The glasses were a much better measuring stick than judging the shadows.

It took me a while to get used to the way the world moved with this night vision. Given that a soft glow emanated from the hole we surrounded, it wasn't working quite as intended.

Adam knelt down next to us, lowering his head. His words were so soft I had to concentrate to hear him. "We need to cloak speedy here in order to get the lights and alarms disengaged before we enter, and so that we aren't blinded by our glasses when the lights go down."

"Okay. Like we did last time?" I almost made the whole sentence without letting my voice wobble. Adam nodded at me and continued.

"Then we need to subdue the occupants and destroy the stockpile. I'll leave that to you, Cleaner and Driver. I'll keep you both under my protection until the first is taken care of." Adam looked at each of us in turn, and only moved on once we'd nodded our understanding. It was on the tip of my tongue. Oh, how I wanted to know what he meant by subdue.

I hated to be first out of the gate.

Orion moved away from me, and my left side suddenly felt the cold. I glanced after him and realized that strange look had returned to his eyes. Like he was resigned to his job. My scar tingled for the first time in days. The unease in my stomach rose, threatening to choke me with bile. I wished these damned signs would just spell shit out already.

Warning: Unstable Portent Reaction. Limit use.

I quickly checked the warning, but that was all it said. I didn't have time for this right now. What the hell was this Portent crap it kept telling me to stop using? There was nothing in any of the information I had at my disposal that let me know what the danger with Portent was. With effort, I pushed those thoughts aside, saving them for the future, again.

Right now, I had my own job to concentrate on. Cloaked by the Driver, I moved in quietly. Luckily, there were shadows abounding in this space. I really didn't want to think about how they got electricity here in the first place. Perhaps a generator.

Concrete was cracked all over the place with greenery struggling to push through. I suppressed a sigh of relief that the electrical breakers seemed to be on the side I'd entered from. I could see two people sitting at a table each. One of them sorted through small bags, but I couldn't make out anything else. The other had some different powders, wires, things that looked vaguely bomb like, I guess. They were skinny and clothed in thick material, but I couldn't see anything else through my glasses. It was too bright.

Except for the dog. It hadn't moved, and I realized it was half asleep with what looked like a bone in front of it. I'd see if he was okay after we were done with everything. Moving along the side of the building was rather easy with the way the wall had fallen to conceal a portion of the room. The shadows were thicker here. So deep I could almost hear them speaking to me, calling my name. Damned imagination.

I could feel the eyes on me, but maybe that was just my team. Wishful thinking only went so far. But the electrical breakers were within reach. I reached out my hand to touch it and closed my eyes tightly before releasing a measured surge of power that made the box snap, crackle, and sizzle. Somewhere outside the makeshift warehouse, I could hear a buzz powering down.

The lights were down, the alarm was done, at least for a few minutes. I didn't think for a minute it called the police anyway. This island didn't seem like it was zoned for explosives and drugs.

The two workers had stood up when the power dropped, confusion spreading across their faces. Even with the tinge of green, I could see the fear begin to rise. Meanwhile, the dog lifted its head, and shrank back, like it was trying to hide itself.

Maybe it had smelled us by now and realized there were too many of us. Or maybe it could see the shadows too.

I watched from my safe spot as Driver and Orion moved into the space. They moved through the space with practiced ease, their footfalls making no sound at all as they approached the workers. Driver reached his hand into his pocket slowly and pulled out something small that I couldn't identify.

But the sound that echoed throughout the metal structure was unmistakable. My stomach flipped and tried to choke me. The gunshot was so sudden and unexpected that I jumped, watching in shock as the worker on the right stood for one second and then began to fall forward as the third eye in his head slowly began to ooze blood.

I watched it all as if I'd somehow slowed time. Every movement precise and enhanced, every sound elongated like a wail. Wait, dealing with them meant killing them? Didn't that make me an accessory to murder? I could feel the blood drain from my face as I grew pale.

The worker's body hadn't even hit the floor yet when I blinked, switching my gaze to Orion. His eyes held a sadness I hated seeing in them and a blankness that scared me. And I knew without him having done anything, what he was about to do.

I watched him as he motioned with his right hand. It was a casual flick of the wrist, like it was something he did every day. Something sleek and powerful shot through the air, hitting the second worker in silence. But it tore through the man's head, blowing half of it away and out the back. Blood spattered all over the small bags the man had been working on, mingling with it, splattering onto the ground like someone had dropped pancake mix.

30

BUDDING APATHY

How could he do that? Why did he have to do that? They could have just knocked them unconscious. Hell, I could have sent enough electricity into them to knock them out like a taser would. It was obvious their instructions had been to kill their targets. And it was obvious Orion had done it before. It explained so much, why it seemed to make him both happy and sad that I was in SC now. Damn it. He couldn't hide the truth from me anymore.

I kept seeing the head, over and over again in my mind. Exploding like a dropped watermelon. Orion had done that. My Orion. Who I'd known for my entire life. Took another's. What if they'd had kids, what if they'd been forced into this? How did we know what their circumstances were? None off it warranted ending their life at all.

Your portion of this task has been completed. You will receive payment and advancement points. Please refer to your interface for more information.

What the everliving fuck did SC have in its programming? Ice cold fucking hearts?

I sat there, huddled in on myself, trying to digest everything while Orion flooded the electronics and explosives, while he destroyed the drugs we'd come to clear off the streets. Sure, that was good. But taking two lives? Two lackeys?

I couldn't wrap my head around it. Oh, wow, what an insensitive comment, even if it was only to myself. My stomach tightened, bile rose, but I forced it back down.

I needed to get out of there, now. Slinking away the way I'd come, I encountered Adam at the back entrance. My head was still spinning. So many thoughts at once. In hindsight, I should have exited out the front. Or just run and boosted myself as fast as I could.

He took one look at me and nodded, before returning his attention to the murderzone in front of him. Of course I didn't matter. I'd done my job, played my part in the massacre. But the dog. I didn't want to risk them finding the dog. They weren't even on the right side of the warehouse for that. And if something happened to it, I feared I'd go all John Wick.

The dog, I could save the dog. I needed to save the dog. So, I rounded the building and crept up to the opposite side from where I'd been. There, right where the building was collapsing on this side, the dog sat huddled under a cabinet. His coat was dark brown, and the same colored eyes stared up at me in fear until I coaxed him out with the peppermint that was stuck in my pocket. I didn't even remember where I'd gotten it. But I grabbed the dog, hugging him and tried to fight back tears that started prickling my eyes. I never cried.

But then again, Orion had never killed anyone in front of my eyes before. He'd never mentioned this. He'd only said he knew that agents could die.

Shit.

He'd also insisted that I wouldn't understand. He was right. I didn't. Not at all. This was why communication was key.

I stood up and staggered out of the building toward the makeshift bridge. My only hope was to keep the night glasses on, or the water would look like pitch black certain death. The lights beyond the bridge, on MLK Jr Drive cast painful spots in my eyes. Everything hurt. My chest, my heart, my brain.

There was only one answer to this. I had to run. So I did. I picked up my pace and ran. I let the adrenaline course through me, the fear and loathing I felt, and let my feet pound the pavement.

Only when I reached the edge of the populated areas, did I remove my glasses and I looked down to realize that the dog had followed me. Maybe he wanted another peppermint. Maybe he knew that we'd just shared something pretty fucking horrific.

Maybe he wanted to know if they expected me to kill people too. Because I sure as hell did. Because I sure as hell wouldn't. And then I'd be the one they killed. Would Orion do that too?

I didn't have a leash, and the dog didn't have a collar anyway. He looked like a mix of some sort. Maybe a bit of a German Shepherd and a sheep dog or poodle. But he stuck to my side like glue as we began to walk further into town, and I welcomed the comforting warmth of his presence.

Should I go home? How would I face Orion? What would I say? I crouched down and threw my arms around the dog again, burying my head in his fur. He licked my hand and wuffed softly into my hair, with a faint scent of rotting teeth and peppermint. "Yeah. I know."

Pulling myself together, I stood up, determined to make it back home and figure out the other shit later. I needed to sleep, even though a part of me wondered if I'd ever sleep again, or if those visions that kept replaying in my mind were just going to be on an infinite repeating loop.

Orion hadn't even hesitated. What had they done to him?

The lights changed before I could cross the street, and I stood there, hands clenched as Wick sat beside me. Maybe it wasn't the most original name, but it was the best I could do at short notice with my brain on strike.

The lights sounded their alarm, allowing me to cross. Which was good, because I hadn't really been paying attention.

But when we got to the other side, two people stood in my way. At first, I thought they might be Adam, or the Driver whose name I'd never actually gotten. But they weren't. Dressed in charcoal grey—thus proving my point that it worked just as well as black—they stood side by side.

"Dare Harvey, we need to speak with you." The one on the left spoke with a foreign lilt that I couldn't place.

"What's this about?" I asked cautiously, scanning the area for a way to run from them. The odds of them catching me was pretty slim. Wick pushed up against my leg, and I could feel more than hear the growl in his throat.

"It's about Second Chance and the partition you have in your mind." The girl on the right spoke. She had blond hair, cut just below her ears. Her expression was so serious it made her button nose a little red. Or maybe that was just the reflection of the streetlights.

It was like the one on the right had just told me we were taking a stroll in the park. I blinked, trying to process the words. How did they know?

"What's Second Chance?" Maybe if I feigned innocence.

But they weren't having any of that. "We all know what we're talking about. We need you to come with us right now, because Nya couldn't explain it to you like she needed to."

"Wait, you know Nya?" Okay, so they knew the program, and they knew Nya. Surely it would be okay to listen to what they had to say, right?

The guy rolled his eyes and crossed his arms, sandy brown hair falling into his eyes, which he impatiently pushed behind his ears. I knew him, I'd seen him before.

"Shane?" I blurted before I could stop myself. He'd been with me in the ambulance way back when all of this started.

"So, you do remember me. Good." He took half a step closer and lowered his voice. "Ever wonder why there are no Runners?"

"You're saying it wrong." The girl interrupted, scowling. "We don't have time to play twenty questions right now."

Shane sighed. "Fine. Dare, you're a Runner, you're an eel. Eels aren't rare, they're just able to control the brain on a level that SC hasn't caught up with yet. It's the one advantage we have. We need you to come with us, to trust us. You'll be home by sun up, I promise."

"Why should I trust you?" Wick ruffed right next to me, like he was punctuating my question, even if he didn't seem quite as put out anymore.

Shane eyed me for a moment and the smile he gave me was filled with sadness. "Because we know a lot more about the questions you're asking yourself. Especially your questions about Orion."

Wait, so these people, one of whom rode with me in the ambulance ride that started this all, knew about Orion? "What do you know about Orion?"

The crack in my voice betrayed me. I was far more upset than I'd realized.

I glanced down at Wick again. His big brown eyes watched me intently, like he was telling me: hey there human who saved me, I'll protect you if this turns out to be a trap.

Shane waited for a moment, glancing up and down the oddly empty street. "We know about the changes in him, and we know how to answer all the questions you have about eel's powers."

"How do I know I'll be safe?" The words came out more confident than I felt. My scar tingled with anticipation. I'd died weeks ago anyway, right?

"You don't." Shane looked a bit sad. "But if you don't come with us right now, your power will burn you from the inside out and take everyone around you with it."

FROM THE AUTHOR

Hi there! K.T. Hanna here.

I want to thank you for taking a "chance" on my new series: Last Chance. I've always been fascinated with characters who have electrical magic, or abilities. Since the human body fires off its own electricity, I've always imagined so many possibilities.

If you enjoyed the book, I ask you, **please** take a moment to leave a review. **Reviews** are an author's lifesblood. Without them, our books sink into obscurity. With them, most algorithms allow well reviewed books to self-promote in some way.

Want to find out more about Last Chance and my other series? Here is how you can keep in contact with me:

Sign up for my Reader's Group (login.somnia-online.com/) and get a short story for free!

If you'd like to contact me, my email is: kthannaauthor@gmail.com I'll do my very best to get back to you

If you'd like previews of what I'm writing, or art I'm commissioning then join my Patreon (facebook.com/groups/SomniaOnline/)!

I can be found in my FB group (facebook.com/groups/SomniaOnline/) fairly often, and also on Twitter (@KTHanna) & Instagram (@kt_hanna).

If you LOVE LitRPG don't forget to join:
The GameLit Society! (facebook.com/groups/LitRPGsociety/)
And of course don't forget LitRPG Books!
(facebook.com/groups/LitRPG.books/)

To learn more about LitRPG, talk to authors including myself, and just have an awesome time, please join the **LitRPG Group** (facebook.com/groups/LitRPGGroup/

ACKNOWLEDGEMENTS

I have a lot of people to thank, who in at least some way encouraged me to write in general, or else to write this book specifically.

Love of my life, Trevor, and my little Kami. It's his fault I found the genre, and her fault I never give up on writing.

I wouldn't be here without the Jami Nord and Owen Littman. I must thank Dawn Chapman, Luke Chmilenko, Michael Chatfield, and Tao Wong for their friendship, guidance, and company on an almost daily basis. And of course Andrea Parsneau for being such an amazing person to go through this with.

Of course, I have to thank a few other people (hope I haven't forgotten anyone)

M. Andrew Patterson

Kylie B.

Amanda W.

Quinton Shyn

Kindra

Dawn Chapman

Bonnie Price

Stephen Morse

Cait Greer

M Evan Matyas

Ian Mitchell

Marko Horvatin

Dave Willmarth

Charles Dean

Daniel Schinofen

Patreon, I thank all of my patrons. You make so much possible and bring me so much joy! Thank you especially to:

Robert

Ma&Pa

Wisp

Pious

www.ingramcontent.com/pod-product-compliance
Lightning Source LLC
Chambersburg PA
CBHW050338190726
48284CB00007BB/2061